AFLAME

LEGACY OF FLAMES
BOOK THREE

EMMA L. ADAMS

1

Dragons, as a general rule, did not enjoy being locked in cages.

The cell the mages had given me was nice, as far as prisons went. Not a dungeon, nor a cramped space like those in the Orion Stronghold, but a small room, sparsely furnished. If not for the bars in the small window atop the door, I might have been able to pretend I was in a hotel and not a jail. That, and the fact that the mages refused to let me out, not even to speak to my little sister.

Compared to some of the places my friends and I had sheltered in, the accommodations were nothing to sniff at. The mages had even brought me new clothes and had offered me top-grade cleansing spells that wiped years of grime off my skin. The Mage Lords had money to burn. Tons of it. Many shifters wouldn't see this as a bad deal, and who knew, maybe it wasn't the worst idea to stay here until London's supernaturals had forgotten their numerous grudges against me. It was a relatively stress-free existence, though a boring one.

But the fire inside me would never be quenched, not until the Orion League was utterly destroyed.

I paced the room one side to the other, grinding my teeth. That I hadn't lost my temper and shifted into a dragon yet was testament to how badly I wanted to avoid pissing off the mages even more than I already had. While the mages' prison was covered in protective wards which might even be resilient to dragonfire for all I knew, they'd never let me speak to Cori if I threw a tantrum and wrecked the place.

That, and I saw the reasoning behind their decision to lock me away indefinitely, considering I'd helped a criminal escape justice and sent him to an unknown location where even the mages couldn't find him. Oh, and I'd deceived them about the location of a powerful magical object because I hadn't trusted them not to steal it for themselves rather than letting me use it to save my sister—or worse, let it fall back into the League's hands.

I stopped pacing as the door clicked open, and Lord Smyth came in. As leader of the Mage Lords in this region, he would probably be quite reasonable to deal with under normal circumstances. As it was, since he'd had the misfortune of having to deal with an attempted assault on London by the Orion League *and* a surprise dragon shifter and her troublemaking allies in the same week, his patience had been thin from the outset. That I'd then lied to his face was apparently one transgression too far.

"Yes?" I tried for politeness, but frankly I had no idea how one was supposed to address a Mage Lord. Lord Smyth was a tall black man in maybe his mid-forties, who wore a tailored suit that probably cost as much as my entire annual income and had two modes: stern and slightly less stern. Today looked to be the latter.

"I apologise for leaving you alone for such a long time, Ember," he said. "We've been busy, cleaning up the aftermath of the hunters' attack on the city and assuring none of their monstrous creatures were left behind."

I doubted the mages themselves had done much cleaning. As per usual, everyone else would left to foot the bill for the damages. It also didn't sit well with me that the mages called the shifters whom Malkin had manipulated to fight on his side using the Moonbeam *monsters* or *abominations*. While I'd used the same terminology myself, shifters typically had a different definition of the word 'monster' than regular humans. And we knew damn well the League thought super-naturals were *all* abominations, the mages included.

"The hunters?" I asked. "Have you found their fortress yet?"

"No, we haven't," he said. "Are you quite certain that's where they were operating from?"

"Absolutely," I said. "Surely there aren't many places to hide a moving island."

"I've learned not to be surprised at the lengths the League will go to in order to conceal their criminality," said Lord Smyth. "I may have some more questions for you later, but I came to give you the opportunity to speak to your sister."

My attention sharpened. "I can?"

Please, let me speak to her. I was Cori's big sister, the only person left to take care of her after we'd lost everyone else in our lives. It was hard not to blame myself for everything she'd suffered recently—first being kidnapped by the hunters, and then when I'd rescued her from the Stronghold only for her to immediately be moved to another cell. That the mages treated their prisoners miles better than the League did didn't mean she deserved to be locked up, not in the slightest.

"Yes. She's fine, don't worry, though she still has gaps in her memory."

"I told you why." My nails bit into my palms. "The hunters

drugged her. She doesn't remember anything up until the moment she was taken prisoner, so she has no information to give you."

"I can see your perspective, Ember, but I need to be sure that you aren't concealing the whereabouts of any other League members. The ones whom you sought shelter with are still at large."

He meant Giselle and Astor. No matter what I said, he and the other mages refused point-blank to accept they'd renounced the League years ago. "They aren't League members. And I have no idea where they are."

"The man found to be impersonating an employee was a League member. I'm sure you understand the dilemma this puts me in. You lied to us when you told us he was killed."

"Because you'd have killed him yourselves without hearing him out," I said. "He renounced the League and helped us get Cori out of their Stronghold. Then he helped us find safety when nobody else would. I owed him my life."

As it was, all I'd been able to do was send him through a magical portal to what I hoped was safety, and the mages hadn't been willing to accept that I really didn't have the faintest idea where he'd ended up. The portal was untested and had been a last-ditch idea out of desperation to save Astor from certain execution at the hands of the mages. All for the crime of having worked for the Orion League. It didn't seem to matter that he'd later renounced them, nor that he'd been manipulated into joining their ranks from the outset when Malkin had staged a dragon shifter attack on his family.

In fact, I was willing to bet a lot of the Orion League's current members had joined under similar circumstances. Malkin used the Moonbeam to take away shifters' free will and ordered them to kill humans. Then he'd send his hunters in to kill or capture the shifter in question and recruited new members from amongst the surviving victims. It was the easiest, most efficient way to build an army who didn't question their purpose. And it was all based on a lie.

Lord Smyth's eyes narrowed. "Your sister can't confirm your story."

"That's because she was unconscious. Have you talked to Will or Becks? They were with me the whole time. They can confirm everything I say is the truth. Kit, too, though he didn't witness all of it due to being Malkin's prisoner, too."

"Yes," said Lord Smyth. "They said the same as you, but I'm afraid I can't trust their judgement to be unbiased. They've lied to protect you before."

"They don't need to," I said. "We only lied beforehand because we needed the Moonbeam to save my sister's life."

"And to save your hunter allies."

"Because they *aren't* hunters." It was like arguing with a relatively amiable brick wall. "I appreciate that the League's actions are unforgivable, but if anyone should hold a grudge, it's me, and I don't."

Okay, I did hold something of a grudge against Giselle, as she was partly responsible for landing us in this mess. When she'd tried to steal and destroy the Moonbeam without caring that I needed it to wake up Cori, she'd ended up falling into the portal the Moonbeam had opened. While the mages had already been searching for her house, the blazing bright light the Moonbeam had created had been a dead giveaway of our hiding place.

"As I said, I'm considering all the evidence," said Lord Smyth. "However, I'd like to offer you the chance to speak with your sister."

"On what condition?" There must be a catch. There always was, with people like him. The mages saw everything as a transaction.

"Only that you tell me the truth. What do you know about the Moonbeam?"

"Not enough," I said honestly. "I didn't even know it could create portals until Giselle fell through one."

"Conveniently."

I bit my tongue, frustrated to have ended up on this subject again. Yes, I'd admittedly tried to repeat the process for Astor when the mages had broken the door down and I'd wished desperately for the Moonbeam to send him somewhere safe. But there was no guarantee that wherever the pair of them had ended up was any less perilous than a house swarming with angry mages.

"I really don't know how it works," I repeated. "I learned from Malkin himself that it can control shifters against their will and also boost their abilities." Not exactly true. It was Giselle who'd told me that, but it hardly mattered now. And I hadn't told him that the Moonbeam might hold the key to finding the other dragon shifters, because I didn't even know what that meant. Perhaps the portal was actually a link to the dragon shifters' home, if such a place hadn't been destroyed a long time ago.

But Malkin implied they were still alive.

I shoved the thought out of mind. Malkin would say anything, tell any lie, to gain the desired effect on his target, whether that were recruiting a new hunter or taking away my last hope of finding my fellow dragon shifters.

"I really don't know anything, sir," I repeated, when Lord Smyth said nothing in response. "If I knew how the Moonbeam worked, I wouldn't have fallen victim to its mind-controlling effects, too. And if Astor hadn't helped me break free of the Moonbeam's spell, you and I wouldn't be having this conversation. We'd likely both be dead."

I didn't need to tell him the specifics. Like how Astor had had the bright idea of *kissing* me in order to bring me back to my human self. I had to maintain some dignity after I'd been stripped of almost everything else.

Lord Smyth looked at me for a long moment, as if weighing up the honesty in my words. "In that case, you may come with me."

He opened the cell door again and beckoned for me to follow him down a corridor whose grey walls had an odd purplish shimmer that gave away the wards built into the surface. Mages didn't always flaunt their power, but it was always present, overlaid with the general aura of wealth and prestige. The Mage Lord had presumably figured out I could snap handcuffs and locks with my bare hands, so he didn't bother restraining me, assuming I'd be too sensible to run.

We passed by a group of black-cloaked mages. Their suspicious eyes followed me, projecting disdain and mistrust. Most mages didn't particularly like shifters. Old prejudices remained, and while they didn't want to hunt us into extinction like the hunters did, they made no effort to stick their necks out for us either. Of course, none of them had ever met a dragon shifter before, and I was pretty sure the Mage Lords had no idea whether to view me as a threat or an ally. Maybe that was why they'd decided I was better off locked up out of the way.

My dragon side raged at the injustice, but the burning desire to see Cori stayed my hand. Ahead, a room beckoned, bisected by glass, and on the other side of the glass sat my baby sister.

Not so long ago, we'd have almost looked like reflections of one another, albeit seven years apart in age. Her bright hair was freshly brushed and bounced past her shoulders, but mine was chopped shorter, and while my roots were already lightening to auburn, the black dye still hid most of the original colour. She looked healthy, unhurt, and not as dazed and shaken as she'd been when she'd awoken. Maybe she'd lost a little weight since being stuck in a coma for weeks, but her smile was practically radiant. It made me want to smile too, despite the circumstances, but the glass prevented me from hugging her as I wanted to.

I'd taken care of Cori as long as I could remember, and I had no doubt that I'd been her protector even during the years missing from my memories. She and I had both had no recollection of the years before we'd arrived in London, carrying nothing but the address of a safe house for shifters, and a notebook containing the little information we knew about our fellow dragon shifters. A notebook that was, to my knowledge, in the mages' possession. As if they hadn't taken enough from us already.

I swallowed my anger and smiled back. "Hey, Cori."

"Hey, big sister." At her grin, tears pricked my eyes. So many times, I'd been afraid I'd never see her smile again. Even after we'd rescued her from certain death in the Orion Stronghold, she'd been comatose and unresponsive for weeks, and we'd had to rely on spells and potions to keep her alive. When I'd finally snatched the Moonbeam from Malkin, I'd literally held her life in my hands, knowing if I screwed up again, I'd lose her forever.

Now she was awake and alert, despite it all. Everything else fell away, including the mages standing guard behind each of us, as I leaned forward until my forehead brushed the glass. "You've no idea how glad I am to see you. Have any of the mages talked to you so far?"

"Sure, they asked me a bunch of questions." Her smile faded. "It sounds like you got yourself into a boatload of trouble while I was out cold. I can't believe I slept through all that."

"Malkin used a powerful drug on you." I hadn't been able to ask about her experiences in the Stronghold yet, and I bloody well hoped the mages hadn't interrogated her about it. She'd been through far too much already. "I don't know how much the mages told you about—well, everything."

"A lot, but I bet half of it was bullshit."

I sucked in a breath and choked on it. "*Cori.*"

"What?" She cast a brief look at the mage behind her, who was studiously pretending not to pay any attention to us. "They didn't order me not to give my opinion. And besides, I don't believe anything a single person says about you that I haven't heard from your own mouth. So, I assume it's all lies."

"Er..." She wasn't *wrong,* and doubtless the mages' account had fudged the truth on more than one occasion, but I'd also skimmed over some details in my own account, too. "If they told you that I stopped Malkin from bringing a shifter army to attack London, that part's true."

"Oh, I believed that." She flashed me a grin. "Because obviously."

I warmed inside despite my lingering worry that the mages would reprimand her for calling them liars. "Before that, we were trying to figure out where Malkin was hiding. We knew the only chance to wake you was—"

"The Moonbeam." Her gaze flashed to the man standing behind me. "Yeah. And the mages *stole* it."

The mage cleared his throat. "It was not stolen. The Moonbeam was not your possession to begin with."

"Technicalities." Cori scowled. "It's not right to lock us up for taking back something that originally belonged to the dragon shifters anyway."

"That's, erm, not why they locked us up." Not the only reason, anyway. "You do remember what happened right before they came into the room, right?"

"Oh." Some of the certainty faded from her expression. "Yeah, the mages asked me a shit-ton of questions about that, and I have no clue what was going on. Looked to me like someone fell into a hole in the floor."

"A portal."

"Astor." She pushed back from the table, bafflement flitting across her face. "I remember his name. I also remember he shot—"

"Cori."

She closed her mouth. Blinked a couple of times. "Uh. He *was* a hunter, right?"

"Ex-hunter." I'd known we'd have to have this conversation eventually, but I really didn't want to do it with the mages listening in. "It's a long story, but he quit the League two years ago and helped us get into the Stronghold to find you."

Confusion clouded her vision. "Are hunters even allowed to quit?"

"Nope. He's wanted dead by both sides, and since he escaped on my watch, the mages decided that we're all to blame." I glared pointedly at my guard. "It's unfair to punish my sister for this, you know. She didn't know any of that was even happening."

"Actually, Ember, they're thinking of letting me go." Cori's teeth worked over her bottom lip. "With conditions. The mages think I can help them find the hunters, since I got to see some of their workings from the inside."

"Shit. Don't do it, Cori. They don't have a clue what the hunters are really capable of." The mages had got a glimpse of the hunters' forces, but they hadn't seen the inside of the Stronghold, nor the ocean-bound fortress they'd turned into their new base.

If the mages dragged my baby sister into danger again, to hell with this. I'd burn them all.

Whoa there, dragon. Where had that thought come from? I'd been cooped up for too long. I didn't want to kill the mages, however much they'd inconvenienced us, and any violent notion I entertained was born of frustration and not reality. I'd been an absolute saint during my captivity, all things considered, but cooperating was the best way to keep Cori safe and for all of us to get the hell out of here as fast as possible.

Cori frowned. "I'm old enough to make my own decisions."

"Cori, they think we're criminals. And they don't know the hunters like you and I do. Malkin… if he lived, he's still out there. He wants me dead."

Her eyes widened. "They said you killed him."

"I wish." I grimaced. "I burned down the warehouse while he was on the roof, but he's a slippery bastard, and I bet he had a few tricks up his sleeve."

"You breathed fire, huh." Her grin was back. "Wish I'd seen."

"Wasn't even the first time." I managed to smile back. "Bet that's why the mages don't quite know what to do with me. Because I might accidentally burn the place down."

She snorted. "You would never."

"I would too." Since her captivity, I'd had a lot of practise at shifting back and forth between dragon and human, enough that the mages would have been lucky to have me as an ally. If I hadn't deceived them.

But the mages would never be our salvation. Of that I was sure.

"Ember, Coriander," said Lord Smyth. "Your time's up."

"It's only been a few minutes," I protested.

"I'm afraid there's an urgent meeting all mages are required to attend in due course. I'll escort you back to your room."

"Huh?" I winced as he pulled me to my feet by my upper arm. "That's not necessary. Ow."

He looked almost apologetic—perhaps he'd thought I was more resilient in my human form than I was—but he didn't let go as he hauled me back towards the cell. Mages rushed up and down the corridors, and the tantalising scent of fresh air wafted through from an open window. Well, air as fresh as you could get in London, anyway.

"What's going on?" I asked. "Not the hunters?"

His lack of response made me turn my head to look at him. "The hunters? Did they attack again?"

"No. From what I gather, we found some of them ourselves."

"You found—" I stumbled when he abruptly let go of me, all but shoving me into my cell again. I fought the urge to shove *him* out of the way to see what was going on, but he was already turning away.

"I have to leave," said Lord Smyth. "I'd ask you not to cause any trouble in my absence, Ember."

"But—" The door to my cell slammed on my protest. "Dammit."

I'd hardly had half a conversation with Cori, though it was a miracle I'd got even that much when she'd clearly been showing zero respect to the mages. Not that it didn't serve them right for locking up an innocent teenager.

And now they were trying to *bribe* her, offering freedom in exchange for repeatedly reliving one of the worst experiences of her life. I'd been through several interrogation sessions myself, in which I'd explained everything I remembered about the escape from the Stronghold. Now that jail was abandoned, the information was all but useless to the mages, but since they hadn't been able to find the hunters' new fortress, they were reduced to asking the same old questions.

Twenty minutes crawled by, in which I amused myself by bouncing a rolled-up ball of paper across the cell and doing handstands against the wall like a kid confined to their room. The mages had offered me a few books, but I was too wound up to focus on the pages. Right now, the only book I wanted to see was the notebook that Cori and I had brought with us to London. The mages had had no right to take it.

I startled at a knock on the door. When nobody entered, I went and peered through the small barred window at the top. "Who's there?"

A green light flickered, and the half-faerie, Kit, smiled at me through the bars. "Hey, Ember."

"Kit. What are you doing here?" I'd half-wondered if my friends might try for an escape at some point, but since we hadn't coordinated a plan before our capture, I hadn't held out much hope.

"This place is weird, isn't it?" he remarked cheerfully. "The walls are purple."

"That'd be the wards. They let you out?"

He nodded, strands of black hair falling into his eyes. "Yeah. They couldn't find evidence I'd committed any crimes, since I was unconscious for most of the action. I think I scared them. They let me go, after making me promise not to come back in."

I raised an eyebrow.

"I didn't have anywhere to go," he said unnecessarily. "So I never actually went outside the building. I glamoured myself and waited until everyone was gone before I came back in here."

Faeries. Unlike the Sidhe, half-faeries could theoretically lie if they wanted to, but most instead chose to deliberately interpret the words of a command in such a way that let them do the opposite. "We did break the law. No way around it. Until they find Astor, we're stuck here, and I don't have the faintest idea where the Moonbeam sent him. Have you seen the others?"

He shook his head. "I slipped in here as soon as the mages left. You're the first person I've seen."

"Why did the mages leave?"

"I don't know," he replied. "Whatever it is, it's urgent."

"Weird." We were supposed to be high-security prisoners, though admittedly the mages had used other methods to keep us caged that didn't require them to be present in person. "I don't suppose you can undo the wards?"

"No. Faerie magic has no effect on them. I've tried."

"Damn." I peered over his shoulder at the symbols etched on the walls, which promised a world of hurt to anyone who tried to break out. "Okay. Listen. Can you do me a favour and check whereabouts they're keeping my notebook? And the Moonbeam?"

"Oh, I know where the Moonbeam is," he said. "The mages keep trying to pass it amongst themselves, and arguing about why it won't work for them."

"Good," I said. "We don't need them using it on any shifters, even accidentally."

"No." He frowned. "It's odd. Malkin never mentioned the Moonbeam when he spoke to me in jail."

"He didn't?" I asked. "I guess he knew it wouldn't affect you, since it's made for shifters."

"Maybe." He tilted his head. "There's someone coming."

He disappeared. Or that was what it looked like to me, since glamour enabled faeries to hide themselves from anyone who didn't have the Sight. In other words, everyone who wasn't fae, which included the mages. Hoping he'd be able to get out without triggering any wards, I sat down on the bench and tried to position myself to look as if I'd been sitting there all along. Was Lord Smyth already back?

A rotting scent reached my nostrils. The smell of the dead.

2

I tensed, body alert as I listened out for approaching steps. My claws itched to slide out, and fire rumbled in my chest despite the warded door between me and my adversary. Nothing but an undead could be the source of the distinct rotten smell permeating the air through the barred window of the door.

There was a scream, followed by a flash of green light. *Kit.*

I let my claws slide out and slashed at the door's lock. The metal would have split underneath my touch if not for the wards overlaying its surface. As it was, an electric shock rang through my nerves, and a yelp escaped as I fell onto my back, red spots dancing before my eyes.

"Bloody mage wards." I jumped to my feet and had another crack at the door. This time, the impact flung me into the air and across the room. I hit the bed frame with a crack that bruised my elbows and brought a new starburst of lights across my vision.

I crawled off the bed, rubbing my sore back, and tentatively poked my claws into the centimetre-wide gap between the door and the wall. A mild shock zapped me again, but I gritted my teeth and refused to yield. *Come on. I'm a dragon. I can deal with a locked door.* The death-smell was worse than ever, and there was a sickening sound of something wet and heavy scraping along the tiled floor. Everyone knew that no living person could bypass the mages' secure wards, but did the undead count?

Cursing the door, I gave it a shove, earning nothing but a bruised elbow. "Ow. Kit, you okay?"

"No," he moaned. "There's a dead man here."

"I gathered. I can't get out the door without being zapped. Are there really no mages left in the building at all?"

"I don't know where they went."

"Brilliant timing." An undead wasn't an overt threat on its own, but they usually travelled in packs. "Can you check on the others? Make sure there aren't more undead near their cells?"

"Okay." He spoke softly. "Someone else is coming. I have to go."

Hurried footsteps rang down the corridor. My heart raced in my chest as I craned my neck, trying to see through the narrow window. Between the tiny gap in the bars, I saw a short, robed figure pause outside my cell.

"Hey!" I called out. "What's going on?"

The mage jumped a foot in the air. From what I could see, he was younger than most mages I'd seen, little more than a teenager. "That's what I want to know," he said, in an apparent attempt at authority. "You're the dragon, aren't you?"

"Yeah. Did you see the zombie?"

"Zombie? That's what tripped the wards?"

"Nothing else smells that foul."

"Hang on. I'll get someone."

He fled. Kit didn't return either, so I assumed he must

have hidden out of sight. Faerie glamour sure came in handy, but even he couldn't break down a warded door.

Neither could an undead, come to that, but a single zombie couldn't have wandered here on its own will. Mostly because the dead didn't *have* any will to speak of. With the veil between this realm and the spirit world unstable since the faeries' arrival, the dead sometimes rose of their own accord, but were effectively brainless. If one had walked in here with purpose, it meant someone had ordered it to, and to my knowledge, the only branch of supernatural with the ability to control the dead were the necromancers.

But why would a rogue necromancer send a zombie to break into the mages' jail? My first thought went to the Orion League, but the necromancers were social pariahs to such a degree that even the League didn't rank them as a real threat. They had guilds, same as the mages, but rather than running the supernatural community, their sole objective was to keep London's dead under control. As we'd all learned the hard way, building the Underground around old plague pits and burial grounds in a city with more dead people than living came with unwanted side effects when the veil between life and death went haywire as it had done in the faerie invasion.

I waited for the mage to return, but he didn't, and nor did Kit. After around five minutes, Lord Smyth opened the cell door, wearing a harassed expression. "My apprentice tells me you saw the break-in."

"Mostly I smelled it. Zombies are hard to mistake."

"An undead?" Lord Smyth glanced behind him. "Unfortunately, our security wards were a little too effective at taking care of the threat before it reached the lower cells."

"I don't follow."

"See for yourself. Come with me, and don't run. Keep an

eye on her," he added to the nervous-looking young man at his side. His apprentice, I guessed.

With most of the mages gone, it'd be easy to take my chances and leg it, but I wanted an explanation. And if the hunters really had been here, this might be my chance to win my way back into the mages' favour.

At the intersection between this corridor and the one that led to the floor below lay a bloody mess shaped vaguely like a person. On either side, gleaming wards shone from floor and ceiling, casting a lavender glow over the messy remains of the intruder. The apprentice pressed a hand to his mouth and looked away.

"*That's* what happens when you run into a security ward?"

The trespasser had dissolved into a puddle of goo. While the undead had already been on the brink of decomposition, I found myself fervently glad that I'd managed to hold my temper in check and refrain from shifting into a dragon.

"If you're an intruder intending harm, yes," said Lord Smyth.

"Someone must have been controlling it," I said. "An undead wouldn't wander in here by accident."

"Precisely." He gestured to his nauseated-looking apprentice to lead the way back down the corridor. "Unfortunately, you seem to be the only witness."

"Me, and the other prisoners." I'd gathered that my friends were imprisoned in a different part of the jail, though, and only shifters had the sharp senses that would have picked up on the intruder long before anyone else did. And faeries, I supposed. I hoped Kit had managed to stay out of the way. "Also, like I said, I didn't see the intruder. I heard it wandering down the corridor. Before it slammed into the ward."

"I see." He turned to his assistant. "Roger, go and tell the others that I'll join them in five minutes, after I speak to Ember."

Tension rippled along my spine. Either he'd changed his mind about letting me carry on with my conversation with Cori—unlikely—or he wanted another favour from me. "Is this about the intruder?"

"In a way." He paused for a long moment as we retraced our steps to my cell. "And also about your hunter friends."

My heart sank. "They aren't my friends."

Giselle certainly wasn't, but Astor…frankly, I wasn't sure a word even existed that accurately summed up our relationship. Allies, yes, but our fraught history ranged from 'mortal enemies' to a level of searing attraction that made it impossible to tell if what I felt for him was human desire or a more animal instinct that would latch onto any potential mating partner if my dragon side felt like it. Since we'd had no chance to talk one-to-one after our battle with Malkin, figuring out where I stood with him had never seemed further away.

Lord Smyth came into the cell with me and closed the door. After seeing the mess the wards had made of that zombie, I wasn't anywhere near as keen to try to escape, but I still gave the wards the evil eye on the way in.

"I don't know where the Moonbeam sent Astor and Giselle," I said. "I told you. There's no more information I can give you."

"It isn't about them," he said. "The truth is, we found three hunters dead in the river today."

"Dead?" I asked. "What, from the battle?"

"More recent. The bodies from the battle were destroyed."

Oh, yeah. The fire mages, as I'd recently found out, had the fun job of cremating anyone who died in the city so that their bodies didn't rise as undead.

Wait a second. I bit my tongue on my suspicion—I wanted to hear the rest of it—and asked, "How did they die?"

"We haven't been able to determine that," he said. "We assumed they drowned, but we found strange marks on their bodies."

My skin prickled. "Tattoos?"

"Not exactly. They appeared to be recent."

"Not claw marks? From a gargoyle, or from one of those shifters Malkin used the Moonbeam on?" Had the gargoyles finally figured out that it was the hunters who'd been killing them off and not my friends?

"No, the marks don't resemble those of a gargoyle kill," he said. "As to the shifters, none of the hunters' creations have been sighted in the area in the past few days."

That didn't mean the city was entirely rid of them, but it would have been nice to imagine the gargoyle gangs had found a new target that wasn't us. "Then what?"

"That's what we're trying to find out," said Lord Smyth. "Ember, I'd like you to be involved in this investigation. Given your history with the hunters, I think you could be an asset."

An *asset.* Like when they'd asked Cori to offer intel on the hunters in exchange for freedom. Seeing a way out, I chose my words carefully. "I can help, but only if you promise to let Cori walk free, and without forcing her to come back in and answer intrusive questions about her imprisonment. She's a kid. She doesn't deserve that."

Sympathy softened his expression. "We've treated her with care. She's remarkably resilient."

"She has to be. She's a shifter." My hands curled into fists. "That's my condition. Cori gets to leave."

His brow arched. "You aren't going to ask for the same for your friends?"

Annoyance flared inside me. "I would, if I thought I had

more of a chance of convincing you than the other dozen times I've asked. Would it help if I said that joining forces with two ex-hunters was entirely my idea, not theirs?"

"It would," he said, "but it's very apparent that the group of you tend to create trouble wherever you go."

I nearly said, *you let Kit leave,* but remembered I wasn't supposed to know. "I caused more trouble than they did. And Cori and Kit had no part in anything we did while they were unconscious."

"The half-faerie has been set free," he said. "And I'll do the same for your sister. Are you her legal guardian?"

"I'm not a legal anything. Her guardian died in the invasion. She's sixteen, which gives her the right to live alone." Not that I was keen on the idea of her roaming the city by herself. I hoped Kit would take care of her, but he wasn't exactly up to speed on the shit show that the city of London had become during the years he'd been the Orion League's prisoner.

"If you want to submit the paperwork—"

"I'm not signing anything." My claws itched to make an appearance. "Let alone with my legal name." Which was hardly legal in the usual sense. The notebook that had accompanied Cori and me to London had only listed our first names, so we'd both taken Rhea's surname, Jones.

"It was a suggestion, nothing more." He sounded vaguely insulted.

I tried to suppress my irritation. He just didn't know any better. "Shifters don't have a pleasant history with authorities. Human or otherwise. I didn't mean to be rude."

He nodded, his expression smoothing out. "Regardless of what your companions decide to do, I'd appreciate your help in determining how the hunters were killed and who was responsible."

"I can try." Starting with figuring out whether the hunters

who'd died were the ordinary human sort or the Elites. The latter were much harder to kill, but I'd taken down plenty myself. "Do you know if the bodies belonged to Elite hunters? They have more tattoos. I think." Most of the Elites' advantages were more visible when they were still alive, their enhanced speed and senses far surpassing regular humans and even rivalling shifters. And yet they refused point-blank to entertain the possibility that they were even adjacent to supernaturals.

"It's difficult to tell."

"All right," I said. "I'll have to get a closer look at the bodies to know for sure, but if they were killed with magic, Will's the expert, not me."

"I'll take that into consideration, but we have spell experts among our ranks, too."

That figured. Maybe I should have tried harder to convince him to let me involve my friends in the investigation, but walking down the prison corridor behind Lord Smyth didn't feel much like freedom. We climbed two staircases before we reached the main reception area.

Cori stood there, flanked by two mages. "Hey, Ember. Ready to go and look at some dead bodies?"

"Not you." I halted. "I thought they were letting you go. That was the deal."

"As if I'd miss this." She fired a wink at me.

I groaned. "Cori, I just agreed to help with a murder investigation so they'd set you free without conditions."

"It's not murder if it's one of the hunters," she said. "Anyway, I want to spend more time with you."

I thawed a little. I hadn't been overly keen on the idea of sending her out into the world without anyone to look out for her except a half-faerie who hadn't even been capable of taking care of himself until recently, and if the mages were distracted by these murders, we might get a much-needed minute to talk alone.

The mages steered her towards a car before I had the chance to break away from Lord Smyth and hug her. Once we were all inside the vehicle, Lord Smyth gave instructions to the driver, and we set off. The mages' neighbourhood was largely a mystery to me, a haven of well-kept streets and posh buildings all but untouched by the devastation that had swept across the rest of the city.

We reached a red-brick building and parked outside. The mages must have swept into a regular police station and taken over, because the entryway was filled with uniformed officers who looked like they weren't sure what to do with themselves. With their long coats and sheer presence, mages seemed to take up twice as much space as normal people did. I'd thought there were fifteen mages or so in the room at the back, but it turned out to be only six. The bodies were laid out on tables, to the clear displeasure of the regular law enforcement. As the Mage Lords were more or less the ruling class, they could evidently disrupt murder investigation procedures as much as they liked, but I doubted it was common practise. These days, the majority of supernatural murders went unsolved if not outright ignored.

Three bedraggled bodies lay before us, each on a separate table with the nearest encased within a warded circle. Lights shone atop the surface, and a female mage paced around the circle's edge, murmuring incantations.

"Lady Wu," said Lord Smyth. "Have you determined the cause of death yet?"

"Not yet." The mage stopped mid-incantation and watched our approach with curiosity. She was more than a head shorter than Lord Smyth, and her features suggested Asian heritage, while her obvious aptitude with the spell-circle meant she must be part witch on one side. Most mages had only one main talent, such as throwing fireballs or conjuring lightning. Witchcraft was less flashy but was more useful in situations like this. I peered at the spell-circle, wondering what Will would make of it.

"It's possible they drowned," added Lady Wu, "but given the volume of water in their lungs, we discerned that they were already dead when they hit the water. However, there are no obvious marks on the bodies pointing to the cause of death. Aside from the usual." She spoke with distaste, indicating the visible tattoo lines on the man's collarbone.

I didn't particularly want to get this close to a dead body, even a hunter, but Lord Smyth's mages stood behind Cori and me, preventing us from backing away.

"It's okay," I whispered to her. "You don't have to look."

"I'm fine." If anything, Cori approached the bodies with eagerness. "Piece of shit deserved it."

I'd had more than my fair share of experience of death, too. I'd never mourn a member of the Orion League, but there was something pathetic about these sopping wet corpses, entirely at the mercy of anyone who wanted to poke and prod at them.

I turned to Lord Smyth. "I thought you said there were recent marks on the bodies?"

"Yes." He nodded to Lady Wu. "Show her."

The witch-mage chanted something under her breath. There was a flash of light, and some of the marks on the man's pale chest lit up like neon paint. I'd never seen a hunter's tattoos up close before—even with Astor, I'd only seen fragments—and he'd never told me their meanings.

The hunter's shirt had been cut away, revealing an expanse of ink partly covered by a circular symbol that had ignited at Lady Wu's command and turned a vibrant shade of green.

"Huh." I peered at it. "What does that mean?"

"The mark is all but certainly supernatural in origin." Lady Wu waved a hand over the mark, and the glow dimmed. "But it wasn't made by a witch."

"Or a faerie." If it had been, the mark would be invisible to everyone without the Sight.

"I can hazard a guess," said Lord Smyth. "If these were ritualistic killings, that would suggest the work of a necromancer. Given that an undead tried to breach our security while we were here, I find the coincidence hard to ignore."

All the mages' eyes turned towards him, and a heavy silence fell over the room. Then Cori spoke up in puzzlement. "Who'd want to raise the hunters from the dead?"

"Good question." No guild necromancer would want to touch a League member. In fact, I was pretty sure they weren't even allowed to summon a ghost without a permit from the guild leader. A rogue, though? I swivelled to Lord Smyth. "Do you have contact with the guild?"

"We do." His gaze sharpened as someone else entered the room, and my heart sank at the sight of Lady Clare. As a mind-reader, she was the most dangerous mage to me on a personal level, being capable of extracting any secret from my thoughts that she wanted. That she'd also been responsible for landing me in jail in the first place didn't help matters either. A pale brunette who barely cleared five feet, she looked surprisingly ordinary for someone who could break your mind without batting an eyelid.

"It would be welcome news if the necromancers decided to take some responsibility for helping to clean up this city," said Lady Clare. "I can contact the guild myself."

"That would be most welcome," said Lord Smyth. "If they can identify these as ritual killings, it would save us a great deal of speculation."

"What was the point in bringing us here?" Cori whispered

to me as the mages broke out in a heated discussion amongst themselves. "Hey, I bet we can sneak out while they're arguing and they won't notice."

I shook my head. "Best not risk it. I'm still their prisoner."

Not that I was much use as a detective. I didn't know the first thing about ritualistic murders, and my knowledge of the necromancers wasn't extensive either. They wore long black coats much like the mages, which sometimes led me to get the two confused, but they lacked that aura of wealth and looked more like wannabe goths playing dress-up. I'd never talked to one in person.

"Ritual sacrifice sounds like the kind of twisted idea Malkin would find appealing," said Cori. "Maybe he's kidnapped a necromancer."

"Why?" Zombies were powerless on their own, though they could be a nuisance in large numbers. Malkin had already proved he wasn't above picking and choosing which forms of magic to use on himself, all the while denying he was anything more than fully human, but ritual magic was a mile away from the kind of technique I'd seen from the hunters in the past. Rituals meant dark magic of the kind that most witches and even necromancers didn't touch, the sort that involved meddling with arcane forces far beyond the comprehension of most people. Including Malkin. I'd thought he was more interested in shifters than the occult.

Shivers prickled my shoulder blades as I scanned the body, finding it hard to make out the circle now that the marks were no longer lit up. The inking within its boundaries looked a little like the glyphs used in some spells, and the circle had been broken by a shallow cut across the centre. Not deep enough to kill, but too precise to be anything but deliberate. A cursory glance at the others confirmed all three bodies were marked within the same manner.

"If they were sacrificed," I said, "then whose orders was the necromancer acting on, if not the hunters'?"

Lord Smyth stepped back from the table. "That's what I intend to find out."

3

Cori and I were sent outside to await further instructions, accompanied by two mage guards. The second we left the building, I wrapped Cori in a hug so tight, she squeaked in protest. "Ember! Can't breathe."

"Sorry." I loosened my hold a little. "You scared the crap out of me, Cori. I thought I'd lost you."

"Like I'd let a few bars get between us."

"I meant before. Everything else." The rollercoaster of the past few weeks, from her capture to her rescue and my subsequent desperate journey to find a cure to bring her out of coma, was impossible to sum up in a few words.

"And I missed all the fun because I was asleep." She wriggled out of my arms. "I'm fine. Better than fine, actually. I don't think I've felt this good since before the invasion. That Moonbeam is something else."

"Too bad the mages confiscated it." I glared at the two mages watching her, who studiously ignored me. "I sure hope it wasn't the hunters who sent that undead, given that it walked straight into the building."

"What, you think Malkin was trying to steal it back?"

That got the mages' attention, briefly, though neither of them said anything other than "Keep your voices down. That's for Lord Smyth to determine."

"He did bring us here." I couldn't get the marks on those dead bodies out of my head. Was Malkin meddling in a new kind of dark magic, now he no longer had access to the Moonbeam to set a shifter army on anyone he wanted to?

"Yeah, I don't get it," said Cori. "Guess we have more experience with the hunters than they do."

"They have all the necromancer contacts they need to confirm if this was ritual magic or not." I gave the mages another pointed look. "They don't need either of us. I've never even met a necromancer."

"I think I bumped into one in a station once," said Cori. "He smelled like grave dirt."

"Figures." I looked for Lord Smyth and spied him talking to another mage in the entryway. "You should take the chance to get out while you can. I'm sure Kit will help you while the rest of us are playing nice with the mages."

Cori scowled. "I don't know Kit. No offence to him, but I want *you*. You're not a criminal. The mages know that."

"Aiding a hunter is a crime. No way around it." A crime serious enough that it would normally merit far worse than a jail sentence. Like a one-way trip to an early grave. "I'll try to negotiate."

If I had any bargaining power left. I'd spent hours in my cell rehearsing arguments in my head, when I wasn't daydreaming about the thousand things I wanted to do when I walked free. Such as finding the other dragon shifters. The problem was, I was pretty sure I needed the Moonbeam for that—not to mention the notebook that the mages had taken away from me.

The dead hunters were way down on my priority list, but

the mages seemed to believe their deaths to have significance. It had taken long enough for them to notice the League was a legitimate problem, and it did not escape my attention that the Mage Lords had only seen the League as worth dealing with when the potential threat to their authority had become evident.

Lord Smyth came out to escort us to the car, ending our discussion. I fidgeted impatiently throughout the journey and suppressed a sigh when we drove to a halt in front of the jail. Back into prison again.

"I thought my sister was allowed to go free," I said as Lord Smyth took me back down the corridor to my cell. "I know we weren't much help, but I've never seen those hunters before. I don't know the first thing about necromancy, either."

"I'm aware of that," he said. "You'll both spend tonight in your cells, then tomorrow, we'll see if it's possible to offer alternative accommodation."

"To Cori? I told you we have a house." Or Will did. Granted, we hadn't stayed there since before the hunters had tried to torch the place, and Kit had never set foot in there at all, but it was the only option short of submitting to the mages' whims. Even if I was a little worried about a teenager and a half-faerie being alone on a street where some of the neighbours had tried to blame us for arson the last time we'd been there.

"Let me elaborate," he said. "I think that the circumstances call for a partnership."

"I told you, Cori isn't—"

"Not with your sister. With you."

My mouth parted. "Do you normally form partnerships with prisoners?"

"A trial," he said. "You'd no longer be a prisoner, but an employee of the mages."

I stared a little. How had he changed his stance so fast? Was he really that worried that the ritualistic murders were the precursor to another power grab from the hunters? That, or the undead trespassing in the jail had rattled him more than he let on.

Regardless, he was offering me a boon. I'd be a fool to turn it down.

"What about my friends? They have just as much to offer as I do."

Namely, not much, as far as expertise on ritualistic murders, but he didn't have to know that.

"I intend to make each of them the same offer, yes," he said. "And yes, thus far the evidence backs up your claim that you were the primary person responsible for the transgressions committed against the mages."

"It's true." Technically, I was the one who'd told him we'd lost the Moonbeam, as well as sending Astor away, but my friends hadn't been totally unaware of my intentions. Still, I was more than happy to take responsibility for my own choices. "If we're your employees, what does that entail?"

"Firstly, aiding in our search for the remnants of the Orion League," he said. "However, it goes without saying that if you see your hunter friend, you'll have to turn him in. If not, you'll find yourself back in this cell."

My heart sank. "I wouldn't have lied to you if you hadn't sentenced him to death without a trial. That might be a fair outcome for an active League member who has no remorse for any crimes they committed as a hunter, but he isn't that. If not for his help, I'd never have been able to destroy the Stronghold, and London would still be under attack by Malkin's shifter army. That's a fact."

"He also chose to work for the mages," he said. "He had the opportunity to come clean, but he didn't."

"Because you'd have *killed* him." Frustration boiled inside me. "And you never gave him the chance to speak for himself. Believe me, I didn't trust him at first either, but the Orion League manipulates their recruits to serve their own ends. Malkin used the Moonbeam to send a dragon shifter to kill his family when Astor was twelve."

Astor would be livid that I'd shared that with the mages, but dammit, I didn't know how else to make his story sound convincing. It wasn't even a lie. Astor had signed up to the League believing shifters to be bloodthirsty monsters who deserved to be wiped out, and the hunters had all been fed the story that it was their duty to exterminate all supernaturals. Then the faeries had attacked this realm, supernaturals had come out into the open en masse, and instead of taking them to war against the invaders, their fearless leader had gone into hiding underground. That had been the final straw for Giselle, but Astor himself had quit because...

Well. Because of me.

Our personal entanglements aside, what struck me the most about Astor's situation was that others had been trying to control his life from the outset. I knew too much about what it was like to be pushed around by forces beyond one's control. After everything he'd given up both for the League and to help us bring them down, he deserved a say in his own fate.

Lord Smyth's brow furrowed. "That's very hard to believe, Ember."

"You saw the Moonbeam's powers," I said. "I'm *not* saying all the hunters are innocent, not by a long shot, but they were manipulated and misinformed. Imagine if the only shifters you'd ever seen were those beasts that he set loose in London. Malkin created them for the sole purpose of indoctrinating the hunters into believing we aren't human, not even a little. They're essentially a cult. You wouldn't execute a member of the regular sort of cult on the spot for being brainwashed, would you?"

"If the person in question committed crimes, they would face the consequences of the law," he said. "Can you conclusively state that he won't attempt to fight against any attempts to arrest him?"

"If he wanted you dead, he'd have already tried to kill you."

I probably shouldn't have been so blunt, but I'd been doing my level best to be honest, if just so that I'd have some cover if he brought in Lady Clare to probe my thoughts again.

"Astor will be offered a choice, should we find him, and if he is willing to submit to a fair trial, he'll get one. Otherwise..."

He's dead. I could read between the lines easily enough. I understood why the mages wouldn't readily trust Astor, and admittedly, I didn't trust him *or* Giselle not to attack the mages if she showed up here. Giselle more than Astor. I mean, he'd gone as far as to take employment under the mages for the purposes of bringing down the League. That he'd deceived them in such a blatant manner was still a sore point with them.

"There's no law for ex-hunters," I pointed out. "Besides, he helped save the city. That's got to be worth consideration. He can also give you insider information on the hunters, and on Malkin. A lot more than I can. I was their prisoner, not their employee."

It might be unwise to make that promise on Astor's behalf, but I could see the shift in the Mage Lord's expression that told me he was starting to wonder if it wasn't worth keeping an ex-hunter around as an informant after all.

"*If* he is to reappear and is willing to cooperate, then we shall see," he said. "Are you absolutely certain you have no knowledge of where the Moonbeam sent him?"

"How can I know? I've been locked up since he fell through the portal. He might have ended up in Switzerland for all I know, so I doubt I'll be able to turn him in even if I wanted to."

Lord Smyth's lips compressed. "Be that as it may, you're responsible for his escape, and if you fail to turn him over, you'll both face punishment."

I folded my arms. "Okay, I get it. Just make sure the other mages know that I can't agree to hand him over if it means condemning him to death."

"I can't make that promise," said Lord Smyth. "Should he be offered a trial, the rest of the council will put his fate to a vote, and his past record doesn't stand in his favour. Even if they were to vote to imprison him, from what I've seen of your friend, he would never willingly submit to captivity."

That's what I'm afraid of. Astor was many things, but submissive was not one of them. Or sensible, or law-abiding, or anything the mages valued. "I'll talk to him. *If* I see him."

That was all I could promise. Hell, I didn't think Lord Smyth was a bad guy. He clearly worked hard to protect his fellow mages and maintain order in a city forever on the brink of splitting at the seams. Unfortunately, his rule-abiding tendencies would run up against a wall pretty quickly if Astor showed up again. I knew I couldn't turn him in one way or another, but once I got out of this cell, I had no intention of ending up back behind bars myself either.

"I hope you're being honest, Ember," he said. "For your sake and his."

I suppressed the growl building in my chest. "I am. And I'll try my best to help you, if you'll let me."

"Good," he said. "In the meantime, forget your friend. I'm

not looking to fight with you, Ember. You could be valuable to the Mage Lords."

Yeah. Like a useful tool. One who'd had enough of being left to rust. "Oh. I had another question?"

"What is it, Ember?" Lord Smyth asked, sounding weary. "If you're concerned about your friends, they will be freed tomorrow."

"Good. Thank you." It was hard to get the acknowledgement out, considering he'd killed my last hope of getting Astor off the hook. "It's more about something that was confiscated when you brought me in. Not the Moonbeam," I added hastily when his eyes narrowed. "There was a notebook. In my rucksack."

"Yes, it contained some curious writing."

Of course he bloody well opened it. Just when I'd started to relax my attitude towards him, at least where me and my shifter friends were concerned. "The notebook's of no use to you. It's important to me, though."

And it's none of your business, whispered my dragon side. The notebook was also the only clue I possessed about my history before Cori and I had come to London. The mages had no idea of its value, and while I didn't want Lady Clare poking around in my head, I couldn't help wondering if abilities like hers would be able to find out who'd erased our pasts in the first place, and why. And why some of the text had been written in the faerie language. Not much, just the inexplicable line that Kit had translated as, 'The rest can only be read by a true dragon shifter'.

"Yes, the notebook is your property. You can have it back. But the Moonbeam stays."

Thought so. "Of course. Have you figured out how to use it yet?"

"We're not the League," he said, a touch of sharpness to

his voice. "I have no interest in testing its power on shifters. As to whatever created that portal, we haven't been able to repeat it. Are you quite sure you don't know?"

"No, of course not," I said. "It just turned on by itself."

A lie. Cori had been holding it, and if the Moonbeam reacted only to dragon shifters, it would explain why Malkin had never used that ability either. That didn't mean he was unaware it was possible, as he'd had another dragon shifter locked up in the Stronghold for years to torture for information.

Regardless, if there was some kind of link between the Moonbeam and the dragon shifters, it was only a matter of time before the mages put two and two together. That knowledge didn't sit well with me, either, but I wasn't about to help them along.

"Maybe Malkin knows," I added. "That's why I was worried about him stealing it back."

He frowned at that. "Your worries are unfounded, though understandable. In any case, you'll stay here tonight, but don't think of yourself as a prisoner. You're free to leave your room, but I'd appreciate it if you stay confined to this floor to avoid tripping any wards. I'd also sincerely advise you not to leave the building."

So I'm basically still a prisoner, but with a corridor to walk in as well as a cell. I held my tongue, the taste of freedom tantalisingly close. "Okay. What about Cori?"

"The same applies to her."

"Thanks," I said genuinely. "I'll try not to accidentally break the law again."

"Or deliberately."

Okay, I liked him a little. But come on, was it too much to ask to be allowed to roam around of my own accord? To talk to my baby sister without mages hovering over my shoulder?

Just a bit longer. Then you'll be free. If this investigation didn't lead anywhere, I'd at least have another chance to win the mages over. Which was funny, because Cori was usually the one who wrapped people around her little finger, like she'd done to our guardian, Rhea.

A pang went through me. I hadn't thought about Rhea much lately, but now I found myself wondering what she'd make of my bargain with the mages. Rhea, the gargoyle shifter who'd taken us in after we'd arrived in London with no memories, had helped countless shifters by operating on the less-than-legal side of the supernatural laws. She'd had no love for the Mage Lords even before they took power. What would she think of us now, running errands for the mages and playing nice with the authorities who'd shown nothing but disdain towards our fellow shifters?

She'd be fine with it, as long as you're alive. These circumstances weren't in any way normal. The faeries' arrival wasn't the half of it. I'd do anything for Cori's sake, as I'd already proven when I'd walked into hell for her, and protective instincts covered my friends, too. Including Astor.

To keep Cori safe, was I prepared to turn Astor over to the mages? Even if it meant his death? I didn't know, but the thought kept me awake long into the night as I tossed and turned on my tiny cot bed, counting down the hours until freedom.

After all, for people like us, not all prisons had bars.

THE FOLLOWING MORNING, another batch of dead bodies washed up by the river. After the guards had brought me breakfast in my room, I was escorted out of the jail and to the entryway of the mages' headquarters. Cori was already there and Will and Becks arrived shortly after, thronged by four mages wearing the long-suffering expressions of people who'd had to spend the past twenty minutes listening to Will's jokes.

"Hey." Will grinned at us. "You guys ready to see a dead body or three?"

"Good to see you, Ember." Becks waved at me, looking more relaxed than I'd seen her for a while. Her medium-brown skin was free from dirt and blood, while her ombre-patterned light-to-dark-brown hair was newly washed, curling to her shoulders. And—huh.

"You got new glasses?" I asked.

"Yep." She beamed. "The prescription doesn't match, so I can't read very well, but it's better than tripping over things every few minutes."

"Really? That seems… generous."

"It's only right," Lord Smyth said. "We're not monsters, believe it or not."

"Some of us are half monster," said Will, and Becks prodded him in the arm. "Anyway, Kit's on his way. He said he had to run some errands."

At least he hadn't been hiding in the jail overnight. I'd been starting to worry he wouldn't leave until we did.

Kit arrived a few minutes later, also noticeably cleaner than before his imprisonment and his silky black hair even more striking. Together with his pointed ears, it would be hard to mistake him for a human, though he was shorter than average for a half-faerie and Will towered over him.

"The crew's all here," said Will. "Excellent. Where are these dead hunters?"

"The bodies are in a spare room," said Lord Smyth. "The human police were understanding of our need to investigate these deaths personally, as they were likely killed by a super-natural."

"How'd you figure that one out?" asked Becks. "What's the cause of death?"

"They had the same markings as the bodies we found yesterday. As you'll see for yourselves." He snapped his fingers, and the other mages swept out of the lobby.

Dramatic, much? The Mage Lords exerted a sense of absolute authority by their presence alone, and it wasn't a surprise to me that the human police had handed over the hunters' dead bodies without asking questions. As we followed Lord Smyth's lead down the corridor, Becks leaned close to me and whispered, "I'm glad you're all right. I figured they'd be harsher on you than us. I've been trying to convince everyone I'm a harmless house cat, and Will's the walking definition of non-threatening."

"I know," I said. "I figured they'd be wariest of me, given that I'm the only one who's breathed fire near to them."

"There's that, too," she said. "I don't think that means the rest of us are off the hook. We've just been on our best behaviour."

I raised my eyebrows in mock astonishment. "So you didn't turn into a cat and try to sneak out?"

"The wards are too sensitive. Not worth the risk."

"Considering they melted a zombie yesterday, you made the best choice."

"I heard about the zombie," Will said. "You saw it?"

"Not until it was in pieces, but I heard and smelled it first." I grimaced. "It walked right past my cell."

Becks shuddered. "Glad it didn't come near mine."

"Wonder how it got that far," Cori muttered, eyeing the wards gleaming on the corridor walls. "I'd say someone found a weak spot."

Clearly, the wards weren't attuned to every intrusion, whatever the Mage Lords claimed. The real question was whether the hunters had been the ones to send the zombie. The body had been in too much of a mess for me to be able to tell if it had been wearing their uniform, but I had to wonder.

We walked down a short staircase and into a room that had clearly once been used for storage. Boxes filled most of the space, some of which had been shoved back to make room for the wooden tables that had been hastily set up to accommodate the latest batch of dead hunters. Their pale flesh was marked with gouges like the tooth marks of a giant monster. One had his intestines hanging out. Ugh.

"Teeth marks," Becks observed. "Maybe one of their pets decided to bite back."

"Might be." I thought of our own narrow escape from a persistent kraken. "Guess it's not the first time Malkin's decided to feed someone to the sea monsters."

"No, but those markings are definitely not witchcraft." Will pointed to a hunter's waterlogged chest, marked with the faint outline of a circle. "Not a sort I'm familiar with, anyway."

"Has Malkin decided to take up necromancy as his new hobby?" asked Cori.

"Non-necromancers can't make ritualistic circles work," said Becks. "Right? It'd be like a non-witch trying to brew up a spell."

"Exactly," Will said. "Anyone can draw a circle and a few squiggly lines, but the hunters wouldn't know the difference between a ritual sacrifice and a witch's spell designed to turn you into a frog."

"We already know the League has worked with witches and gargoyles in the past," said Becks. "Maybe the necromancers were the only ones who'd pick up the phone this time."

"All of this district's necromancers are accounted for," said Lord Smyth. "However, I can't speak to those who operate independently to the guild."

"Nobody else could have done it," I said. "Unless someone's flaunting the guild's rules, I'd wager there's a rogue operating from the outside."

"A foolish one," Will said. "And one who knows full well what they're doing. You don't *accidentally* summon up a bloodthirsty spirit."

"Is that what the spell is for?" asked one of the other mages. "You seem to know a lot about it, young man."

"I'm a witch, not a necromancer," Will retaliated. "Witches have more sense than to screw with the spirits beyond the veil. Also, we have better dress sense."

The mages eyed Will suspiciously. I prepared to jump in on his behalf, but Kit chose that moment to bound up to the table. "There's no glamour on them," he announced. "Just in case you were wondering. I'd be able to see it."

From the mages' startled expressions, the thought hadn't even crossed their minds, and was yet another example of their tendency to overlook anything that didn't relate directly to their own branch of supernaturals. In fairness, I understood their wary reaction to Kit's tendency to appear and disappear at will whether he used glamour or not. Really, it was impressive how he'd bounced back from his encounter with the first undead, and he didn't appear bothered by the hunters' corpses, either. Then again, none of us were particularly sorry they were dead.

What worried me more was the possibility that Malkin was screwing around with supernatural forces he didn't understand. For that reason, we needed to find the source, preferably before our rogue necromancer did something dangerously irreversible. Ghosts and undead were the least of what the veil had to offer.

"Anything else?" asked Lord Smyth.

"Yes, I think we need to find the spot where they were killed," Will said. "Necromantic summoning circles are difficult to hide. They stir up dark forces whenever they're active, and I'd say our rogue isn't the sort to cover his tracks. An actual necromancer would be able to pin them down more easily, mind."

"There are thousands of ghosts in the city, and possibly even more undead," said Lord Smyth. "Tracking a disturbance in the veil might work in a smaller place with less history, but not London."

"Fair point," Will conceded. "We can still pin down the site of their death using a tracking spell. That's the best I can do, but I'll need some time to brew one up."

"We already have some." Lord Smyth indicated to his assistant to hand a spell over to Will. "We've tried four already, but you might be able to see something we didn't." His tone was doubtful, but it was clear that Will had the expertise here.

"I can try," said Will. "Should I try a spell on each body until I get a reading?"

"Start with one." Lord Smyth pointed to a clear spot on the nearby table, where dried blood had leaked from the corpse.

The spell, shaped like a band, expanded into a circle upon activation. Shimmering glyphs washed over Will's arms as he put his hands in the circle and leaned forward as if watching a screen visible only to him. Tracking spells were imprecise and lost their effectiveness with time, but the best way to track a specific person was to use a small piece of them like a strand of hair or a nail clipping. Blood was rarely used because of the ick factor, but the guy was dead, and adding his blood to the spell would enable any witch to watch the last few moments of his life. Or death, as it were.

After a few seconds, the circle collapsed into fine powder and Will took a step back, his gaze coming back into focus.

"They didn't die near the river." He shook bits of spell-dust off his hands. "They were dragged from somewhere underground before they were dumped into the water. The spell didn't show the moment of death, either."

"But where underground?" asked Becks.

"I don't know." Will's expression turned grim. "But I'm almost certain it was one of our tunnels."

4

"He knew," Will said quietly as we left the mages' headquarters shortly after. "If the mages already used four tracking spells, they can't possibly not have known the bodies came from inside a tunnel. I bet they know they're the same tunnels the shifters use, but they wanted to send us in there, so they don't have to get their own hands dirty. Literally."

"Sounds plausible," I admitted. "But hey, we're allowed to go and investigate on our own without the mages tailing us. I'd say the freedom's worth it."

"Not if we don't find somewhere new to live," said Cori. "They were talking about sticking me in an orphanage, seeing as I'm under eighteen."

I stopped walking. "*What?* You never said."

"I wasn't gonna bring it up in front of them," hissed Cori. "Also, they have someone following us."

I turned around to see a figure wearing a long coat slip out of sight behind one of those old-fashioned public phone boxes. Even *that* hadn't suffered any damage from the invasion.

"Of course they do." I dug my hands in my pockets, irritated with the mages for already trying to circumvent their promise to leave Cori out of any plans they might have for the rest of us. Maybe they'd made the orphanage suggestion before Lord Smyth and I had come to that arrangement, but still. I wanted to keep Cori safe, and letting the mages dictate her life did *not* fit that definition. "If they try to pressure you, let me know. I'll try to sort out our living situation as soon as they stop breathing down our necks. Unless you think we'd be safer in their accommodation than Magic Avenue?" I wanted to let Cori herself have a say in this, after all.

"You didn't think I'd say yes?" Cori hit me in the shoulder. "You should know me better than that, Ember. I'm staying with you. Even if it's in the gutter."

"Of course." A lump rose in my throat as it struck me again how fragile our freedom was, and how we were dependent on the mercy of people who hadn't given a shit about us not long ago. "At this rate, our tunnels are going to stay off limits forever."

"Typical," said Becks. "If you ask me, the hunters dumped the bodies in there on purpose. They don't want us to forget they know our hiding places."

"Yeah, I'm sure they couldn't resist," Will said. "From what I saw through the tracking spell, the guy was already dead when they dragged him out of there."

"I bet the ritual didn't take place too far from the entrance," I said. "I don't see the hunters dragging a corpse for miles through tunnels swarming with ghosts and undead."

Will had identified the tunnel entrance he'd seen in the vision as one we didn't use too often, mostly due to its proximity to the river. Because only two of us could fly—and we didn't want to risk running afoul of the gargoyles again— we'd opted to walk from the mages' part of the city directly to the waterfront. It was nice to have a little air after spending nearly a week in solitary confinement, but the stench around the river was the exact opposite of refreshing. Here, it was difficult to forget that the hunters had been smuggling witch supplies over the water on Malkin's orders without the mages being any the wiser. That they'd also killed any gargoyles who'd got too suspicious and left us to take the fall was another reason that I found myself wishing the hunters had picked somewhere else to conduct their creepy rituals.

I kept half an eye on the sky as we made our way closer to the river, a familiar tension clenching my gut when I spied a winged shadow below the clouds some distance away.

"They aren't looking for us," Will murmured. "I think Malkin's monsters scared them away from the river. They don't leave their territory as much these days, I've heard."

"Good," said Becks. "I'm sick of having to avoid half the city because of those bloody gargoyles."

"Me, too, and I'm one of them, technically," Will said.

Kit gave him a puzzled look. "I thought you weren't part of one of their clans."

"I'm not," said Will. "As a half-witch, I'd get beaten on all the time anyway. It wouldn't be worth it. Plus, they have *no* sense of style."

I snorted. "They have no sense of smell, either, if they used to enjoy flying around this place."

Granted, the air was a little more breathable in the sky, but it was hardly a tourist hotspot. Though we avoided the warehouse in which the mercenaries deposited the dead fae they picked up before the bodies were destroyed, the stench still reached us, and I kept expecting to hear the rumble of an engine. That the hunters had made a habit of stealing trucks full of dead monsters was the least of their depravities, and I shuddered to think of what purpose they'd used them for.

The smell eased off a bit as the river came into view and the usual milder stench took its place. Like most of our tunnels, the entrance by the waterside was hidden down an alley between two run-down blocks of flats that went more or less unnoticed by human eyes.

I reached the entrance first and manipulated the hidden panel that caused part of the brick wall to slide back.

"Ugh." Becks's nose wrinkled. "It smells like the dead in there."

"It does." Not that I'd expected any less. "Should I turn on the light spell or wait until later?"

"I can help." Kit glided ahead, his outstretched hands glowing faintly green. While the light wasn't as vibrant as a witch spell or a manmade creation, faerie magic was subtle enough that we'd still have some cover if something jumped at us out of the darkness.

I left the tunnel entrance open behind us as we walked into the gloom. Becks transformed into her cat form to act as our scout, while Will and Kit walked ahead of Cori and me. For a brief time, it was just like the old days.

Until we heard the screaming.

A high-pitched noise arose from nowhere and pursued us through the darkness like someone suffering horrific torture. Its owner appeared so suddenly that we all came to an abrupt halt. As the ghostly figure passed through all our bodies, still screaming, a horrible icy sensation trickled down my spine like someone had upended a bucket of ice over my head. Ghosts couldn't usually cause physical harm—not if the veil was functioning the way it should—but this one seemed determined to blast out my eardrums.

I reached into my pocket and grabbed the saltshaker Lord Smyth had given me before we'd left. It didn't work as well on ghosts as it did on undead, but just shaking it sent the ghost scooting away from me, uttering a final wail as it vanished through the earthen wall.

"That's one unhappy spirit." I kept the saltshaker in hand as we continued through the tunnel. "That wasn't the guy who died, I don't think. I bet the hunters hate supernaturals too much to even consider rematerializing as a ghost."

"I thought the necromancers were meant to be exorcising the dead from underground," said Cori.

"There's too many," said Will. "Kit, are you okay?"

The half-faerie had gone still, staring at the spot where the ghost had vanished. "She's *dead.*"

"Yes." Will sounded puzzled. "That's kind of the condition of being a ghost."

"She tried to deafen me," muttered Kit. "I don't like this."

"None of us do," said Becks, back in her human form again. "For god's sake, how are we meant to find anything down here?"

"If there's a big summoning circle with satanic rites scrawled all over it, I think we might have found our mark."

"Dammit, Will, this isn't funny," Becks said through clenched teeth.

Kit, however, cracked up laughing, the sound echoing off the tunnel walls. Will grinned at him.

"Shush," Becks said. "We don't want to wake the dead."

"Literally," I added. "How are you holding up, Cori?"

"I'm fine. You're being overprotective again." She squinted dubiously ahead. "I don't think there's a summoning circle around here. Will, is this definitely the right way?"

"There's only one entrance, and we haven't hit any forks yet," he said. "I couldn't see the details of the tunnel because it was too dark in the vision. Maybe we'll find some clues further in."

Becks swore quietly. "How far? Are the mages trying to get us killed?"

"Quite possibly," I said. "I mean, Lord Smyth is definitely fed up with me, but I don't see him trying to bump off London's only dragon shifters."

"Because we're such vital *assets*." Cori gave an eye-roll.

"He said that to you, too?" I lowered my respect level of the mages by another percentage point. "He should be glad we agreed to help at all."

"Yeah…" Cori trailed off. "Do you hear that?"

"Hear what?" The tunnels carried echoes of every step that all but smothered any other noise, and it took a moment for me to isolate the fainter sound of dragging footsteps somewhere nearby. "Ah, shit."

"Zombies." Becks all but tripped over her feet in an effort to get behind the rest of us. "We shouldn't have come in here."

"I'd say the living are more dangerous." I lifted the saltshaker again as a shadow appeared at the tunnel's end. Dragging footsteps followed, carrying a rotten stench, and the first undead shambled into view.

The most irritating trait of undead was that they didn't react to pain, and only salt could effectively neutralise them. Otherwise, they'd just keep going no matter how many pieces fell off them. Left to their own devices, they had no self-awareness to speak of, but a necromancer could order them to follow simple commands. Apparently, this one had been told to carry a knife. And so had the other three looming behind it, their rotting faces sunken inward and their flailing limbs jabbing blindly at anything in their paths.

I shifted my hands into claws and gripped the saltshaker awkwardly as I poured a line of salt onto the tunnel floor. It wouldn't keep them away outright, but it'd be much harder for them to gain the advantage if their feet rotted underneath them.

"Good thinking." Will threw a handful of salt and caught

an undead full in the face. It fell down, the salt eating through the flesh remaining on its bones, while Becks cowered against the wall, moaning under her breath.

Even with the first batch down, the undead kept coming. The glowing light from Kit's magic illuminated a wall of zombies between us and our destination.

"Where the hell did they come from?" My dragon's desire for bloodshed warred with my rational knowledge that outright physical attacks wouldn't do much to slow them down. Each of us only carried a single salt canister and we needed to reach the necromancer who'd called them back to life to put a stop to this. Assuming they were still in the tunnel.

The undead advanced on us, stepping on the corpses of their fellow zombies as they did so. Salt flew from my fingertips as I kicked an undead's legs out from underneath it, and Cori's foot stamped down on its skeletal arm. "Dammit, Cori, you were supposed to stay back."

"As if. I have weeks of fighting to catch up on."

I shook my head at her, but I knew I was facing a losing argument. Together we took two more dead apart, while Kit and Becks huddled at the back and Will attempted to fend off three zombies with a single salt canister. Cori and I ran in to help, my claws easily slicing off a zombie's head and my feet kicking at its legs. Brittle bones snapped, but its hands kept scrabbling at the ground until I stomped them flat. Bloody persistent zombies.

Cori brought down the second zombie, and Will kicked the third away. The undead went down in a pile of shattered bones, and another handful of salt took care of the rest.

"Is that all?" Kit asked tremulously. "I almost preferred the ghost."

"Believe me, this isn't how I wanted to spend today

either." I kicked the bony mass aside to clear a path through the tunnel. "Will, can you see the ritual site?"

"No, and I don't want to go any further, frankly."

"I can't hear anything up ahead," said Cori. "And if we turn back, I can guarantee the mages will use it as an excuse to give us shit."

"We didn't agree to clear out the tunnels for them. That's the necromancers' job." Not that the necromancers were known for being attentive to their duty. Moreover, from what I'd gathered, most weren't talented enough to do more than raise the odd spirit, and they'd be as easily overwhelmed as the rest of us if faced with a horde of undead.

That meant whoever had sacrificed those hunters had been uncommonly powerful. And while I'd be tempted to pin the blame on Malkin, it seemed an odd choice for the League to sacrifice their own soldiers when their numbers were dwindling already.

"Those aren't League members." I made my way around the twitching bodies. "That means they weren't part of the ritual."

They'd probably been drawn here by the disturbance created by whatever the necromancer had done. Since the faerie invasion had permanently screwed up the veil between life and death, any spell that touched the afterlife was liable to draw a horde of ghosts and undead from miles around.

"I still don't want to go any further," muttered Becks. "This is creepy as hell."

"It's also our tunnel." A surge of annoyance rose inside me. "What claim do the hunters have to it?"

"None." Will nodded in agreement. "As to the undead, it's not like this is the first time we've found them in here. I'd say we keep going."

"What?" Kit yelped. "Have you both lost your minds?"

"Probably," said Will in cheery tones. "But damn, I missed being underground."

I had, too, though I'd freely admit that it was probably weird for a dragon to enjoy walking in a confined space. The tunnels had always been our haven, a place that belonged to the shifters alone.

"Same," Cori said. "Fuck the mages. This is our territory."

Some of my resolve faded a little, but Cori had kind of had a point when she'd accused me of hovering over her. While I'd come a hair's breadth from losing her forever, she remembered none of it, and she was a fierce fighter in her own right who didn't need a babysitter.

No more undead materialised as we walked on, and after a few moments, I realised we weren't far from the entrance to Magic Avenue.

Cori brightened, recognising our surroundings, too. "We're going home?"

"Might as well take a look," Will said. "Though I'll raise hell if the hunters have set up a summoning circle in my house."

"House?" asked Kit. "I thought it was a shop."

"Both," said Will. "It's shut down at the moment because those dickhead hunters tried to set it on fire, but since it's the only non-compromised shelter we have, we'll have to set up base there."

"It's that or stay with the Mage Lords forever," I added.

"I don't think they want us to stay with them," said Becks. "They wouldn't have tried so hard to get us trampled by undead if they did."

"Yeah, but we'll have to report to them if we don't want to get on their bad side," I said. "And ask Lord Smyth for the notebook back. I forgot to do that earlier."

"He has our notebook?" Cori sounded indignant. "Why do the mages need that? It doesn't mean anything to them."

"He did promise to give it back." I slowed when we came into view of the door that led into Will's basement. A faint thud came from the other side. "Oh, hell. There's someone else in there."

"Hope it's a some*one* and not a some*thing*," Will said. "Ah, well. It's my house. I can throw out squatters if I want to."

"Not if they're undead," said Becks. "Hope they haven't swarmed Magic Avenue while we were gone."

Another scraping noise came from the basement. Tension rippled through our group.

"I'm going in. On three." Will took a step back, readied to run for the door. "One, two—"

The door sprang open, and someone came hurtling out into the tunnel. Will tripped back over his own feet and Becks shifted into cat form, leaping on the intruder. The man swore, hitting out at her. He wore dark clothes, his pale face was dirt-smudged, and strands of chestnut-brown hair fell into his curious green eyes.

"Astor?" I gasped.

Becks leapt off him and shifted into a human again. "What the hell are you doing in here?"

"Very good question." Cori glared at him. "This is *our* shelter, dickhead. Get out."

Astor scowled. "You're the ones who abandoned it."

"Shit, it's actually him," said Will.

"Dammit, Astor, you scared me half to death." I pressed a hand to my thumping heart. "What are you doing here? *How* are you here?"

"If you'd let me get a word in edgeways," Astor said, "I've been here since you sent me through a portal that dumped me several hundred feet underground."

"The portal took you into the tunnels?" I'd been thinking about sending him somewhere safe, but I'd never guessed that the Moonbeam would be able to open a portal somewhere I wasn't sure it had ever been. "I assumed you left the city."

"Chance would be a fine thing." A scowl appeared on his face. "This place is a bloody maze."

"She was trying to save your life, arsehole," Cori put in. "Don't think I've forgotten what you did."

Ack. I'd tried my best to fill her in on some of what she'd missed, but the last time she'd seen Astor before her recent awakening had been two years ago when he'd been clad in a hunter's uniform and trying to shoot at me with his gun.

Astor's jaw locked. "And just where have *you* all been for the past week?"

"In jail, where else?" Will said. "Since, you know, we let a wanted criminal escape and lied about it, and the mages aren't big fans of that kind of thing."

"You seem to be walking freely right now," Astor said. "All of you."

"Because we took on a job," said Becks. "Did you know the tunnels are swarming with zombies?"

"Yes." Astor pushed open the door to the house's basement. "It's lucky someone left salt in the cupboards. They've tried to break into the house at least a dozen times."

"The word you're looking for is *thanks*," said Will, as we crowded after him into the small basement. "I'm the one who left the salt in the cupboards, on account of this being *my house*."

"You haven't been here in weeks," countered Astor. "I had to throw away half the food before the stench attracted the dark fae."

"You've been tidying my house?" Will gave him a pitying look. "You poor assassin. You must have been bored out of your mind."

"Better than dead." He reached the ladder and placed a

foot on the bottom rung. "I had to fight off at least a dozen attacks from undead that came through from the tunnels."

"Sounds like a great party," said Will. "Housework and zombies. Please tell me you vacuumed as well."

"No," said Astor.

"Pity."

"Why," asked Kit, "are we talking about housework? I don't want the mages to arrest us for abetting a criminal."

"They won't arrest us," I said, "because we aren't going to tell them we saw him."

I'd never truly intended to betray Astor to the mages, but I also hadn't expected to run into him this soon. I'd assumed the portal had sent him far outside of London, and the sight of him had sent my thoughts into a tailspin.

"Did they really send you to clear zombies out of the tunnels?" Astor asked over his shoulder as he climbed the ladder.

"No, we were sent to find the site of a ritual where some hunters were sacrificed." I climbed after him. "Or that's what we think. Their bodies showed up in the river with necromantic markings on them, and a tracking spell led us into the tunnel."

"But all we found in there were regular zombies," Will put in, letting Cori climb the ladder first and then Becks and Kit. When Will had joined us, he closed the trapdoor behind him.

"Regular zombies are bad enough on their own," said Becks, with a shudder. "Creepy fuckers."

"Yet we didn't find the ritual." I looked at Astor, but he seemed oddly reluctant to look me in the eyes. "Did you see or hear anything while you were in the tunnels?"

"I wouldn't know what a ritual even looked like." He walked ahead through the short corridor. "Also, that door down in the basement isn't secure. I tried jamming it shut, but the undead got through anyway."

"We weren't followed." Will pushed open the door to the shop. Aside from the musty smell and the broken front windows, the house was in decent condition considering it had been abandoned for more than a fortnight. "It's safe to say the shop won't be re-opening any time soon, but we might just be able to salvage the shelter."

"Good," said Becks. "I don't care what the mages say, I'm not living on their charity."

"Nor me," I said. "They wanted to take Cori into care or dump her in a human orphanage, on account of her being under eighteen."

"Which is ridiculous," Cori cut in. "I'm old enough to live alone and work full-time, for crying out loud. Who even keeps tabs on these things?"

"The mages do." I followed Astor's lead into the living quarters at the corridor's other side, which consisted of a small kitchen adjoined to a living room laden with second-hand furniture. "Like everything else. Anyway, the hunters haven't been seen in the tunnels, right, Astor?"

"Not by me." He positioned himself against the back wall with the sort of sentinel-like countenance that only someone trained by the Orion League could achieve.

"Wait, isn't Giselle here, too?" That should have been my first question, really, but his appearance had thoroughly scrambled my thoughts, and the fact that he was acting like I was carrying a contagious disease didn't help my confusion. "I thought she was sent to the same place."

"Apparently not," said Astor. "I did look underground, but like I said, the tunnels are a maze. She might have ended up anywhere."

Not encouraging, and Giselle would be livid to find out the mages had got hold of the Moonbeam after all. "And you really haven't seen any hunters. Living or dead."

"I told you I haven't," he said with a touch of impatience. "As to this ritual, what exactly *is* its purpose?"

"I don't know, but anything that requires a human sacrifice is nasty business," I said. "Which kind of goes without saying, even if the people being sacrificed are hunters. Two groups of bodies have shown up in as many days."

If I didn't know better, I'd say he looked a little discomfited, but his default blank expression made it difficult to tell if my words had had any effect on him or not. A lot of people who were otherwise fearless had an aversion to the dead, even if they were a more common sight now than they were before the invasion. Like everyone else, Astor would have seen the ghosts flooding the city after the veil between this realm and the spirit world had gone haywire, but there hadn't been another incident on the same scale since then.

"It's either a rogue necromancer or some new trick of Malkin's," I added. "I can't say meddling in the arcane arts sounds much like his usual strategy, but we know he experimented on shifters, faeries, everyone he captured. It wouldn't surprise me if he had an interest in necromancy as well."

"Bearing in mind nobody but a necromancer can raise the dead," added Becks.

Astor's jaw clenched in irritation. "Maybe. I don't know. I never heard anyone mention necromancy while I was a member, and it's beyond me to figure out what he's been doing since Ember nearly torched him."

"You think he lived, then."

"Obviously." Now he met my eyes, hate simmering in his gaze. "Someone like him would crawl out of his own grave if possible."

"He's not the only one, given those zombies." Shivers prickled my arms. "I don't know where else to look if the ritual wasn't conducted inside the tunnel itself. Lord Smyth will have to send in the local necromancers if he wants answers."

"So you're going back to the mages?" Astor's tone carried a sharp edge, as if he dearly wanted to call me out for hypocrisy after I'd criticised him for doing the same.

"They have my notebook," I said. "I'm going to ask for it back."

"And the Moonbeam," added Becks. "Should we sneak in and rob them while we're there?"

"Hell, no," I said. "Did I tell you what the mages' defensive wards did to that zombie? I don't want to get liquefied."

"They do have the Moonbeam." Astor's eyes narrowed. "Of course they do."

"I wasn't kidding about the wards," I said to him. "They turned a zombie into paste. I wouldn't get within a metre of the Moonbeam without becoming a dragon-shaped print on the floor."

"The Moonbeam's safer with the mages than the hunters," said Will. "We have that going for us."

"Not much safer, if they figure out how to make it work," said Becks. "Besides, what if that undead was sent to steal it?"

"I wondered the same," I admitted. "But the zombie didn't even get close."

It made sense for the League to send an undead scout to test the mages' wards, and it undeniably worried me that it had slipped through at least one layer of security. Not enough to risk stealing it back ourselves—yet.

"Regardless, we should probably come to a consensus about whether we want to burn bridges with them or not," said Will. "I mean, if we don't mention Astor, we're running the risk of being locked up as soon as we set foot near that mind-reading Mage Lord who hates Ember so much."

"Mind-reading?" Astor queried. "It's true?"

"Yeah." My hands fisted. "Lady Clare. She probed around

inside my head to find proof of my innocence. I think she enjoyed it a little too much."

"Bitch," Cori said. "No, it's not worth trying to play nice with the likes of her."

"Doesn't mean we have to alienate the others either," I said. "We might have to fight alongside each other again before long."

The mages might not be our friends, but even I had to admit that it was the Mage Lords who'd held the rest of supernatural society together and saved humanity from absolute anarchy in the weeks following the invasion. Yes, their methods were sometimes questionable, but if Malkin succeeded in striking them down, the effects would ripple throughout the city and none of us would be spared from the fallout. Having the Moonbeam in their possession made it even more likely that Malkin would target them again, and soon.

"Get the notebook first," Cori said. "Then say we have our own plans and we don't need their employment. They can't argue with that."

"Except they know our address," said Will. "If the mages figure out we're moving back here, I wouldn't put it past them to send in a spy. They'll almost certainly be on the lookout for Astor."

"Right, of course. I'm their mortal enemy." A smirk twisted his mouth. "If they want to waste their time on the likes of me when they have a horde of genuine enemies out there, I suppose it's their prerogative."

"Seriously, they have all the resources and connections to make our lives a misery if they wanted to," I said. "They're the only people in the city who *can* legalise a supernatural registry. Our only saving grace is that they hate the League more than they dislike shifters."

"And they also hate being fooled." Astor's eyes gleamed

mockingly. "I'm sure that's at least part of the reason they'll be happy to witness my death."

"I talked Lord Smyth out of executing you on the spot," I said. "He said you'll get a trial."

"How very generous of him."

"I didn't say it was a fair offer. Only that I tried." Maybe I shouldn't have said anything at all. Seeking a change of subject, I asked, "Aren't you bothered about where Giselle went?"

"Not really. She knows what she's doing."

And she's probably safer out there. I'd have no problem turning *her* over to the mages, if it came to a choice between my friends and her, seeing as she'd pointed a gun at me and tried to destroy the Moonbeam before I'd had the chance to use it on Cori.

"Are we going back to the mages today?" Cori wanted to know. "Because it'll take a while to walk to their base, and we were supposed to report in this afternoon."

"I know." I worked my teeth over my lower lip, thinking. "Astor—"

"Don't bother," he said. "As I said, I can hide."

"Everyone seems to have forgotten this is *my* house," Will said.

I gave him a pleading look. "The mages want him *dead.* You let us stay, after the invasion."

"Oh, for crying out loud." Will rolled his eyes. "I don't give a crap if the assassin decides to hide in my basement. But if you touch my hat collection, Astor, I'll murder you."

And that was that. I was more worried he'd sneak out and make the decision for me, but the presence of my friends kept me from speaking openly to him. Not that I actually knew what I might say if we were alone, either. *I missed you? I'm glad you didn't end up transported across the globe? I promise not to let the mages kill you?* I had the distinct impression he wanted to hear none of those things.

He didn't even want to look me in the eye.

Never mind that. We had more important things to worry about. Like getting the notebook back without Lady Clare reading my mind and figuring out that I'd once again broken a promise to the Mage Lords.

5

———

Unease chased me down to the basement and back into the tunnels below the city. The mages hadn't sent us a cab, so we had to walk, and we'd voted on the tunnels as the quickest route. The general mood was optimistic, overall. Our old hideout was almost habitable, and we were the closest we'd been to rebuilding our lives in weeks. Oh, and we'd found Astor safe and unharmed. Yet his behaviour bothered me, and so did the knowledge that I'd thrown out my bargain with Lord Smyth within less than a day. Even though my alliance with the mages had always been a conditional one, I found myself wishing I'd promised them nothing at all. No reward they offered was worth Astor's life.

It always came back to him. No matter what I did, he was bound up in my life as surely as every one of my friends. However odd he'd been acting earlier, he'd chosen to stay at Will's house out of all other options, and the guy was so good at disappearing that he'd hidden under the mages' noses for weeks without them knowing who he was. He had no end of fake identities and could easily leave the city altogether if he got his hands on a car. That left two reasons he might have stayed: to find Malkin, and to find me.

Of course, there was one little-sister-shaped obstacle in the way of me asking which it was.

"Why?" said Cori, for at least the seventh time. "Why on earth would you put yourself at risk for *him?* I know I missed a lot of shit while I was asleep, but the last I saw, he wanted us dead."

"He quit the League two years ago, I told you." I was trying to be patient with her. I really was. "Not only that, but he worked against Malkin from the inside and helped destroy the Stronghold. I'd never have got you out of there without him."

The others might have backed me up, but Becks was scouting ahead in cat form to make sure there were no more undead, while Kit and Will seemed content to leave me to answer all of Cori's questions alone.

Her forehead scrunched up. "So what, he just showed up on the doorstep one day and you let him in?"

"Actually, we took him prisoner, thinking that he was working with the hunters who captured you," I said. "Like I said, we had something of a rocky start."

"Major fucking understatement."

"Language." I hoped the old joke would relax her a bit, but she scowled even more.

"You *do* remember how he sneaked into Magic Avenue and tried to befriend us, don't you?" she said. "This all might be part of another game. He's a professional-grade liar."

"I thought the same at first," I said. "Then I witnessed him take a bullet for me. Amongst other things. You don't have to like him, but he did help save your life. Not just in the Stronghold, but I wouldn't have been able to get my hands on the Moonbeam without his help either."

Her jaw worked. "I get the gist of what happened. I know

he helped you. But he… he's killed shifters. I can't forget that."

"I know he has." I'd always known this conversation, whenever it came along, wasn't going to be easy. "I'm not asking you to forgive him. Shit, I'm not sure I do either, but don't forget *I've* killed shifters, too."

"Oh—Ember, I don't care what *you* do. You're my big sister, and you'd never kill someone in cold blood."

Maybe I would. My dragon side's instincts were unpredictable, divorced from the rational human side of my brain. That was why I had a hard time judging Astor for his past when I knew damn well that had I been born human, I might easily have ended up in the same position.

"I've killed plenty of hunters without batting an eyelid," I said. "Astor can't undo what he did, but he wants nothing more to do with the League. You don't have to like him, but he's an ally."

It was unreasonable to expect Cori to accept Astor right away. She'd never give him up to the mages, I was sure, but guilt gnawed at me for making her complicit in my lawbreaking even if I hadn't had much choice.

I couldn't make myself not care about Astor. Not after what we'd been through together.

"All right." Cori grunted, pacing ahead of me. "I'll *tolerate* him. But if he's a dick to you—*ahhh!*" She cut off in a scream when a skeletal figure emerged from a side tunnel, pawing at her with a hand.

"Get the fuck away from my sister." I dug in my pocket for my salt canister while the others came hurrying back to join us.

"Zombie!" Kit yelled unnecessarily, as I took aim and swore when only a few bits of salt came out of the canister.

"Get *off* me." Cori threw her own salt in the undead's face.

Its papery skin melted off its skull, followed by its neck, and Will brought it down by kicking it in the back of the knee.

As the twitching corpse stilled, I recognised what it was wearing. Plain black clothing, topped with a jacket. A hunter's uniform. "Shit."

"Where in hell did that thing come from?" Will said.

"Walked out of there." I pointed to the shallow opening in the wall, which at a closer glance revealed a half-collapsed tunnel. "Or crawled. Anyone want to find out if there are more?"

"Becks can probably fit in," Cori said.

"God, no," said Becks. "I'd rather swim in the river."

"Me too." I shivered. "Another leftover from the ritual, do you think?"

"Should we take it to the mages?" said Cori. "At least then they won't be able to accuse us of shirking our duty."

"I'm *not* carrying a corpse around." Becks shuddered all over.

"Wish Lord Smyth had given us a tracking spell," Will said. "This guy's fresher than the bodies from the river."

"Yeah, true." Cori reached out and took hold of the zombie's decaying arm, which broke away from the rest of the body. "Ugh."

"Careful with that." I took the arm from her, revulsion rising in my throat when the arm twitched a little. "You know what, I think we *should* take it to the mages."

"I'll carry it," Will offered.

"No," said Becks. "You just want to use it to tap us on the shoulder while we're walking."

"Damn, am I that obvious?"

"Yes." I marched forward with my gruesome accessory. "Come on. We need to get back to the mages before this thing goes past its sell-by date."

"Think it already has." Cori mimed vomiting. "By the way, Ember, if you poke me with it, I'll put it in your bed."

"I'm not that mean." I was also already starting to regret carrying an arm that kept twitching as if it very much wanted to claw my face off. "Tread carefully, guys. There might be more of them. Cori, get in front of me."

"I'm *fine*," said Cori. "You can't treat me like a weak link forever."

"I know, but you scared me. Again." I was overreacting, I knew. She'd been through a lot, but she was resilient as hell. I was the one who needed reassuring, not her.

"Well, I for one don't want to stay in the dark and wait for more zombies to show up," said Will. "Right, Kit?"

"No!" Kit shuffled around him. "I don't think I want to carry the arm either, thanks. What if it tries to strangle you?"

"I'll keep it at arm's length. Get it?"

Everyone groaned. I glanced down at the arm and nearly dropped it when its fingers twitched as if it had somehow overheard Kit's comment. "Anyone want to volunteer to cut the hand off?"

"No," chorused four voices.

Great. I shifted my hands into claws and sliced the zombie's hand off. "Happy now?"

"No," said Kit. "It's cold, and I can hear whispering."

"That'd be the ghosts," said Will, with a grin. "I have a story—"

"Don't," I told him. "No ghost stories until we're rid of the zombie arm. Let's go."

"WHAT TOOK YOU SO LONG?" asked Lord Smyth expectantly, as we gathered around his desk in his ground-floor office at the mages' headquarters. It was the first time I'd seen his actual office; the manor house that served as the mages' main base had at least four rooms for receiving visitors, which seemed a bit excessive to me. Like the rest of the headquarters, the place was pristine, all wood-panelled walls and mahogany furniture and framed portraits of past Mage Lords watching imperiously from above.

"Zombies. To be precise, hunter zombies." I waved the hunter's dead arm at him. Lucky it wasn't crawling with maggots yet, though the smell was foul enough to make his apprentice take a step back, gagging.

Lord Smyth raised an eyebrow at me. "Is there any particular reason you brought that into my office?"

"To use a tracking spell," I said. "The trail we followed led to a dead end, but his body was fresher than the ones you pulled out of the river, so I figured he came from the ritual site."

"I see," said Lord Smyth. "Roger, go and ask Lady Wu for a tracking spell."

His apprentice scurried from the room with visible relief. As silence followed in his wake, I said, "Lord Smyth, you promised to give me my notebook back. I forgot to ask earlier."

"So I did." He opened a desk drawer and gave me the notebook, though he angled his grip so that our fingers didn't touch. Didn't want to end up smelling of zombie, I guessed. Though from what I'd seen, the mages used cleansing spells whenever anyone so much as sneezed in the vicinity.

"Thanks." I slid the notebook into my coat pocket, feeling more awkward than ever about hiding Astor's survival from him. At least Lady Clare wasn't around to read my mind and expose our lies. "You brought it here? Did you do the same with the Moonbeam?"

I probably shouldn't have asked so overtly, but I'd never

confirmed whereabouts they'd put their most valuable new possession.

"Yes, for now," he said. "In a few days, we'll be moving the Moonbeam to our secure storage facility. I think that's the best place for it."

Given the break-in, I mentally added. If he put the Moonbeam in some secret storage chamber known only to the Mage Lords, I could say goodbye to ever setting eyes on it again.

To my relief, Roger soon returned with the tracking spell and set it up on Lord Smyth's desk. I gladly put the dead arm down. Lord Smyth wrinkled his nose, but if he hadn't wanted to do this in his office, he could have easily said so.

Light flooded the desk as Will activated the tracking spell. He leaned in with his head bowed, watching the vision the spell showed him. When the circle collapsed into dust, he stared at the desk for a moment in apparent confusion. "Huh."

"Anything?" I asked. "Did you see the ritual?"

"No," said Will. "All I got were a bunch of images of dark tunnels."

So much for that idea. Lord Smyth looked disappointed, too. "Didn't you search thoroughly when you were underground?"

"We did, but the tunnels are extensive and a bunch of them have been out of use for years." Not a lie. Everyone knew which areas to avoid, but if the hunters had dug out their own route, we might need to probe deeper. Either way, undead hunters wandering underground stank of foul play. Literally. "What happened to the bodies from this morning?"

"They've been destroyed, naturally."

Good. "Have you contacted the necromancers' guild?"

"We did, but they said they can only use the veil to track ghosts, not the undead," he said. "They also claimed there's simply too much overall instability in the veil to be able to tell if anything out of the ordinary has taken place in the area."

That sounds to me like they're trying to wriggle out of any responsibility. Which fit with what I knew of the necromancers, to be honest. "Is there anything else we need to do?"

That was the politest way I could think of to ask, *Can we go home now?* Preferably without signing a contract of any kind.

Lord Smyth, however, didn't seem concerned at our lack of progress. "Come back to the office tomorrow. I'll let you know if there have been any more developments."

My mouth parted. I could see Will shuffling awkwardly from one foot to the other out of the corner of my eye, but if we backed out of the investigation, the mages would naturally conclude that we'd decided to reopen the shop. We couldn't afford for them to know we'd gone back to the Avenue until Astor was far away.

What a mess.

"I'm not sure we can be of much help," I hedged, cursing myself for hesitating. "Except pressure the guild to do more, and I doubt they'll listen to us."

"I'm sure it'll be of interest to your fellow shifters if the League is operating underground," he said. "Given the tunnel network you mentioned."

I'd told him the bare minimum, but he made a good point. I sure as hell didn't like the idea of letting zombies run amok down there, let alone turn my back on someone conducting necromantic rituals using the hunters' corpses.

"Okay. I'll see you tomorrow." If more zombies showed up in the night, the necromancers would have to take an interest, but after what I'd heard from Astor, I was a little concerned the dead would pay another visit to Will's house instead.

"He definitely just told someone to follow us," Becks muttered as we left the Mage Lord's office. "I saw him sending a text message when he thought we weren't looking."

"Sure he did," Will said. "Doesn't mean they'll be able to keep up."

"Uh, Ember," said Cori, glancing at my pocket. "Did I mention that I found out what that odd text in the notebook is? It's the faerie language. Kit told me."

"He told me, too," I admitted, "but you were still unconscious at the time. All it says is 'The rest can only be read by a true dragon shifter'."

"Uh, what?" Will blinked at me. "Do you not count as a real dragon shifter?"

Becks looked equally bewildered. "Who's supposed to be the judge of that?"

"No idea," I said. "I mean, the Moonbeam itself can only be used by a true dragon shifter, so you'd think that'd be enough proof for whoever wrote it."

"Wish we'd been able to keep it for longer," said Cori. "I bet it can help us figure out what the text meant."

"Yeah." I glanced behind us at the closed office door. "Wonder which room he put it in?"

"You don't think…?" Cori trailed off suggestively, her eyes gleaming beneath her overly long fringe. She needed a haircut. So did I, if just so I'd look a bit less ridiculous with my hair half red and half black. I was starting to wonder if I should forego the hair dye altogether, since everyone knew what I looked like now anyway.

"I don't think we should push our luck," said Will in a low voice. "I've spent enough time in prisons lately, and I want to get my house back before our grumpy friend decorates it with corpses."

"Shh." It was unwise to allude to Astor in any capacity

while within earshot of the mages. "Becks, what do you think?"

"I can have a look around. Will, did you bring a shadow spell?"

"When have I had any time to brew anything in the past few hours?" Will said. "Come on, let's go."

"But…" How many other chances would we have to slip into the room containing the Moonbeam? If it was due to be taken away in a matter of days, the only time we might see it again was if the hunters stole it back. Doubtless that was Malkin's exact plan, and there was no guarantee that the mages' secure storage facility was any safer than the jail.

Kit waved a hand, and the others all disappeared in a flash of green light. "There. We're invisible."

It was a good job there was nobody here, because the first thing I did was trip over Cori's foot and fall flat on my face. Wincing, I got to my feet. "Kit, can't you make it so we can actually see each other, like you did when we were in the car?"

"Never mind," Will said. "I prefer it this way."

Becks yelped. "Will, cut it out."

At a guess, he'd poked her or trod on her foot. "Guys, be sensible. Please."

I hoped the mages didn't have security cameras. I hadn't seen any so far, and technology and magic didn't always play nice together. Their wards were sufficient on their own, and were set to react to anyone the mages perceived to be the enemy. Which didn't include any of us… yet.

"All right."

Kit's glamour faded enough for me to see my friends, and Becks shifted into cat form and took the lead. We waited as she pushed against each closed door and peered into every room before vanishing upstairs.

She returned with a promising *meow*. Kit led the way upstairs to join her, and the rest of us followed.

We're not going to steal it. We're not going to steal it. I repeated the words in my head in case it helped, though I wasn't entirely certain how the wards sensed intent when they couldn't read minds like Lady Clare did.

Luck was with us, and we reached the upper floor without tripping any alarms. A wide, carpeted corridor beckoned, and Becks led the way to a half-open door.

"Wait." Will halted. "Someone's in there."

Sure enough, voices drifted out. My blood went cold when I recognised Lady Clare among the speakers. *Of course it's her.*

"I told you not to touch it," she was saying. "You're lucky it isn't warded like the cabinet is."

Curiosity got the better of me. I nudged the door open enough to slip through and found myself in a room full of glass cases and cabinets. Their contents gleamed invitingly, ranging from elegant jewellery to carved pieces of stone, but my eyes were immediately drawn to the faint white glow circling the middle of the room. The fist-sized piece of black rock inside the cabinet lay dormant, and Lady Clare stood glaring at a skinny male mage who looked about sixteen.

"I—I wasn't," the mage stuttered.

"You can't hide your thoughts from me," said Lady Clare. "You should know better."

"Sorry," said the mage sheepishly. "I was just curious. Are you really going to put it in storage without seeing what it does?"

"A team of mages has been assigned to examine it before we transfer it to the facility," said Lady Clare. "Not you. Your duty is to guard it until the others are here."

Of course she'd put herself at the head of that team. As if she had any right to meddle in our business. As her gaze skimmed over our location, I held my breath, hoping she couldn't hear my racing heart. At least I was reasonably confident that her mind-reading talents didn't work if she couldn't see the target. Out of the corner of my eye, I glimpsed Will backing away from the room and out of sight.

"Of course, Lady Clare," the mage murmured. "I didn't mean to disrespect you."

"See to it that you don't have any more lapses," she ordered. "If I find you touching that stone again, I'll have you replaced."

From her tone, I wasn't entirely sure if she meant in the security guard sense or as an apprentice. If the kid was *her* apprentice, I felt sorry for him.

There was a sudden crash, like the sound of filing cabinets toppling downstairs, and a flash of purple light outside indicated the wards responding to a threat. *Damn. I hope it doesn't see Will's pranks as on the same level as that zombie.*

The mage apprentice startled. "What was that? An intruder?"

"I'll take care of them." Lady Clare marched ahead, and her apprentice hurried behind. "Not you!" she snapped when they reached the door. "Go back in there."

He did so, but the instant Lady Clare was outside, Becks shot underfoot and tripped him. He fell sprawling, his gasp cut off when Becks planted herself on his face, preventing him from crying out for help. When Lady Clare's footsteps faded, she jumped off him.

The apprentice lurched to his feet. "What—?"

Becks gave him a shove, sending him tripping over the threshold out of the room. Once outside, the door closed in his face. Kit waved a hand, and a film of green light settled over its wooden surface, rippling like a curtain.

"There." He beamed at us. "I made the room soundproof.

It won't hold up if a stronger mage comes in, but we'll still be invisible."

"Damn." Cori eyed him with admiration. "I didn't know you could do that."

Becks meowed approval but didn't turn back into a human. She sat by the door, a clear indication that she intended to take over watch duty in case Lady Clare found a way back in.

I trod closer to the Moonbeam. I didn't quite dare touch it yet, but an impulse told me to take out the notebook. As I opened the cover, the Moonbeam's glow flared into life.

The book reacted, too. As the Moonbeam's light shone over the pages, they seemed to shine from within. I flipped through to the blank pages at the back and found to my astonishment that writing now covered them from top to bottom, shimmering in the Moonbeam's glow.

Cori inhaled sharply. "Can you see that?"

"Yes." I leaned closer to the page—and the world disappeared in a haze of light.

6

Cold air whipped past as my wings beat a steady rhythm. Below lay a fringe of snow-capped peaks. I'd never lived near mountains, but the undulating shapes nudged at my memory, like an image out of a picture book I'd had as a kid. Forbidding peaks that few humans would dare to climb were the perfect habitat for a dragon.

Wait… wasn't there something else I was supposed to be doing? Where was my sister?

At the thought, the low-lying clouds closed in around me, and the cold, clean air was abruptly replaced with London's thick smog while the mountains warped into Victorian terraced houses. My memories jerked back to the present, and I gasped, causing Will to almost drop me. I had no recollection of him picking me up. The last time I'd been aware of my own senses, I'd been crouched on the floor in the mages' headquarters, not being carried down a London high street.

"She's awake!" Will placed me down on my feet. "Unless you're gonna zone out again?"

"No." I shook my head, my head fogged. "Where's Cori?"

"She passed out, too." Becks walked up to us with Cori

draped in her arms. "We only got you outside because you were still hidden by Kit's glamour. The mages came back into the safe room. It was too risky to stay."

"Damn. Thanks for getting us out." What had I seen? A vision, or a memory? It had been like watching a screen, albeit through the eyes of a dragon. Not myself. I'd only ever shifted into a dragon while in London, far from any mountains, so whose eyes had I seen through?

Cori stirred in Becks's arms, coming to alertness. "Ember?"

"Here." I peered at her face and saw my own confusion reflected back at me. "Are you okay?"

"Yeah. How'd we get out of the mages' place?"

"Kit dragged you out of the upstairs room when the mages started swarming up there," Becks explained. "I went to fetch Will, and he came to help carry you out. It's lucky we didn't trip any alarms."

"Lucky," I repeated, looking at Will. "What did you do this time?"

"Well, firstly I knocked over a few cabinets," he said. "Then when I realised you weren't coming downstairs when the alarm went off, I may have put some adhesive on Lord Smyth's office door to stop him from following you."

"You did *what?*" I said.

"Relax, he didn't see me," he said. "He thought the door got jammed. There was some astonishingly creative cursing from in there. I'd have stayed to enjoy more of the show, but Kit was freaking out upstairs. He thought you'd died."

"You weren't moving," said Kit solemnly. "Your eyes were open, but it was like you weren't here."

"Oh." I thought back. "Shit, where's the notebook?"

"I put it back in your pocket," said Becks. "What even happened there? It's like both of you went into a trance."

"I think I did." Reaching into my pocket, I flipped open

the notebook and was greeted by a string of words on a page that had once been blank. Although the glow had faded, the text the Moonbeam had conjured was still there. I hadn't imagined it. I began to read. *I have hidden this text...*

"Whoa there." Will tugged at my sleeve, and I stepped aside as a small group of people came around the corner. Humans, teenagers by the look of things, packed together as though they might protect themselves from the monsters in the streets by sheer numbers.

Shoving the notebook back in my pocket, I faced the others again. "The Moonbeam made text appear on the blank pages."

"I saw it, too," Cori murmured. "It's still there?"

"We'll have a proper look when we're back home." Becks and Will were both watching us curiously, and Kit's pointed ears were pricked in alertness, too. None of them knew much about the notebook except that it was the closest thing Cori and I had to a guide for surviving as a dragon shifter. We'd rarely mentioned it otherwise, but if the Moonbeam had revealed unseen text, what else might the pages be hiding?

We returned to Magic Avenue via the same route as before, encountering no undead but plenty of rats. For once, I was glad to avoid a fight. My thoughts were a million miles away, soaring over mountains with my wings spread wide. Had I seen the present, or the past? Surely not the future— that wasn't possible for any supernatural, as far as I knew— but if the other dragons lived in the mountains, it'd explain why nobody had found them. Except the hunters, apparently.

Lost in thought, I startled back to the present when Will opened the door to the basement and revealed Astor waiting on the other side.

"You lot make enough noise to wake the dead," he

commented. "I was half convinced there *was* a horde of undead coming in."

"What have you been doing in here?" Will remarked as he followed Astor up the ladder. "Decorating again?"

"Looks more like fortifying." The door leading into the shop was entirely blocked by an armchair, which Astor must have dragged out of the living quarters. "You didn't see anyone suspicious outside, did you?"

"No, but I did hear a sound that distinctly resembled a gargoyle landing on the roof."

"And you didn't confront it?" said Will. "Doesn't sound like you. Do you even have any weapons?"

"Only what I was carrying before the mages swarmed into Giselle's house." He led the way into the living quarters, which he'd also rearranged, having dragged another armchair in front of the sole window. "We need to be ready for anything."

What's bothering him? I doubted he'd admit anything while the others were in earshot, and I had a more pressing mystery to solve. That of my own history.

I pulled out the notebook and placed it on the floor. A nervous flutter of anticipation went through me when I saw the others watching. It was a strange reaction—I kept no secrets from my friends—but reading words written by dragon shifters felt different. Intimate.

"Is there any particular reason you're all staring at a page?" Astor said.

"That text wasn't there before." I gestured to the shimmering symbols. "It's like the Moonbeam revealed it to us."

"Really?" Astor wore an odd look on his face. "Your eyes are glowing."

"They are," Will put in. "Cori, yours, too."

We looked at one another, my sister and I, seeing the

same white glow that mirrored the light of the Moonbeam. Then, as one, we turned our gazes back to the notebook.

Cori rested her elbows on the carpet. "The opening says, *If you're reading this, you've fully shifted into a dragon and have been entrusted with the secrets of our kind.* I mean, *I* haven't shifted, but I guess that's when we were meant to read it."

"Rhea always said when I shifted into a dragon, it would prove that I was ready to find the others," I murmured, with a twist of guilt. "I sometimes wondered if she was just trying to humour me."

"I mean, *she* couldn't read this." Cori's brow furrowed as she read on, and so did I.

I have hidden this text so that there is no risk that you should stumble upon these secrets before you're ready to seek us out again. However, I don't know how many of us will be left by the time you read this, and it's possible they may have already reduced us to extinction.

"They who?" Cori fidgeted. "Well, no shit. The hunters."

"Yeah." I read on.

In truth, it's too risky for me to share the full story even with the text hidden, in case this notebook should fall into the wrong hands. As it is, I will only say that I am deeply sorry for sending you away. It is unsafe for anyone who is too young to fight to survive among us any longer, and in truth, I grow increasingly pessimistic that there will be any of us left by the time you gain your fire. When that occurs, and if you wish to find us, go to...

There followed a name and address. "Samuel Birke. Doesn't sound like a dragon's name."

"His address is in London, so it can't be." Cori's head lifted. "That was it? All that secrecy for nothing but a name?"

"Looks that way." Part of me felt like a kid again, abandoned on a train with my baby sister in my care and nothing to guide our way but a notebook written by someone I didn't remember. I hadn't really expected to find any other text in the book at all, let alone to glean answers about our pasts, but somewhere deep down, I'd hoped for more. It didn't even sound like the other dragons *wanted* us to find them.

I let the book fall to the floor, my hand suddenly shaking with irrational rage at the writer for being so damn cryptic, for leaving us with more questions than we'd started with.

"Oh. There's more." Cori leaned over my shoulder. "I can see it through the paper."

I took in a calming breath and turned the page over. Sure enough, a few more lines had been scrawled mid-page as if the person writing it had been in a hurry.

I apologise for my vagueness, it read. *I fear the enemy already knows our intention to send you away, and if you were to be discovered, all our lives would be forfeit. It would be better for you to forget about us until the opportune time.*

We might be on the brink of extinction, but the Orion League cannot eradicate us all. One day, we will rise, one way or another, and reduce them to cinders. Should you wish to join the fight, I look forward to the day you attain the true fire of a dragon.

I stared at the page. "Well, shit."

"Yeah." Cori ran her finger down the lines of text, her lips parted. "Damn. Wish *I* could shift."

"You will." It'd be a few years yet, though, and I was reluctant to drag Cori into the battle as she was now. Still, I saw no harm in seeking out this Samuel guy, if he'd survived the invasion. The person who'd written this text couldn't possibly have seen *that* coming.

"Let me get this straight," Becks said, having listened without commentary as we made our way through the text. "You have a name and address, but not belonging to a dragon shifter. And you still don't know where their hiding place is?"

"I think they were worried Malkin would get hold of the book before we figured out how to read it." I pushed to my feet, my knees cramping from crouching on the floor. "A fair assumption, since we needed the Moonbeam to reveal the text in the first place."

"Yeah, *that* makes no sense," said Cori. "Malkin had the Moonbeam for years, right? How did they expect us to see the text without access to it?"

"Maybe Rhea knew." Certainly, her promise that I'd be able to seek out the other dragons when I learned to fully shift hadn't been an attempt to placate me after all. Shame seared me for doubting her.

Will cleared his throat. "What else did it say? Any clues about who wrote it?"

"Only that they were a dragon shifter," I said. "Someone who thought it was unsafe for Cori and me to stay with them as long as the League was a threat."

"No shit," Cori said. "Who'd want a couple of kids running around with the hunters shooting everyone on sight?"

"Isn't that exactly what they were doing in London, too?" You'd think the others would have known that the League was *always* a threat to shifters, no matter where we went. "It's *worse* here, with the Stronghold right next door. Why the hell did they send us to London, of all places?"

"Because it's the easiest place to hide?" Becks suggested. "You don't lose your mind at the full moon, either, so it's not like you'd give yourself away to humans. And the underground network in London is second to none."

"Before the faeries, this was one of the safest places for shifters in the country," Will added. "You two would stand out like beacons in a small village."

"That's right," Kit said, having watched our back-and-forth silently. "They were in every major city, too. That's how they got me."

"All right," I relented. "I wonder how the Moonbeam fits

in, then. It seems to react specifically to dragons, but it's not like we can take it with us to see this Samuel guy."

"Why not steal it from the mages?" Astor asked. It was the first thing he'd said since Cori and I had opened the notebook.

"Because they have wards that can melt a zombie?" Will said.

"Only if you intend harm," Astor corrected. "You already got your hands on it once."

"We didn't touch it," I said. "It was in a sealed cabinet. It's too late, anyway. The mages are transporting it into storage soon."

Astor's tone was flat. "Then it'll be back in Malkin's hands by the week's end."

"Tell that to the mages, not me." It was a cheap shot, and it didn't surprise me when his eyes narrowed. I hadn't meant to snap at him, but the message inside the notebook had unearthed a positive treasure trove of old insecurities and questions that had plagued me throughout my teenage years. "Lord Smyth will have probably taken more precautions after the stunt we pulled earlier."

"Exactly." Becks yawned. "I don't know about you, but I'm done with the mages. I'd say we go to Lord Smyth tomorrow and officially cut ties, then go in search of this Samuel dude."

"I'd rather ghost the mages altogether," Cori muttered.

So would I, but if more dead hunters showed up—or their zombies—I would rather find out from the Mage Lords than by one of them breaking into the house.

In the end, we agreed to help Will set up some alarms and other defences around the house in case another gargoyle decided to land on the roof, and also laid out a line of salt behind the door to the basement to slow down any undead.

I also raised the suggestion of taking it in turns to watch the door in case of an intruder, but Astor stepped in and said he'd already been spending nights down there. I couldn't say I was keen on the idea of leaving him alone in the basement, but he was insistent, and after an already exhausting day, I didn't have any will left to argue.

Besides, this was the first night all of us had spent under the same roof since Cori had woken from her coma. I wanted to treasure that and spend time with my friends, especially if things turned bad with the mages and we needed to run. Then tomorrow, we'd seek out Samuel and learn the truth of where the other dragon shifters were hiding.

I only hoped the hunters hadn't found them first.

It took considerable effort to keep the guilt off my face when I met with Lord Smyth the following morning. We'd debated skipping the meeting altogether, but while no undead had burst into the basement during the night, I wanted to confirm if there'd been any new developments on our mysterious necromancer.

We piled into Lord Smyth's office with varying levels of apprehension, with the obvious exception of Astor. And Kit, who slipped away before we entered, perhaps in case we changed our minds about committing a robbery after all. Lady Clare wasn't anywhere in sight, but I didn't dare ask if the mages had moved the Moonbeam as planned or if it was still in its case upstairs.

"There have been no new developments." Lord Smyth looked and sounded incredibly tired. Possibly some of that was because he'd had to pry off his own office door after Will had sealed it shut the previous day. If *he'd* been able to read our minds, we'd have been screwed from the outset. "The necromancers are looking for anomalies in the veil, but the whole *city* is built on anomalies. Between ancient graveyards, plague pits, generations of bodies buried under our feet, it's impossible to isolate the site of a single act of necromancy."

"But you still think it took place underground," I said. "We did check, but there are other tunnels all over the city, and some have caved in."

"I see," he said. "The necromancers are running more tests to isolate the area that was likely used for the summoning, but the best we've been able to do is pin down a five-mile range."

"Five miles is still a long distance." Stating the obvious, maybe, but the tunnels were a maze, and I wasn't convinced that anyone other than the shifters knew how deep they went.

On the other hand, I'd come here intending to nicely talk our way *out* of employment with the mages, not get ourselves further ensnared.

"Yes, exactly," he said. "If you can think of any places you haven't already searched, it would be most welcome."

"I don't think we have." I took in a breath. "And I was thinking that there's not much we can do to help you with this necromancy business. We haven't been any use so far, really. It's a necromancer you need."

"You want to terminate your trial with the mages?"

He didn't say *already,* but it was implied. Really, I shouldn't feel this guilty. It wasn't like I'd signed a contract or anything. I hadn't even got paid yet. "I—"

"I was under the impression that you wanted to join forces to seek out and destroy the remnants of the Orion League," he added. "Which is our intention."

"I did, but the League isn't here. Or not in the open." I was doing a shit job at this, but I'd come in without the intention of burning bridges, and the mages were dangerous enemies to make. "I don't want us to waste your time, that's all."

I might have added *and money,* but the mages were loaded.

They could pay us a full salary for sitting on our arses all day and not even notice the difference. Which I might have considered taking advantage of, if I'd had less of a conscience than I did.

"If you want to earn your keep in another way, that can be arranged," he said. "We're currently engaged in a clean-up of some of our supply rooms here in the headquarters, and we'd appreciate any assistance in sorting through the rooms' contents."

Supply rooms? He couldn't mean the one containing the Moonbeam, surely.

"You mean your spell supplies?" Will guessed. "I can tell which spells are expired or broken, if that's what you need."

"That's what I had in mind, yes."

He wasn't serious, was he? I looked to the others, but Cori was grinning, and Becks wore a neutral expression that usually signalled boredom or indifference.

"Cool," said Will. "We'll start right away."

As Lord Smyth's office door closed behind us, I caught Will's elbow and hissed, "What are you doing?"

"Some of these spells are rarer than gold," he muttered back. "I want to see how they work."

"We're not here to indulge your inner mad scientist, Will."

"Some of the spells might be useful," Becks put in, speaking in an undertone. "I mean, if nobody's going to check up on us, it might be worth slipping a few in our pocket."

"No," I said flatly.

"If they're broken, it's not stealing." Cori skipped ahead, and I suppressed a groan. *We're supposed to be finding the dragon shifters, not tidying cupboards.*

I kept a lid on my temper as we sorted through boxes of spells and Will declared which were usable and which weren't. I was pretty sure he smuggled a few into his pockets that weren't deteriorated in the least, but it would be much easier for the mages to replace them than it was for us to buy all the ingredients from scratch. Besides, stealing a few spells was the least of our transgressions.

"I'd say getting paid in spells isn't a bad deal," Will remarked as we made our way back through the tunnel to the house. "Some of these can be fixed with a bit of help. And others I've never seen before."

"You're lucky Lord Smyth didn't ask you to turn out your pockets." And luckier still that Lady Clare hadn't made an appearance. "Now we're done being unpaid interns, we need to go and find this Samuel guy."

"I looked up the address," Cori put in. "It's miles from here, on the other side of the river. We'd need to drive."

"Or fly." Since our only potential driver was Astor, I'd put our odds of him agreeing to this at fifty-fifty, given that we'd left the house earlier that morning on the assumption that we'd be severing ties with the mages. He would not be thrilled that we'd gone back on our word, even if it hadn't been my idea.

We found Astor waiting on the other side of the basement door. "Where exactly have you been?"

"Will decided he needed to raid the mages' stores."

His brows shot up. "You have the Moonbeam?"

"No," Will said, walking past him to the stepladder, "but we do have a significant collection of high-grade spells that might come in handy if the hunters are waiting at this dude's house."

"What?" I hurried after him, climbing the ladder into the hall. "Why would the hunters be there? Malkin can't possibly know who he is."

"Can you confirm that?" Astor queried.

"We're talking about people who are paranoid they can't even give us specific information in invisible text in case the hunters manage to read it," I said. "And it already can only be read under the light of the Moonbeam."

"We can't confirm that either," Astor said. "That's how *you* read it, but don't forget Malkin had another dragon shifter held at his mercy for years who might have given away their location."

My heart sank a little. He wasn't wrong, but the Moonbeam was ours alone, and it shouldn't have let Malkin access the same information. "We already know the hunters have been waging war on the other dragon shifters for years. That doesn't mean they found this Samuel guy."

Though there was a decent chance he'd been killed in the invasion, along with half the population of the city. The only way to know for sure was to go to his house and see if it was still standing.

"If I were Malkin, an informant with links to the dragon shifters would be one of my first targets."

"Malkin didn't even know *we* existed until two years ago." It seemed to me that Astor was just arguing for the sake of it. "Besides, it sounds like his new focus is amateur necromancy. We stand more of a chance of stopping him this way than by fishing bodies out of the river."

Astor's arms folded. "It's a fool's errand."

"You don't have to come," said Cori. "Some of us would prefer it if you didn't, actually."

"Cori." I nudged my sister. To Astor, I added, "This is personal to us. You can come if you want, but we're going regardless."

"If you want to drive, I'm obligated to play chauffeur, aren't I?" he said. "You can't be considering flying out in the open."

"Yeah, about that," said Will. "I don't have any shadow spells, and for some reason the mages don't have any in storage either. Guess they don't do much in the way of sneaking around."

"Not like they need to rob banks or anything," Becks said. "Well, shit. Ember, Cori, can you both fit on Will's back at the same time?"

"Nope." I turned to Cori. "You—"

"I am *not* staying behind," she said, sticking out her chin in true stubborn teenager fashion. "I'm owed answers as much as you are, Ember."

Dammit. "If I shift—"

"Oh, for god's sake, fine," Astor ground out. "I'll steal you a car. Again."

7

───────

Ten minutes later, we all piled into the small black car that Astor had procured. We'd chosen a tunnel exit at a safe enough distance from Magic Avenue that we were unlikely to be followed, and the lack of undead in the tunnel bolstered my nerves somewhat.

"Maybe Malkin has already ditched his new hobby," Will suggested as we got into the car. It smelled strongly of cigarettes and air freshener, suggesting it had recently been in use. At least it didn't belong to the mages.

I took the seat next to Astor, out of habit, and the others crammed in the back. Squashing four people into a seat made for three didn't make for a comfortable ride, though Kit opened the sunroof and kept up an ongoing commentary on any strange clouds he spotted. The others were silent, for the most part, including Astor. Any attempts I made at conversation hit a dead end. We had to take a circuitous route to reach the other side of the river to avoid the bridges that had been damaged in the battle with Malkin's shifters, and I held my breath all through the areas controlled by the gargoyles, too.

I breathed out a little when we reached the other side of the river. Astor seemed to know where he was going, to the extent that I almost forgot it was Cori and me who were supposed to be leading the way. The car slowed when we pulled up into a street lined with terraced houses.

"Doesn't look like the invasion made much of an impact here," I said, eyeing the neat gardens and roads free of debris.

"Maybe this Samuel guy has some secret talent that he used to fight off the faeries," Cori said hopefully.

"Nice neighbourhood." Will bounced out of the car first. "Hey, assassin, what are you doing? Put that gun away."

Astor had one hand at his belt, where I glimpsed a familiar metal sheen.

"I didn't know you kept that."

"It's loaded with fake bullets, but it still works."

Will scoffed. "You're more paranoid than whoever wrote Ember and Cori that hidden message."

I left the pair of them bickering and followed Cori through the narrow garden to the house.

After one knock, the door opened. A white-haired man peered out in a way that suggested he couldn't see very well. "Can I help you?"

"I hope so." I took in a breath. "Are you Samuel?"

"That I am." The old man looked down at us with an expression of vague bewilderment. "You look familiar."

Did that mean he'd met other dragon shifters? Hope stretched tentative wings inside my chest. "I'm Ember. This is my sister, Cori."

His expression showed no recognition of our names, and the tentative hope began to recede. He certainly didn't look as if he was in any position to fight off the hunters.

"Can we come in?" Cori asked. "We were given your address by someone we trusted."

"Rhea," I added, and this time I saw recognition flare in his rheumy eyes.

"Oh." He nodded vigorously. "Do come in. Are those people with you, too?"

"Yes. My friends will behave," I added hastily, as it sounded like Will was in the process of calling Astor an array of inventive names. "Come on, guys. Let's go in."

I regretted that decision as soon as I set foot in the hallway. The entire house appeared to be crammed floor to ceiling with antiques, and all of us except Astor tripped at least twice on the way to the living room. If there was any furniture in there, it was buried underneath a collection of trinkets ranging from crockery to ornamental animals. And spiders. Lots of spiders. I coughed when I inhaled a wave of thick dust, wondering how in the world anyone could live in this environment.

Samuel pottered around in the equally cluttered kitchen for a bit, and I accepted a mug of lukewarm tea and took a seat on the edge of a sagging sofa draped in enough hand-knitted throws to suffocate someone. My friends also sat, while Astor entered the room last. If I didn't know him, I'd say he was moving slowly to avoid knocking anything over, but it was more likely that he was checking every corner for hidden threats. Easier said than done. There could be a whole squad of hunters hiding under the crockery and we'd have no idea.

Samuel went to fetch a plate of stale biscuits, and I surreptitiously poured my foul-tasting tea in the nearest plant pot as I dug around in my pocket for the notebook. Figuring I might as well get straight to the point, I held it up and asked, "Do you recognise this?"

Samuel peered over my shoulder, his gaze clouded. "My eyesight isn't what it used to be, but it looks familiar. Am I right in assuming that you're the two dragon shifters who were sent to London as teenagers?"

Cori and I exchanged surprised looks. "We are," I said. "Does that mean you know the person who wrote this?"

"At one time." He put down the plate and sank into a seat. "Unfortunately, we haven't been in touch since the invasion."

"Who is it?" Cori said. "Wait, you knew Rhea, too? But you're not a gargoyle. Or a shifter. Are you?"

"I'm a witch," he said, confirming my guess. "Not a talented one, mind, but I had a gift for illusion, and I was entrusted with the means of contacting the dragon shifters some years back. I've been in hiding since long before the invasion, but the League wouldn't ever suspect an old man like me might be a threat to them."

Astor made a sceptical noise, which I ignored.

"You have the means of contacting the dragon shifters?" I leaned forward in my seat. "How? Where?"

"There's a slight problem." He rose creakily to his feet. "You'll have to come with me so I can show you."

As Cori and I stood up, I glanced over at Astor. He hadn't sat down, but his expression was as blankly dangerous as if he was about to cut someone's throat. Plainly, he didn't trust this guy, but if four shifters and a half-faerie hadn't picked up on any bad vibes or hidden threats, I figured he was just being paranoid.

Samuel led the way down a staircase so rickety that I worried his shaky legs would give way beneath him. The basement was smaller than Will's and instantly made me claustrophobic. Cori and I barely fit into the space, and the others didn't follow us at all.

Samuel reached a mirror that rested against the back wall, covered in dust and with a deep crack down the centre. "There was a quake the night the faeries came, and the glass cracked."

"You brought us here to show us a mirror?" said Cori.

"Not a mirror. A portal." He took in a quavering breath. "The other, its partner, was at the home of the dragon shifters."

My breath caught. "A portal... to the dragon shifters?"

A sigh caught in his chest. "I did try my best to fix it, but it hasn't worked since then. I heard tell of another object that carries the same properties, called the Moonbeam, but I was told that it was in the hands of the enemy, far from the dragon shifters' reach."

"The Moonbeam." Another blow hit my heart. And a question. If the Moonbeam also linked to the other portal, was that where it had sent Giselle?

"You know of it?" he said. "I'm afraid the Orion League stole it a long time ago, as far as I know, but it was said to be able to open portals to any location when held in the hands of a dragon shifter, not just between the mirrors."

I trod closer to the mirror, examining its surface, but the crack travelled straight through from top to bottom and thin lines spiderwebbed out in all directions. Nothing remotely magical caught my attention.

"It's not with the Orion League," Cori said. "The Moonbeam isn't. How else would we have read the notebook?"

Confusion furrowed his brow. "When you shifted into dragon form, how else?"

"We were supposed to read it *while* shifted into a dragon?" Nobody had told us that. Maybe Rhea had known, but she'd opted not to tell until one of us had achieved a full shift.

None of us had known that I'd only shift on the day of her death.

A familiar sorrow knotted my chest. We'd all thought we'd have more time than we did. So much more.

"Yes... does that mean you have the Moonbeam?" Hope shone in his eyes.

"We don't." I didn't need to give the details. "Are you sure the mirror can't be repaired?"

"It's possible…" He looked thoughtful. "If the Moonbeam was brought into close proximity to the mirror, their connection might be able to restore the portal to functionality. Otherwise, there's no other way to reach the dragon shifters' home."

The dragon shifters' home. My heart began to thump against my ribcage. *I have to fix it.*

"But you had contact with them?" Cori asked, a suspicious note to her voice. "Why should we trust your word? We'd be risking our lives in a major way if we tried to get the Moonbeam back. The League tried to kill us with it before."

"Your sister's sharper than you are, Ember," said Astor from the top of the stairs, making me jump and hit my head on the low ceiling.

"Dammit, Astor." I spoke between clenched teeth. "Do you mind showing some patience? This is important."

"Your friend can come in, if he likes." Samuel gave him a benign smile, but Astor glowered at him as he descended into the basement.

When he reached the bottom, I elbowed Astor in the ribs. Hard. It wouldn't kill him to try not being obnoxious towards someone who wanted to help us. I didn't make a habit of putting my trust in strangers, either but the person who'd written the text in the notebook had known Samuel, and the other dragon shifters were on the other side of that portal. If I believed him.

Samuel spoke again. "You don't have to tell me where the Moonbeam is currently located. And it's your choice if you want to try to fix the mirror."

"Is there really no other way?"

He shook his head. "These portals can only be used to their full extent by dragon shifters. Your kin created them, after all, and as far as I know, its partner is located in the only village in the world inhabited almost entirely by your kin."

It's true. My mind whirled. If he was right, then we could use the Moonbeam itself to get to the village without using the mirror… but that still meant trespassing in the mages' headquarters.

I looked at the mirror's dusty glass, indecision gripping me. I didn't know any experts in magical artefacts, but if it was truly unique among its kind, the odds of finding someone capable of fixing it were low. Which left us with one choice.

We said goodbye to Samuel without confirming our plan one way or the other. We'd need to talk it over as a group first, but the mages' intention to move the Moonbeam elsewhere put a time limit on our decision. Our other options were thin on the ground, short of living with the knowledge that we'd given up our last chance to reunite with our fellow dragon shifters and abandoned them to the hunters' wrath.

Astor hung back to give the old man one last glare before he closed the door.

"You." I hit him in the arm. "Next time, I'm flying here with Cori and leaving you to sulk in Will's basement."

"He's with the League."

I snort-laughed. "No, he isn't. I'd know if the hunters' stench was all over his house, trust me."

Will turned back. "What's the problem?"

"Mr Sceptical here insists Samuel is with the League and tricking us into thinking he's on our side," said Cori.

"What?" said Becks. "How'd he figure that one out?"

"Assassin logic," I said. "Trust nobody."

"I think it's a good principle to live by." Astor strode up to the car. "Malkin's been hunting down any link to the dragon shifters for years. What makes you think he's never used the Moonbeam to travel into that portal himself?"

I'd feared the same, but if anything, that only gave me more of a reason to find out what had become of the other dragon shifters.

"He said only a dragon shifter can use it to its full extent," Cori put in. "And the Moonbeam only opened the portal for Ember and me. Not him."

"That's right," I said. "Why would he have left Samuel alive if he'd already found his hiding place?"

"Because an elderly witch who collects old junk isn't a threat." He climbed into the front seat. "And because Malkin knew that he'd be the first point of contact for any new dragon shifters who arrived in the city."

"I mean, he's not wrong," said Becks. "I don't think Samuel's a villain, but I find it hard to believe the hunters never knew the Moonbeam was a portal."

"Maybe not." I opened my own door. "But I'm not going to assume he's out to get us with no proof."

"He asked for the Moonbeam back," said Astor. "If that's not suspect—"

"He thought the hunters still had it," I said. "And they did, until less than a week ago. Anyway, if he's right, we can use the Moonbeam to get through the other portal without coming back to his house at all."

We argued all the way back without coming to any real consensus. By the time we'd covered the winding route back to the house, our only agreement was that we needed to decide whether to take the Moonbeam regardless of whether we trusted Samuel or otherwise. To get away from the noise, Will went out on a supply run and came back with the news that half of Magic Avenue seemed to have heard about our role in the battle with the monstrous shifters. Or mine, at least, since I'd exposed my dragon form in full view of the city.

"The good news is that they don't seem to think we're the bad guys anymore," he said cheerily as he walked in laden with bags of spell ingredients, food, and other supplies. "The gargoyles are staying quiet, and it's hard to call us a bunch of evil arsonists when everyone who was watching the sky on that day saw Ember protect all of us from those shifters. Even if they didn't see her push Malkin off a roof."

"That doesn't mean we need everyone knowing we're back here," Becks said from the sofa. "And what of the gargoyle who landed on the roof the other day?"

"Maybe it was just a huge pigeon and Astor was being paranoid," Cori suggested.

Astor scowled. His mood had not in the least improved since our return from Samuel's house. "I know what I heard."

Will got some spells brewing, and we continued our debate over whether to go after the Moonbeam or play it safe, and when was the best time to avoid being seen. While it was easier to sneak around under cover of night, that was also when the nasty fae came out to play.

"Not in the mages' part of the city," said Cori when I mentioned this. "I bet that place is warded to hell and back with iron barriers."

"Good point." We could do it tonight. My reservations remained, but meeting Samuel had banished some of my guilt over deceiving the mages. I wasn't doing this for myself, but for the other dragon shifters. However well-meaning he might otherwise be, Lord Smyth couldn't ever understand. "We can go out later, if Will can get those shadow spells finished."

"I'm working as fast as I can," he said from the kitchen. "What will you even do once you have the Moonbeam, bring it here? You don't think the mages will show up at the door five minutes later?"

"Depends how long it takes them to notice it's gone." We'd have to be careful. "I know. It's not ideal. We could take it to Samuel, but…"

"But Astor thinks he's with the League," Cori said.

Astor himself did not contribute, but he'd made his opinion clear. We ran the risk of the mages chasing us down no matter where we went, but our first priority was to find the dragons on the other side of the portal.

"Can't you use the portal without actually removing the Moonbeam from their property?" asked Becks. "Like when you two went into that trance?"

"I think one of us needs to be touching it, like the last time," I said. "I bet their wards stop it from working properly, too. It wouldn't surprise me."

"They don't have a damn clue how it works," Cori muttered. "What else do we need? Anything we can use from the spells Will took from the mages?"

"I bet there is." Will paced to the middle of the living room and turned out his coat pockets, exposing a collection of pieces of what any ordinary person might assume to be expensive jewellery. "We have a sleeping spell—might come in handy—and a few spells that cause mild confusion. Oh, and cleansing spells."

"What for?" Becks raised an eyebrow.

"You never know. Things have a habit of getting messy when we're around."

That was true. "And explosives?"

"Already had plenty of those," he said. "I'll handle the diversions."

"I think I should go in first, as a cat," said Becks. "Just to make sure it's still in that room."

"We'll also need to undo the wards around the cabinet," I

added. "We didn't have a problem getting close to it, but if we'd tried to touch the case, we might've got zapped."

"We're dragon shifters," said Cori. "It's *ours*. And I think the Moonbeam knows that, too."

Astor gave a faint scoff that caused everyone to look at him.

"What?" said Will. "If you have a problem with our methods, assassin, you're welcome to leave."

"Hang on. Astor, can I talk to you alone?" Whatever his problem was, we needed it out in the open before we made any move to steal back the Moonbeam. I had a suspicion it went deeper than his dislike of the recent risks we'd taken, both with the mages and with Samuel.

I half expected him to refuse outright, but he shrugged and left the room without argument. I followed him out into the hallway and closed the living room door behind me.

"What the hell is wrong with you?" I said. "If it's about Samuel, we can use the Moonbeam without involving him at all. As for the mages, you never wanted them to take the Moonbeam in the first place. I thought you'd be happy we're claiming it back."

"I also don't remember advising you to take up employment," he said. "I never should have put the idea in your heads."

"It was that or stay in jail until they found your hiding place." I stared him out. "Also, it was Lord Smyth's idea to join forces. He didn't get it from you."

"It's not like you to willingly let yourself be manipulated."

"Excuse me?" I folded my arms over my chest. "I put my freedom on the line because it meant Cori was able to walk free. That was my condition, since he wouldn't agree to let *you* go. And if you expect me to choose between the two of you, forget it."

"Isn't that exactly the choice you're facing?" He gave me a

searching look. "If you go through that portal, the Moonbeam will be left behind, leaving the rest of us to deal with the consequences."

"Then come with us. It might be where Giselle ended up, too."

"That's exactly the problem—you don't know where you sent her," he said. "And now you're doing the same to yourselves."

"I'm not thrilled at nobody giving us a straight answer either, you know, but that doesn't mean you need to take it out on everyone else. You're not exactly endearing yourself to my little sister, either."

"She doesn't trust me, with good reason. I expected no less."

I ground my back molars. I'd anticipated the same, but it was no less frustrating to witness. "It's not just that, you're being an arsehole for no reason. And I know for a fact you aren't just staying here to keep yourself safe from the mages, so—"

"It was my being employed by the mages in the first place that got you into this mess."

I stared at him incredulously. "What? You think it's your fault?"

"It *is* my fault. They'd never have known the Moonbeam was out in the open if not for—"

"Me. *I* told them, because they wouldn't have taken Malkin's threat seriously otherwise." I met his eyes defiantly. "And I'm not sorry for it. We'd have died otherwise."

"Malkin wouldn't have set the shifter army loose in the city if I'd caught him sooner."

"You're determined to take the blame for this, aren't you?" I said disbelievingly. "I didn't agree with your decision to work for the mages, but that's ancient history. It doesn't matter."

"I trusted Giselle. That's what I regret."

There it was. The real source of his disquiet. Giselle's actions had led to our arrest—and he blamed himself.

"We all trusted her, too. Provisionally. I left my *sister* with her."

"And I didn't see the obvious. She hated the Moonbeam. She mentioned it needed to be destroyed more than once."

"I wouldn't have minded as much if she'd let us use it on Cori before she flipped out," I said. "I didn't know it was a portal at the time, did I?"

"No, but it wasn't her decision to make," he said. "I knew how volatile she could be, but I let you take shelter with her regardless."

"That's not your fault." I had to make that clear. I never thought I'd ever see him doubt himself. I'd assumed his hunter training ensured he never let emotions get in the way of his judgement, but that was before he'd left.

Before he met me.

I moved towards him until our bodies were inches apart, close enough for me to hear his rapid breathing. "You said once before that I got under your skin. That doesn't make you responsible for everything bad that happens to me, whether it be at the hands of the League, the mages, or your questionable friends. I make my own choices."

I brushed my lips against his. I half expected him to draw back, but he returned the kiss in a brief moment of connection that nevertheless sent a buzz of electricity through my nerves.

All too soon, he stepped back. "We don't need to traumatise your sister."

"She's resilient. And she's going to have to learn to like you at some point."

"Isn't that up to her?"

"Yes, but *I* like you, and she knows I have good taste."

"You like me."

"Against my better judgement. Why? You knew that."

"I don't think you've ever said it aloud." He glanced at the living room door. "I don't expect the same of your friends. I'm not a team player. I never have been. I was taught to look out for my own survival above everything else. All of us were conditioned to work alone and leave our dead behind. Friends were not an option."

Except Giselle, but mentioning her would not help my argument. "Well, my friends like you." At his obvious scepticism, I added, "Kit was terrified of hunters when you met, but he's fine being around you now. Becks sees you as an ally. And I can tell Will to stop calling you 'assassin', but he gives pet names to people he likes. He called me 'fire-breather' when we first met."

Astor followed my gaze to the door. "I won't argue with you. But I can't go with you. The mages' wards respond to threats, and I can't think of the mages as anything other than our enemies."

That was fair. "I hope they don't think the same of us."

"You really think you have to do this."

"What else do I do, give up on the other dragon shifters?" I shook my head. "The League is still hunting them, Astor. What if Malkin found his way there? I *have* to know they're okay. They're all I have left of my family, aside from Cori."

His expression smoothed to blankness. "Then I won't stop you."

My heart dipped a little. Maybe he thought I'd chosen the other dragon shifters over him, but that wasn't it, at all. "I'll try not to get caught."

I expected Astor to slip away after stating his intention to stay behind, but he came back into the living room with me. The others watched him curiously, as if wondering what we'd been discussing.

"Good, everyone's here," said Will. "I give it an hour until the shadow spells are ready. I'm only making two, but Kit can use glamour on anyone else."

"Astor isn't coming," I told him. "Since the mages' wards will see him as the enemy. I'm not sure they won't do the same for us as soon as we open the cabinet. Will, do you have anything that might help us unlock the door?"

"I have a spell that can dissolve concrete," he said. "That's not what it was originally meant to do, mind, but I accidentally found out when I dropped it on the floor earlier. It was one of the mages' broken spells."

"You think it'll work on the cabinet locks?" I guessed.

"Or the entire cabinet," he said. "It doesn't seem picky. And I have five different improvised neutralisers you can try on the wards once the cabinet's open. Failing that, you could always stick your hands directly onto the Moonbeam and hope that your scary dragon powers let you take it out of the cabinet intact."

"Scary dragon powers," said Cori with a snort. "Might work. We're doing this tonight?"

"We'll have to," I said. "Then, I don't know. I really didn't want to burn bridges with the mages."

"Getting burned is an occupational hazard for anyone who chooses to work with a dragon," said Astor. "The Moonbeam isn't their property, and they should know that. It's yours by right."

Cori looked startled. The others were clearly surprised, too, but not one voice of dissent spoke as we gathered our things ready for the mission.

My thoughts churned, my heart pounding in my chest. I was so close to finding my fellow dragon shifters. More than I'd ever been before. To step into the Moonbeam's portal was to leap into the unknown. To a world I'd only dreamed of, but that had haunted my entire life.

I was ready. Cori and I were both ready, to find the other dragon shifters, and to go home.

8

We reached the mages' part of the city under cover of darkness, encountering few other people on the way. We had to take a couple of detours to dodge roaming fae creatures, including a pack of bloodthirsty redcaps lurking in a disused tube station. As soon as we reached the mages' corner of the city, the streets became notably clearer, but my apprehension only grew with each passing moment. When we neared the street where the mages' headquarters lay, the smell of smoke tickled at my nostrils.

"Is it just me," said Cori, "or is something…?"

"On fire?" A strong breeze brought a stronger whiff of the burning smell. "Yeah. And it's not one of ours."

We resumed walking and I soon saw the flames issuing from the hands of two mages standing at the roadside. Nearby, lightning crackled over the roof of the mages' head-quarters. A storm raged further along the street, upending buckets of rain on top of what at first glance appeared to be a large hulking statue. When it moved with a slow, mechanical grind, recognition set in.

"Automaton." I hadn't seen one of those things for a while. "Guess someone else got here first."

The hunters had come for the Moonbeam, yet I didn't see any uniformed individuals behind the giant mechanical warrior. Maybe they'd sent it to break the doors down first, but in doing so, they'd unintentionally done us a favour. By drawing some of the most powerful mages outside, we had an open route into their headquarters.

I reached for my shadow spell. "Ready?"

"Do we even need a diversion?" Will said dubiously. "I mean, I'd be happy to contribute to the chaos, but I don't think it's necessary. If we go in through one of the side doors, I bet they didn't even turn on the wards."

"I'll check the Moonbeam's in there first." Becks shifted into cat form and ran towards the manor, returning within moments with a meow of confirmation.

Go time. "All right. Tread carefully."

I directed this mostly at Cori, who rolled her eyes at me. I hadn't seen Lady Clare yet, after all, and she was the mage who was the most dangerous to all of us.

I moved towards the headquarters, switching on my shadow spell. It had an hour's use, so I'd have to move fast to make the most of being unseen. As most of the mages had assembled at the front, we crept down the side of the house until we came to a small door. Like Will had guessed, it was closed but not locked; the mages had dashed out of all the building's exits at once to deal with the threat.

I reached for the door first, feeling the hum of wards against my fingertips. "It's warded."

"No problem." The door began to emit a buzzing noise, but the sound swiftly ceased with a sputtering noise that sounded like Will had set off one of the neutralising spells he'd brought. Hoping he saved some for the cabinet, I held my breath as I crossed the threshold into the manor.

Mage wards lit the carpet up in blue and purple streaks, but nothing on the inside reacted with more than a faint buzz. I still moved quickly, trying to touch the floor as little as possible as I followed Becks's soft footsteps to a stairway to the upper floor.

Nobody was upstairs, but a new layer of shimmering wards covered the door to the room that contained the Moonbeam as well as a padlock.

"Anyone got a lockpick?" Cori whispered.

"Let me try." I reached out a tentative hand and felt the buzz of resistance as I tried to push. "Right. I have one unlocking spell."

Will had the rest, and I had an inkling that a single spell wouldn't cut it against the wards. Sure enough, the lock clicked, but the door still refused to move inward.

"Will." No response. Had he gone elsewhere to create a diversion? "Becks?"

A faint meow from the stairway told me she was keeping watch. I kept pushing at the door, but the wards refused to give. Mage wards responded to intentions, and we didn't mean them harm, but that didn't mean they'd allow thievery.

We're trying to protect the Moonbeam, I thought firmly. I was strong enough to kick down a regular door, but the wood might as well have turned to stainless steel for all the impact I made. A frustrated growl caught in my throat as I kept pushing at it, and then I took a startled step back when Will popped into view.

"Gotcha." He held up a stick-like instrument that resembled a wand, the sort used by stage magicians and not actual witches. "I thought Lord Smyth would leave this lying around. *His* office is much easier to get into. I think he had to take the wards down when I sealed the door shut."

"Shh," I whispered. "What even is it?"

"Spell detector." Will prodded the wand against the

wooden surface. "It's supposed to reveal and negate minor hostile spells, so I thought it'd tell me what's blocking the door."

"And does it?" asked Cori.

He peered closer. "Ah, shit. It's a permanent seal. My guess is it's set to turn on every night so nobody can get in after dark, mage or otherwise."

"So what do we do, wait until morning?" The mages would never leave an opening like this again. If I didn't know better, I'd have suggested the hunters had been trying to do us a favour by setting the automaton on them. "There must be an off switch."

"I have one." Kit appeared in a flicker of green and lifted an object that resembled a blockier version of the wand-like instrument Will held with buttons that put me in mind of a remote control. A single click of a button and the door's surface shimmered purple, then turned back to solid wood.

Will's mouth fell open. "What *is* that?"

"I saw the mages using it on the wards in the jail." Kit sounded extremely proud of himself. "I had time to sneak around after they let me go and figure out where they kept it."

"When did you plan to tell us that?" Will shook his head. "You're a marvel."

Kit flushed brick red. "If I'd known we might need it, I'd have mentioned it sooner."

I cleared my throat. "C'mon. Let's get in there while we can."

This time when I pushed open the door, I encountered no resistance. The various cabinets were still locked, but I had eyes only for one. The Moonbeam sat bathed in pale light which swiftly brightened at our approach, reacting to the presence of two dragon shifters. The glow beckoned, calling me like a siren song.

I extended my palms over the cabinet and felt the buzz of resistance within the glass. "Will? Do you have the—?"

All sound was obliterated in a faint roar that seemed to come from within the Moonbeam itself. The brightening light sliced through the cabinet, bisecting the floor, and shone upon the spot where Cori and I were standing. My skin burned, a familiar fire roaring under my skin as the dragon in me came to life.

Brightness obscured my vision. I gripped Cori's hand and braced myself as the ground lurched away beneath us.

———

THE LURCHING sensation stopped as abruptly as it started, but I didn't let go of Cori. Though I couldn't see her face in the gloom, she was a solid anchor in a place I no longer recognised.

"Holy crap," she whispered. "Where are we?"

"Very good question." I reached for my wrist and turned off the shadow spell, mostly to reassure myself that I was here at all. Wherever *here* was. The tight space looked like a cave in the little light that filtered through from a narrow gap in the packed earth above our heads. Cool air brushed my face, mingling with the earthy scents. I inhaled deeply. I'd never smelled such clean air in London.

Was this another vision? Last time, there'd been a sense of disconnect, and I hadn't been able to see myself *or* Cori. I'd been seeing through the eyes of a dragon. Now, solid ground lay beneath my feet, and as Cori flickered into view, she sucked in a breath and whispered, "Look behind you."

A mirror leaned against the back wall. Not cracked like Samuel's but whole, intact, and emitting a faint white glow.

"We came out of there," I murmured. "We're in the right place."

Why would the dragons have buried the mirror underground? They'd used it to contact Samuel, but that had been more than two years ago, and it was anyone's guess what might have happened in the interim.

"Maybe they buried it to stop anyone from finding the Moonbeam." Cori reached towards the gap above our heads. "I bet I can pull myself out."

"Wait." A faint noise came from somewhere overhead, and my dragon instincts flared to life. A giant shadow fell over us. My skin chilled, a bone-deep tremor travelling through my entire body when an equally giant eye stared at us through the gap in the cave's roof.

An eye that could only belong to a dragon.

"Hi." My voice came out as a quiet squeak, half fear, half awe. *Another dragon.* Blue scales covered its majestic head, and though I couldn't see the rest of him, I knew he was male, and that he was a full-grown adult bigger than me. Bigger than the dragon I'd seen in the jail, too. Questions bubbled up in my throat, words tangling as I tried to figure out which to ask first. Cori gaped at him, too, rendered speechless.

The dragon roared. The sound sent Cori staggering back against me, and I grabbed her hand, my skin burning like it was on fire. My dragon side yearned to burst out of my skin, but my instinct to protect Cori stayed my hand. When the roar faded, I nudged her and whispered, "Stay here."

Then I reached up to the gap in the earth and pulled myself out into the open. My legs straightened, and I looked up at the biggest dragon I'd ever seen. He was somehow even more giant than I'd imagined, towering over me like a god descending to bestow judgement upon us mere humans.

I didn't have the chance to blink before the dragon's claw shot out, embedding deep in my chest. The world slowed, my body numbing, shock ringing through my mind. The claw withdrew, and the spray of bright crimson seemed to linger in the air for an endless moment.

Then I was falling, and the air turned to cinders and smoke.

9

When I came to awareness, my hand immediately jumped to my chest. An exhale of relief escaped at the lack of pain. Someone had used a healing spell, but I didn't recall anything of the past few moments except a fall into light, then darkness. And blood. A lot of blood.

My blood.

I jerked upright, gasping, eyes scanning the room. Not a cell. A bedroom. The mages hadn't caught us, but how had I got here?

"You're lucky to be alive." Astor appeared from the shadows near the door. "Cori thought you were dead."

"Cori." I breathed out her name. "Where is she?"

"She's downstairs," he said. "She was hysterical. Will had to give her a potion to calm her down, and she passed out there and then on the sofa. I advised against bringing her upstairs until we knew for sure you were going to survive."

"But..." I pressed a hand to my chest again. "Healing spell?"

"Yes, but the others had to get you out of the mages' head-quarters first," he said. "Becks and Cori brought you back while Will cleaned up the mess. It's a good job he stole all those cleansing spells, because if he hadn't, the mages would have seen the blood and worked it out."

I flopped back on the pillow and groaned. "Fuck. *Fuck.*"

"They haven't shown up on the doorstep, though. I don't think this is the worst outcome, all things considered."

"It's pretty damn close." Yes, I was alive, but we'd never have an open shot at the Moonbeam again. Oh, and my fellow dragon shifter had tried to *kill* me. "Where's the Moonbeam?"

"Still with the mages. Did you expect your friends to focus on that with you bleeding out in their arms?"

"Damn." My skin prickled. "I barely even felt it. Happened too fast."

"How do you feel now?" He sounded genuinely curious.

"Tired. Lightheaded. I could use a glass of water." I saw someone had placed one on the bedside table, drank the whole thing in one gulp, and found him watching my every move. "What?"

"What else?" He moved closer to the bed, each motion controlled, careful. "What happened over there?"

I put down the glass, my eyes on the floor. "Another dragon."

He sucked in a breath. "A dragon did that to you?"

"Guess I shouldn't have expected a welcoming commit-tee." I couldn't look at him. My thoughts were a maelstrom. "We came out into a cave with another mirror like Samuel's. I think the other dragons must have hidden it from the hunters. Or hidden it because they don't want visitors. Samuel had a lucky escape, if you ask me."

"That's fucked up."

I exhaled agreement, my heart heavy. "Yeah. It is."

I didn't know what else to say. The longing for my people I'd felt for the first year after my arrival in London reared up inside me, consuming, aching. I'd always, always wanted to find the dragon shifters' home. Everywhere else, Cori and I would be outsiders, adrift, without a true home.

Now that home had rejected us, leaving me unmoored, reeling. Sudden rage gripped me, and my fists clenched on the mattress, claws rising to the surface.

"Ember." The sound of my name from Astor's lips drew my eyes to his face. "I don't blame you in the least, but savaging the bed sheets won't solve anything."

Oops. The soft fabric had given way beneath the sharp claw points. I pulled them free, grimacing.

Astor placed a hand on my arm.

I stiffened. He hadn't touched me like that—with tenderness—in all the time I'd known him, and as his face hovered inches from mine, the raging anger instantly quelled, replaced with a familiar need, and the steadying knowledge that I didn't want to have any more regrets.

I tilted my head upward, our lips inches apart. Heat rose to the surface, a frisson of electricity dancing between us as we came together. I forgot all about my exhaustion. A growl built in my throat as my now-human hands locked on his shoulders and pulled him onto me, consuming, demanding. He responded in kind, his touch searing me through my too-tight clothes. I growled with lust and frustration, all but tearing his shirt off. His hands tore at my clothes with equal abandon, ripping off what was left of my top. The sight of my own blood brought a moment's hesitation—and then I saw his unmarked skin, without a single tattoo marking his chest or arms.

The tattoos hadn't been covered up, but they'd vanished in a way which shouldn't be possible. Not without leaving a mark behind. My gaze slid along his collarbone, looking for tally marks that should have been present but no longer were. Nothing but a spell was so precise, but Astor could barely bring himself to use a healing spell, let alone something of this level of complexity. It was confusing enough to distract me from the urge to rip the rest of his clothes off and take him.

Astor's eyebrow arched. "Yes?"

"You got rid of your tattoos." Was now a bad time to mention it? Probably, but he couldn't expect me *not* to notice that every blemish had vanished, even the puckered scars from the myriad times he'd been shot by the hunters' bullets. "And a lot more besides."

He moved off me, his pale skin gleaming in the faint moonlight streaming through the thin curtains. Not a single tattoo remained. Why would he get rid of them? He'd carried the marks of his past around for the last two years since he'd renounced the League.

I swiftly reached out a hand to grab his arm. "I just want to know why."

"Why do you think?"

"Because you don't want to acknowledge that the League did something to you that you don't understand. That they made you…" Supernatural. *Unnatural.*

He sat down on the bed, without making eye contact with me. "It's not out of shame. Not for the reason you're thinking."

"What, not because you don't want magical powers?" He must have had to swallow a hell of a lot of pride to ask for a spell, even discounting his usual aversion to all things supernatural. And the only other reason was that he didn't want *me* to look at them and remember his past as a hunter. So I'd want him with no repercussions.

I'd never expected him to do something like that for me. Never.

He rose from the bed again. "Whatever kind of *abilities* I have are as natural to me as breathing, now. It's not something I can undo."

"It's more the visual reminder you don't want." I reached for his hand again. "I'd do the same. No judgement here. Get back in."

"Should I take that as an invitation?"

"Yes." I tugged on his hand. He obliged, but he refrained from resuming our former activity, instead sitting down as if the notion of climbing *into* the bed was beyond him.

"You should be resting," he said without looking at me. "You nearly bled out, and I… shouldn't take advantage."

I burst out laughing and pulled the covers over my chin to stifle the sound. "Sorry. I just. *You* take advantage of *me*."

"You didn't see what you looked like earlier."

"Oh, come *on*." I reached out from under the covers and grabbed his thigh. "Fine. If you're going to be like that, then we can sleep. In here. Together."

He hesitated. "That's all?"

"Yes. Get in."

He climbed into bed beside me. The lack of resistance surprised me, but it wasn't particularly comfortable to fit two people into a bed made for one. His body was all sharp angles and pointy elbows and *freezing*.

"Your feet are like ice, Astor."

"That's because you're on fire."

"Ha." I wriggled aside to make more room, and his arm snaked around my waist, pulling me closer to him. He was cold as I was warm, his body hard against mine. In more than one way.

I felt his readiness between my thighs, but he didn't press

further. Alertness spread through my body, waking up every nerve. I squirmed against him, and he growled.

"You're killing me, Ember." His fingertips circled my hipbones, moving to my bare waist where he'd torn my shirt off. I didn't tell him to stop.

"Speak for yourself." I breathed fast, hard, his rough breathing in my ear driving me close to the edge. "Touch me."

His hand slipped between my legs. I moaned into the pillow, flames licking through me as he ignited a new nerve with every touch. I hadn't been touched like this—intimately, slowly, by someone concerned with my pleasure over their own—in what felt like years. His assassin's hands were surprisingly gentle as he flipped me onto my back to better access me. Then his tongue replaced his hand, and I let go of the last thread of sanity, gripping the bed tight, waves of pleasure lapping through me. At last I collapsed, boneless, more tired than before but a thousand times happier.

———

I woke to dawn nudging through the curtains, Astor's body pressed against my back, and an ungodly hammering on the door.

"For fuck's sake, tell me you two have clothes on now," Cori yelled.

"Shit." I sat up so abruptly that the top of my head collided with Astor's head, and we both dissolved into a stream of curses.

The knocking abated. "Get downstairs. Now."

"Guess I deserved that one." I rubbed the back of my head, looking at Astor in bemusement. "Better make ourselves decent."

"This isn't decent?" He ran a hand over my hips. The fire inside me stirred, guiding me towards him.

"Astor." I grabbed for my clothes. My bloody, torn shirt was a lost cause, so I rummaged in the wardrobe for a spare one. "I want to shower, but we should probably settle this first."

"*You* should settle this. She's your sister, not mine."

"Oh, you're not off the hook." I ran a hand through my tangled hair and found auburn curls where there should have been black dye. "The fuck?"

"What?"

"My hair. The dye's gone."

"I thought you knew," he said. "You came back through the portal like that. I was more concerned with the blood than the missing hair dye."

"No shit?" I sank back onto the bed and lifted a curl, finding that it had grown back to its original length, too. Had the Moonbeam somehow been the cause?

"Come on." Astor nudged the door open.

After checking for any more wayward articles of clothing on the floor, I followed him out into the landing. I had to envy his ability to keep a straight face. He walked as casually as if the pair of us were returning from a shopping trip, while I could feel my entire *body* flushing as we entered the living room to find ourselves with an audience of everyone except Kit.

Cori strode up to me and gave me such a jab in the chest that I stumbled back a step. "I thought you were *dead.*"

"You were out cold." I leaned away from her. "Also, you just poked me in my wound. I might have still been bleeding."

"Don't change the bloody subject!" she fumed. "You must have been just fine if you spent last night acting as you did. My eyes might never recover."

"You might have knocked," was Astor's contribution.

To my astonishment, Cori then strode up and poked *him*

in the chest. "I thought my sister was dead, you inconsiderate prick."

I heard Will snickering and glared at him.

"Cori, I'm sorry," I said. "Astor is, too."

"No, he isn't." Cori paced away from us, throwing up her hands. "After yesterday turned out to be a shitshow on every level, of course you spent last night fucking a *hunter*."

"Cori!" I raised my own hands. "I said I'm sorry. What more can I say? Yesterday *was* a shitshow. I didn't mean to make you worry."

Talk about role reversal. I'd spent so long stressed beyond belief on her behalf that I hadn't expected our positions to flip on their heads in a blink. Or a stab of a dragon's claw.

All my defensiveness faded as the memories of what had led up to the moment of my near-death made a return. "You brought me back."

"Through the mirror." Cori nodded, her eyes swimming with tears. "You fell back into the cave, and I pulled you through the portal. I didn't know if you were even breathing."

"You both reappeared in the mages' storeroom," said Will. "Made a hell of a mess, too."

"Astor told me you cleaned it up." I turned to Will. "Thank you. And for the healing spell. You saved my life."

"Oh, it's pretty much my job to keep you lot alive at this point," he said. "Becks is the one who was the real lifesaver in the end, when Lady Clare came back into the headquarters right when we were trying to get you out."

I sucked in a breath. "If she finds out we were there…"

"We're screwed, but what else is new?" Will sounded absurdly cheerful. "Honestly, I think we got off lightly with the mages. The hunters, too. I think they only sent the one automaton."

"And didn't come in person?" I frowned. "What was the

point in that? If they wanted the Moonbeam, they'd have sent some actual hunters to steal it. The robots won't even fit through the door."

"Maybe it was a test run," Astor suggested. "To gauge the mages' defences."

"Hope not," Will commented. "Because they made a pretty piss-poor showing."

"They did," I said. "Is Kit still asleep?"

"Last I checked," said Will, going into the kitchen. "When he's here, we'll all make a plan."

"Before anything else, I need a shower," I said. "Since, you know, I did get stabbed yesterday."

"In more than one way," Cori said, and I flipped her off over my shoulder. It wasn't exactly an endorsement of Astor, but she'd acted pretty much the same every time a guy and I had hit it off in the past and it was a marked improvement on her former hostility towards him.

I took a quick shower, scrubbing off the blood and marvelling again at my newly regrown hair. The Moonbeam was still full of secrets, and as long as it remained within the mages' clutches, I'd have no hope of learning them, nor why the other dragon had reacted the way he had.

I returned downstairs, and Astor went to shower next. Will raised an eyebrow at me as I nonchalantly wandered over to the cupboard in the kitchen and poured myself a bowl of cereal. "I didn't have the misfortune to look in your room, but I sure heard some interesting sounds last night."

"Drop it." Evidently, Astor and I had been less subtle than I'd thought. In my defence, I hadn't exactly been paying much attention to how much noise I made. The man was good with his hands.

When Will had left the kitchen, I opened the medicine cupboard and was relieved to find we still had an ample supply of witch-brewed contraceptive spells. My knowledge of dragon shifter fertility cycles was almost zero compared to other kinds of shifter, but I figured it was best to avoid any unnecessary complications.

I joined Cori and Becks on the living room sofa and dug into my cereal to avoid talking about the assassin-shaped elephant in the room.

Becks watched me over a stack of toast she'd placed on the coffee table. "Ember, what in hell happened to your hair? You came out of the Moonbeam and…"

"And the dye had gone, I know," I said. "I have no idea when it happened. During the crossover, apparently."

"It happened the first time we went through the portal," Cori said quietly. "I didn't see at first, since it was so dark in that cave."

"Cave?" Will came into the room and claimed an armchair. "Was that what was on the other side of that portal? Except, you know. Stabby dragons."

"Will," Becks reprimanded, when Cori flinched. "Sorry. Both of you. It must have been awful."

"I'm fine." I didn't *want* to discuss the subject, but my friends deserved to know, and besides, maybe they'd be able to help me make sense of it. "I didn't necessarily expect a warm welcome, but he just stabbed me without even letting me speak."

"Damn," said Will. "That's rough. Dragons are territorial, aren't they? You probably scared him by appearing out of thin air."

"I don't think he was scared, he was mad." I shivered at the memory, looking down into my cornflakes to avoid the others' eyes. "He was *furious* that we showed up. I don't know if he thought we were human intruders, or mistook us for the hunters, or—what."

"Probably the latter," Becks said. "They must know the hunters had the Moonbeam for years, right? So they assumed that anyone who came through the portal must be an enemy."

"He might have *asked* first," Cori said. "Dickhead."

"Yeah." Pain pulsed through my chest that had nothing to do with the wound. "I don't understand, but the dragon shifters' home... it's still the only place with answers about our pasts."

The whole point in the whole endeavour was to find whoever had wiped our memories. To learn what had happened to our families, as well as securing our future. Eradicating the hunters would be a bonus. But all this time, I'd thought the other dragons *wanted* to find Cori and me. They'd sent us away because they felt they had no choice, but they'd wanted us to come back when we were ready. They wouldn't have left us the notebook otherwise.

Was it all a lie?

Kit glided in, breaking the awkward silence. I looked at him, relieved *one* person wasn't staring at me, and saw I wasn't the only one who'd undergone a transformation. His overgrown hair had been trimmed to a respectable length, though admittedly in a manner that suggested a short-sighted person had clipped it haphazardly. Since when had Becks taken up playing hairdresser?

"What happened to your hair?" I asked him. "It looks like you had an accident with a pair of sheep shears."

Kit flushed bright red. "Uh. It wasn't me who cut it. Will did."

"I thought it was Becks."

"Even my eyesight isn't that bad," said Becks.

"Have you ever tried cutting someone's hair when they're constantly fidgeting?" Will turned away, but not before I saw he was blushing, too. "I happen to be a great stylist. You all have too high standards."

"What, and it has nothing to do with being infatuated—

ow." Cori slid off the sofa as Will leaned over and kicked her under the coffee table. "You're all bullying me."

Huh. I looked between Will and Kit, making sense of some of their interactions in a new light. I raised an eyebrow at Becks, who shrugged in such a way that implied she thought I was dense for not picking up on the obvious.

"Ember." Cori pouted at me. "You're my sister. You're supposed to come to my defence."

"Oh, no, you deserved that one." I picked up my spoon again, and for a few moments it was just like old times. At least until Astor came into the room.

"Grab a seat," I told him when he hovered near the door instead of properly entering. "Come on, we don't bite."

"Some of us bite." Becks glanced at me with a grin.

I gave her the evil eye. "So, what else did I miss while I was sleeping?"

"Sleeping." Cori made quote marks with her hands.

I flicked a piece of cereal at her. "Yes, sleeping. Since, you know, I got stabbed."

"We're past the point where you can use that as an excuse, Ember."

I didn't really blame Astor for keeping his distance, but I waved him over again anyway. "Seriously. Did the mages handle the automaton?"

"Last I saw, it was lying in pieces all over the road," said Will. "Doesn't mean the hunters won't send another."

"They might have come in person last night," Becks added. "We didn't see."

"Then there's a chance they already have the Moonbeam." I didn't blame the others for not sticking around to check, given the state I'd been in.

"Depends if Malkin went there himself," Cori said. "I hope that portal was still open if he did. Let him get a taste of being stabbed by an angry dragon."

"Assuming they aren't allies." I put my cereal bowl aside, my appetite gone. "That's the thing. We can't prove Malkin *didn't* force the other dragon shifter to use the portal to help him travel to their hiding place."

It had been my worst suspicion, but I hadn't wanted to believe it. Hadn't wanted to believe there was any chance the other dragons wouldn't welcome us home as family. My eyes stung with the indignity of it all.

Cori scooted closer. "Who needs them, anyway? Bunch of dickheads, if you ask me."

The brittle note beneath her voice told me that the rejection hurt her as much as it did me, yet she was trying to make *me* feel better. If anything, that made me want to cry even more.

I blinked hard. "We need answers. Samuel knew the dragon shifters, didn't he? He might have some ideas."

"He might be dead," said Astor. "If the worst assumption is true and the hunters did steal the Moonbeam back."

And use it to repair the mirror. Would Malkin have known how to do that, though? "If they did, they might not know Samuel existed. The portal only opens for dragon shifters."

"That's not exactly what he said." Cori fidgeted with her sleeve. "He claimed only a dragon shifter can use the portal to its true extent, but if he was using the mirror himself, it must work for regular people, right?"

"Before it broke." The Moonbeam, though, opened portals only for dragon shifters. I was sure of it. "I know there's a chance we're running into a trap, but I do think we should see Samuel again, if just to warn him the hunters might show up at his house."

"And if they're already there?" Becks said. "We can't fight off the League *and* a horde of hostile dragon shifters at the same time."

"What's the alternative, go back to the mages?" I asked. "And hope we don't run into Lady Clare at the door?"

"We can at least see if the hunters succeeded in stealing the Moonbeam last night," said Will. "I'll fly there alone, if it's less risky."

"No, we'll all go," I decided. "Then whether the Moonbeam's still there or not, Samuel has some explaining to do."

10

I knew the worst had happened when I saw the police cars. Flashing red and blue lights led the way down the residential district neighbouring the mages' headquarters, and we had to skirt around a group of officers to get through. Debris littered the way, several ruined cars lay at the roadside, and several houses bore the sort of damage that suggested a giant had ripped a chunk out of the wall. Or an automaton. The hunters must have marched straight through this area on their way to attack the mages.

I slowed when we neared the headquarters. "Oh, damn."

The front windows were smashed in, the fences had been trampled, and an alarming amount of blood smeared the road near a few misshapen chunks of metal that had presumably once been the automaton.

Shivers sprang to my skin. "Is much of that blood mine?"

"Some, but… damn," said Becks. "I almost wish I'd come back to help fight."

"Me too," Will said. "I had no idea the hunters broke in."

"How?" They never should have been able to get past the wards.

"Ember." Lord Smyth strode towards us, his clothes gleaming with what I assumed was a recently applied cleansing spell. "I'm afraid I can't invite you into the office today. There's been a break-in."

My heart lurched at the almost defeated note to his voice. "Did the hunters…?"

"They took the Moonbeam."

I wanted to scream. "I thought you used wards. Protections."

"We should have moved it to our secure storage unit sooner," he said. "Five mages were killed in the fighting. Malkin himself must have had a hand in the attack. In addition to the mechanical beast he sent, there were dozens of Elites."

My hands fisted. Had we unintentionally weakened the defences when we'd gone in to steal the Moonbeam for ourselves? Guilt churned inside me. The lines on his face made it clear he'd known the mages who'd died, and he grieved them.

"Did you see where the hunters went afterwards?" asked Cori hoarsely, her face stricken with the same horror I felt myself.

"No. Some of us tried to chase them down, but they split into separate groups, and we lost track of who had the Moonbeam. Lady Clare is questioning witnesses who might have seen from their windows."

Shit. The one mage I couldn't afford to run into. "We'll go. I don't think there's much we can do here. And if Malkin has the Moonbeam, I doubt he'll wait long before using it openly." The entire city might be in danger if he used it on any shifters, but I never had found out where he'd been hiding since he'd left his seabound fortress behind.

"Then I hope you'll be careful, Ember." His grave tone matched his eyes, though I also detected a hint of suspicion, too. Probably he'd guessed we intended to go after Malkin. I hoped that was why, because we were fucked ten times over if the mages figured out the role we'd played in the burglary.

"Well, I feel like a piece of shit," Will said in an undertone as we walked away from the mages' headquarters towards where Astor had parked the car he'd 'borrowed' the previous day. He stood in front, one hand resting on the gun at his belt as if he expected a fight.

"They took it." I didn't need to say more. "I don't know where they are, but I'd say we need to head for Samuel's right away."

"Flying is faster than driving," Astor said. "If you think he's there."

"I brought enough shadow spells for all of us this time," Will put in. "They should last long enough to get us there and back."

Except that then left the question of who would carry whom. Will could only carry one person—or two, if Becks shifted into cat form—which would leave Cori and Astor with no option but to both get on my back at the same time. If, of course, Astor wanted to come with us at all.

Taking in a breath, I turned to my sister. "You—"

"I'm coming, Ember. No arguments."

"I was going to say you'll have to fly with Astor. Unless he wants to stay behind."

"No." Astor's jaw set. "I'm not letting you get into trouble without me again."

"What use would you have been yesterday?" When I shot her a warning look, Cori added, "Just saying. We were miles away."

"And we'll know better this time, but I need to be able to fly to Samuel's house without worrying you'll try to push each other off my back. Can you please *try* to get along?" I directed this mostly at Cori, and she rolled her eyes.

"Sure, but only because your brain's addled from sex at the moment."

"Cori." I decided to let that one slide. "Right. Let's move."

Our first challenge was finding somewhere to shift into a dragon which wasn't in public view, so the others would be able to climb onto my back while I was still visible. We ended up walking the short distance to Hyde Park and finding one of the areas the fae had claimed, which resulted in Cori having to wave a knife at a group of redcaps that tried to pick a fight with us. Maybe they smelled the blood from mage territory.

The last redcap ran off with a shriek as I shifted into dragon form, my wings scraping against the close-growing trees around the patch of grass I'd chosen to shift in.

Cori watched my transformation with admiring eyes. "I want to be able to do that."

"You will." The words came out as a growl, but she got the sentiment.

Flying to Samuel's place was much faster than driving but was considerably wetter once we were on a level with the clouds. Cori grumbled about the rain while Astor maintained his usual silence until we dipped lower over the rows of terraced houses.

There were so few people in the streets that the sight of two black-clad figures walking down the road drew me to a screeching halt.

"Fuckers aren't even trying to be unobtrusive," Cori hissed. "Do they have the Moonbeam?"

I couldn't tell. I flew down, the air current of my wings hitting the two walking figures in the back, but not strongly enough to knock them over. I wanted to see how many hunters were present before I unleashed my fire.

As I suspected, their path took them in the direction of Samuel's house. I followed, having to pay careful attention to make sure my wings didn't knock anything over and blow our cover. One of them halted briefly when the air gusted into his back, looking around for the source, but seemingly found none. He then followed his companion up the steps to Samuel's home.

I hovered, invisible, as Samuel opened the door to them. "Are you ready?"

"Of course," said one of the hunters in a low voice. "You're certain two of us is enough?"

"Are you too cowardly to perform your duty?" Samuel enquired in a cold voice that didn't sound like him at all. It sounded, in fact, like someone else altogether.

"No." He reached for the gun at his belt. "We're ready."

"Then let's not delay." Samuel beckoned them into the hall.

Through the door, I could see the mirror propped against the wall. From the glow encasing its surface, it was easy to tell that the surface was no longer cracked, but whole.

The mirror's glow expanded, and one hunter stepped through the portal and then vanished. The other followed in his path, disappearing in a white flare.

I touched down, claws digging into the road, flames ready to burst from my lungs and set the house alight. *The other dragons. The hunters are coming for them.*

"You can come out now, Ember," said Samuel, looking directly at me.

Fire roared through my veins, demanded to be unleashed, but I didn't move. Exposing myself would also expose Cori and Astor, and if people could walk into the mirror, they could also walk *out.*

Cori shifted on my back. "Burn the fucker," she hissed. "Go on."

Samuel bared his teeth in a smile. "You want to go after them? It's too late, Ember. And is that your sister there, too?"

The heat burst from my chest in a torrent of dragonfire. Flames licked up the front of the house, and the old man momentarily vanished. Yet through the white haze, I could see him standing there, unharmed. The ground beneath his feet smoked, flames licking at the house's door frame, but his clothes remained unsinged and his smile didn't waver a bit. He didn't fear me at all.

"You should have done as you were told, Ember." The tone of voice he used left no doubt as to who really wore Samuel's face. *Malkin.*

An instant later, the old man's face flickered out of existence and revealed the one I expected. He must have used an illusion spell, perhaps stolen from the witch himself. Now he wore his real clothes, fake army uniform topped with more spells or tattoos that made him impervious to magic. Even a dragon's flames.

Or was it the Moonbeam that protected him?

"Very useful, this contraption. Both of them." He gestured to the mirror with the same hand that held the Moonbeam. He'd probably tortured all the information from the real Samuel before killing him. "I have to thank you for leading me here. Tracking spells *are* useful, aren't they?"

"You have more witches working for you, do you?" Astor's tone dripped with derision. "You still can't see the hypocrisy of being dependent upon the very supernaturals you claim to despise so greatly?"

"I merely choose to make full use of all the tools at my disposal."

"I bet you do, wanker," Cori called to him. "Not going through the portal yourself? Too scared of what you'll find out there, are you?"

A growl of warning rumbled through me. Malkin had locked up my sister. Tortured her, put her into a coma. She deserved retribution, but the guy was bulletproof in a literal sense and even my fire couldn't touch him.

Or rather, couldn't touch the Moonbeam.

I released a storm of fire, this time aiming at the house. The windows shattered, the remnants of the fence crumpled, and even the brick walls quaked as flames far hotter than any natural creation rocked the street to its foundations.

As the last of the fire left my mouth, I flew upward, trying to see where Will and the others might be.

"Ember," Cori hissed in my ear. "The bastard's taking aim at us!"

A powerful blast hit me from below, catching my wings like a ferocious air current. Cori screamed in my ear as I fought to regain control, to fly lower, my wings dragged sideways against my best efforts.

I caught a glimpse of Will caught in the air current, too, fighting it with all his strength. He dropped in a spiralling arc, Becks's cat form clinging to his back, shrieking in fear. As Samuel's house vanished beyond the rooftops, I regained my balance in time to reach and grab Will's wing and stop him from plummeting to the ground.

Steadying him, I aimed for the nearest patch of green and descended in a few shaky wingbeats.

Will landed upside-down in a bush, turning human again. "What in hell was that?" He lifted his head feebly. "Kit, you okay?"

Kit flickered into view, lying on his back with Becks sprawled across his chest. "That was powerful magic. How did Malkin do that?"

"It was a defensive ward," said Will. "One of the old man's. It must have activated when Ember attacked the house."

Once Astor and Cori got off my back, I turned back into human form again and landed beside them. "I hope it hit Malkin, too."

"Bastard's wearing too many protective spells." Will righted himself, picking leaves out of his hair. "We shouldn't have come."

"What choice did we have?" I asked shakily. "He killed the real Samuel and stole the mirror. Now he's sending hunters through there, and…"

The other dragons. If they hadn't been in imminent danger from the hunters before, they were now.

"Would you say a protective spell is the same as a ward?" Kit asked, breaking the grim silence. "Magically speaking, that is?"

"What on earth does that matter?" Then I saw he held the remote-control like device he'd taken from the mages. "You still have that?"

He ducked his head. "I almost put it back earlier, but we need it more than they do."

"Will it work on Malkin?" Cori asked dubiously.

"I don't know, but I'm wondering if it's the Moonbeam that protected him from dragonfire, not a spell."

"Because we created it," Cori said. "Shit, I bet you're right. Knock that thing out of his hand and we can burn him."

And then take back the mirror and the Moonbeam both.

I shifted into a dragon again, and the others climbed onto my back. I didn't bother with a shadow spell this time. I wanted Malkin's eyes to be on me, and not the others.

He stood in the same place I'd left him, feet planted in front of Samuel's ruined house. "That was a powerful spell. Pity it didn't activate until after the old fool was dead."

I growled, but I refrained from breathing fire. Instead, I waited for the gleam that told me Kit had got close enough to touch his target.

Malkin's eyes widened in surprise when the half-faerie reappeared, leaning over Will's back to throw the anti-ward device at him. Rather than bouncing off an invisible shield, the device hit him in the chest.

As he staggered, I flew at him. I didn't breathe fire but instead crashed into him, feeling a satisfying solid crunch when my scaled body hit his fragile human one. The Moonbeam spun away from his feet, its gleam drawing me in.

"Let me down," Cori said. "I'll grab it."

I did so, bloodlust surging through me at the sight of Malkin lying in a bloodied, broken heap. Near the ground, Cori jumped down and reached for the Moonbeam. Spiralling light ignited, flooding over Cori and then me. I shifted to human again and ran to grab her arm.

Several voices shouted our names. Then we were gone.

11

The sensation of falling overwhelmed me, and for a short time, I couldn't see anything but dazzling white light. Then came solid ground beneath my feet as the Moonbeam's light dimmed to an overcast sky. Cool air filled my lungs, too clean to belong to a city. This time we hadn't landed in a cave but on a grassy slope.

My sister's sudden scream had me on my feet in a flash. Cori lay some five feet downhill from me, pinned beneath the claw of the dragon who'd attacked me before. His huge fearsome head bent over Cori, teeth curling from his wide jaw. Blue scales covered his large body from head to toe, tent-like wings were tucked against his back, and his muscled legs were planted on either side of Cori's body.

I shook off my shock and let my claws slide out. "Get the fuck away from my sister."

The dragon opened its mouth and roared. I braced myself, digging my claws into the earth to keep from being knocked aside. Any other shifter would probably have been rendered immobile, and even to me, the instinct to flinch threatened to overwhelm my stronger impulse to attack, to defend my sister.

Instead, I shifted into a dragon myself. Clawed feet planted on the hillside, a roar of my own escaped, sending a clear message. *Let her go.*

The dragon growled without moving an inch. Cori lay absolutely still beneath his claw, frozen in terror.

I roared again, jabbing my claw in her direction. The dragon remained unmoved. *You're trespassing,* his body language conveyed.

We didn't come here to harm anyone. We came with a warning. But dragons weren't mind-readers, and the brute still refused to move. I wasn't sure I could win a confrontation with a creature of his size even in my own dragon form, but I had to get him away from Cori.

I walked closer, lifting my front claw. The other dragon mirrored my movement and my claw locked with his, the momentum threatening to tip me over. He was so much stronger than me, and there was real power in his grip, enough to tell me that I hadn't done nearly enough training in dragon form to fight another of my kind.

I used my powerful back legs to push off the ground, shoving the dragon's scaled side and unbalancing him. Cori seized the chance to roll away from his claws and rose upright, reaching for a knife at her belt, but I shook my head in warning. *Run, Cori.*

My moment of distraction cost me, and the other drag-on's claw struck me in the face. Warm blood gushed down my cheek, and I hissed in pain.

"Stop!" Cori shouted at him. "Don't hurt her. We're not here to fight. We're dragon shifters, like you."

The dragon's other claw disentangled from mine and then jabbed at my ribs, glancing off my tough scales. Cori let out a hoarse scream, and I followed her gaze to the sky. Two more dragons descended and landed upon the grass with a tremor that caused the whole hillside to shake.

"We're not enemies!" Cori yelled. "Tell him to stop attacking us."

The dragons exchanged a series of growls then grabbed Cori between them. Fury overtook me, and I tried to push past the large blue dragon to reach them. *Let her go!*

He struck me again, this time in the leg. I roared as his claw pierced the joint underneath my scales, and the shock of the pain sent me sliding downhill.

The other two dragons took flight. Cori yelped and kicked as their claws locked around her waist and lifted her off the ground. I kicked off with my uninjured leg and took flight, the other leg hanging limply beneath me.

The dragons carried Cori over an unfamiliar landscape of forests and rolling hills. Taller shadows on the horizon indicated mountains, like the ones in the vision I'd seen. We couldn't be anywhere near London anymore, but within less than a minute, the other dragons began to descend. A settlement waited ahead, a small village of stone buildings.

The first dragon overtook us, holding something in his claws that dazzled my eyes with a vibrant glow. *The mirror?* Was he taking away the only route home? I flew faster, my leg streaming blood, and landed behind the other dragons on a cobbled street.

Stone houses that didn't look to have been updated in the past century lay on either side. Before I had the chance to wonder how in the world a dragon possibly fit through the doors, our three companions shifted into humans. They were all male, large and muscular, and the one holding the mirror was built like a wrestler or bodyguard. His battered-looking leather jacket and jeans struck an odd contrast with the ancient-looking buildings.

Cori squirmed free from the other two and ran back to

me, her eyes huge and her limbs shaking. "Ember. Are you okay?"

I turned human and stumbled when my leg nearly gave way beneath me. "I'm fine." Levelling a glare at the big man, I said, "Are you going to hear us out now?"

"Rogues." He spoke with a faint Scottish accent. "What do you want from us?"

"We came here with a warning." I glanced at Cori, hoping she'd let me do the talking. This guy seemed to have a short fuse, to say the least. "From London."

I'd hoped that might stir a little recognition, but none came. The big dragon narrowed his eyes. "Warning, is it?"

"The mirror—the other mirror—has been taken by the hunters." Or I thought it had, unless Astor and the others had managed to get it out of Samuel's house. "The Orion League. Two hunters came through that one not five minutes ago. You know the League, right?"

The dragon snorted, more with disdain than amusement. "You smell of humans. Yet you think to bring a warning to *us*?"

"We won't bother next time, then," Cori said. "Thanks for nothing."

I moved closer to her, conscious of the threat the dragons presented even in human form. "We also came here because we were under the impression that someone from here sent us away to London as children and told us to only return when we had the ability to shift."

"That one's still a child." He eyed Cori, who glared back at him. "If you want us to help you attain your fire, we don't have time for that, little girl."

"That's not what I asked you for." I didn't want to tell this aggressive stranger our life stories, but hostility was the last reaction to our arrival I'd have expected. "We lived here when we were younger, but someone wiped our memories and sent us away. We came back to find out who."

None of the other three dragons showed the slightest sign of recognition. My heart sank into my shoes. I hadn't expected everyone in this hidden colony, whatever it was, to know who we were, but how many dragons were left in the world? And why look at us like we'd committed some awful crime just by showing up?

The big dragon studied us both. "If you are who you say you are, come with me. I want to ask you some more questions."

I swallowed down harsh words, the throbbing pain in my leg tempering my anger. Cori's safety was paramount, and this guy held the only means of getting home. He carried the large mirror ahead of us down the cobbled street. My injured leg hurt like hell, but I refused to show weakness. Every house we passed brought the impulse to knock on the door and ask if the inhabitants knew my parents. Maybe someone here had been the one to put Cori and me on that train to London, but certainly not our current companions.

We reached a stone building larger than the others. The leading dragon shifter stepped inside, placing the mirror down in the narrow hallway. He then beckoned us into an equally austere room set out more like a cave than anything. Fitting for a dragon, in a way, but I found it hostile, as unwelcoming as its owner. The large room carried the cold air in from outside, cooling down the heat of my transformation.

The dragon shifter gestured for us to sit in two of the slab-like seats that comprised the only furniture but didn't do so himself. "Tell me who you are."

"I'm Ember, and this is my sister, Cori," I said. "We're from London. Who are you?"

"My name is Lorne." He spoke the name like it was more

of a title. "You should not have come here. We're not open to sheltering strangers."

"We aren't strangers," I objected. "I'm almost certain we used to live here, or at least among other dragon shifters, when we were children. Our memories were erased. I want to find out who did it."

"We had a notebook," Cori added. "Whoever gave it to us wrote instructions to come through the mirror when we were ready. We assumed our memories were wiped so that the Orion League couldn't torture us into giving away the other dragons' location. So, *your* location. You should be thanking us, you—"

I half-rose from my seat in case he struck her for impertinence, the movement sending another spike of pain up my leg. "That's the way we understand it. If we're wrong, we'd appreciate hearing the full story. I know that mirror of yours used to be linked to London, before the faerie invasion."

I hadn't seen any signs of the faeries in the village so far, but the area was isolated enough that it might have escaped with minimal damage. Or else the dragon shifters had sent the fae packing. This guy sure looked capable of punching out a Sidhe lord. No matter what I said, no warmth or understanding shone in his gaze. His eyes were cold.

"You're young, untrained, and unequipped to be part of our clan," he said. "You'd be a burden on us, nothing more."

Cori bristled. "A burden? We want answers, not charity, arsehole."

"And you have no respect for authority," he added. "I should have you put to death for insolence."

"You stabbed my sister for no reason," Cori objected. "Twice. We did *nothing* to you. Insolence is the least of what you deserve."

"Enough." Flames flickered in his eyes, and blue scales gleamed on his hands. "I will be merciful, though it goes against my instincts. I will give you the chance to leave of your own volition and return to London."

"But if you'd let us explain—" I began.

"You already did. We've wasted enough time."

"The League is *here*. Their bullets can kill even a dragon in a single shot."

His hands shifted to claws, and I tensed, sweeping Cori behind me with a hand. Eyes dancing with white fire, he drove us out into the hallway, where the mirror waited. Its glow formed a pillar against the floor.

Cori dug in her heels. "You can't do this to us. You haven't told us a damn thing. Why are you here, and what gives you the right to stop us from talking to the other dragons?"

He lifted his claw warningly, forcing her to take a step back into the light. I reached for her, shielding my eyes, and the brightness consumed us both.

12

This time, Cori and I landed on soft carpet when we fell out of the stream of light. We were greeted by Will's loud voice as he came hurrying over, brandishing a healing spell. "Oh, good, you aren't on your deathbed this time."

"Not quite." I cast my gaze around the room in confusion. Becks and Kit watched us from the sofa, and even Astor was present, albeit standing on the other side of the room and not seated like the others. A relieved sigh escaped as the healing light spread over my leg. "How'd we get here?"

Cori cleared her throat and gestured to the coffee table. The Moonbeam lay gleaming in a pool of greyish light.

"You got it away from the hunters?" I asked. "Wait, is Malkin dead?"

"I doubt it." Astor's jaw tensed. "Your friends wanted to get the Moonbeam back to the house in case you came out of it bleeding to death again. You didn't disappoint."

"I'm fine." I felt a little dizzy from the blood loss, but I'd got off lightly this time. "And the mirror?"

"Samuel's house collapsed on it," said Becks. "I take it the dragons weren't any friendlier than the last time you met?"

"Yes, tell us how Narnia was," said Will.

"Narnia?" echoed Kit. "Is that something else I missed in the last two years?"

"Not quite," I said. "It was certainly cold enough and there was snow on the mountains. Way up in Scotland, I assume."

"And somewhere that's stuck a few centuries in the past," Cori added. "The village didn't even look like the invasion touched it."

"The guy who spoke to us was wearing modern clothes, though," I reminded her.

"Same guy who stabbed you the last time?" Will guessed. "What did you *do* to the other dragons? Did you make a habit of robbing little old ladies and kicking puppies when you were a kid?"

"I wish I knew." I sank into an armchair, my head swimming with dizziness. "This big dragon dude—Lorne, he called himself—refused to answer our questions and then sent us home. He wouldn't even let us speak to the other dragons."

"That's so weird," said Becks. "You'd think they'd be glad you showed up."

"Apparently not." Between the two of us, Cori and I filled the others in on our experiences while we grabbed a late lunch and otherwise cleaned ourselves up. Malkin's fate loomed in the back of my mind, but I needed to rally a little before I went back to Samuel's house to see if he'd survived.

"He must have known," said Astor, who'd been silent through most of our discussion. He'd also seemed reluctant to meet my eyes, but I'd seen his jaw tighten every time I mentioned the other dragons, especially Lorne. "If he had the mirror."

"It was buried in a cave until Cori and I showed up," I said. "Now it's in the bastard's house, so going back to pay a visit will be all but impossible."

"It also means any hunters who use the other mirror will come out in his house," Cori said. "Serve him right if they shoot him on the spot."

"He can't be afraid of them." Astor spoke in the same clipped tone as before. "No, I'd wager they're allies. Maybe they always have been."

"How'd you figure that one out?" said Cori. "The hunters *killed* the dragon shifters. Unless you're making excuses for them."

I gave her a warning look. "If Lorne does have some kind of agreement with Lorne, that doesn't mean the other dragons share it. We only saw three, and the other two were Lorne's cronies."

"Three?" Astor's voice carried the same edge as before. "They didn't know you?"

It occurred to me that part of him—maybe even unknown to himself—was *jealous*. That he wondered if I might have decided to stay with the other dragons, given the chance. Which was far from the truth, but I could hardly run off with him now to prove I hadn't forgotten last night. We had more important things to worry about.

"The person who wrote the notebook seemed certain that the other dragons would be there to welcome us back," I said. "The guy running the show said he didn't even know who we are."

"Unless he lied," said Cori. "He basically said he didn't want to take on responsibility for a pair of inexperienced young dragons. Which is bollocks. We weren't asking to stay at his house, for crying out loud."

"Only answers." My skin prickled. "Maybe one of the others will talk, but how are we supposed to get them alone when the only route into the village is through Lorne's house?"

"It might not be." Astor sounded like the words pained him to speak, and he kept his eyes on the Moonbeam rather than on us. "I went through the Moonbeam's portal myself and ended up underground, remember? It doesn't just link to the mirrors."

"Shit, the assassin has a point," said Will. "I bet you and Cori can control the direction the portal sends you in."

"And we never did find Giselle," I said slowly. "I sure as hell didn't see *her* in the dragons' village."

"They'd have killed her." Astor's tone was carefully neutral. "Even if they didn't attack her outright, she would have provoked a fight."

He was probably right, but I knew that he had mixed feelings on Giselle's recent actions. That didn't mean she deserved to die at Lorne's hands, though.

Surely a dragon that proud and strong would never cave in to the hunters. The only way the League had been able to subdue me was by suppressing my shifting ability by drugging me, and Lorne certainly didn't have that problem.

"We'll go back," Cori said decisively. "Make sure we're prepared this time."

"You *want* to go back?" Of course she did. Even our near-death encounter didn't change our shared need for answers. "I know we need to figure out what's going on, but that guy is volatile as hell."

"He can't stop us talking to the others." Cori lifted her chin. "They're our people. And if we use the Moonbeam like Astor said and land somewhere far from Lorne's house, we can avoid him."

Astor himself looked somewhat surprised that she'd acknowledged his idea.

"We'd need to use shadow spells," I said. "And hope his

allies don't sniff us out. Plus, you know, there's a chance everyone in the village is working with him."

"I bet they aren't," said Cori. "Everyone around will have heard your fight. I bet they'll be curious to meet another dragon shifter after years being cut off from us."

"I hope you're right." The risks were high, but she was right. This was too important to ignore. "Will, how many shadow spells do you have?"

"I can use glamour," Kit offered. "That'd last longer."

"And I can create diversions, too," Will added. "I have this new spell which makes it rain spiders."

"Hang on," I said, alarmed. "I didn't say you should all come with us."

"I wouldn't miss this for the world," said Will.

"And I'd like to see the other dragons," Becks added. "We're coming, Ember. Deal with it."

"We can't all go," I protested. "Also, the only way back home to use the mirror, remember? We'd have to sneak into Lorne's house no matter what."

"I'd say that gives us more reason to come and help," said Will. "Kit has his anti-ward device, and I have the mages' spell detector."

"They're dragons, not witches or mages," I pointed out. "We don't need—"

"Unlocking spells? A powerful itching spell that'll give that Lorne character a real distraction while we sneak around his house?"

"Hell, yes," said Cori.

"Stop it!" I knew I was losing the fight, but the notion of all my friends ending up at Lorne's mercy repelled me. "Guys, it's not a holiday. There's an angry dragon shifter and his horde of minions up there and possibly the hunters, too. We never did find out where the ones who went through the mirror landed."

"We know that," said Becks. "We're still in."

My shoulders slumped. "Fine, but please take this seriously. The other dragons will be wary of outsiders. If Cori and I do manage to get an audience with them, we'll need the rest of you to take charge of securing the way back home. I don't know about the others, but Lorne hates humans, and it wouldn't surprise me if he hated other shifters, too. He seemed the intolerant type."

"Sounds like a charming guy. Can't wait," said Will.

Another thought hit me. "And someone will have to stay with the Moonbeam. We can't all go."

"I know who'll volunteer." Will lifted his head. "Maybe not. The assassin's gone."

My heart swooped as I lifted my gaze to the unoccupied corner. "Did any of you see where Astor went?"

"Maybe to find someone else's house to crash in," said Will. "About time. He's been sulking in the corner the whole time you've been gone. Real mood-killer, that one."

"Sulking?" I frowned. "You're not serious, are you? He did look after the house while we were in jail."

"He's a shitty housekeeper." But there was no real heat to his voice. "I don't mind that, since it's apparently my job to take in any wayward individual we run into, not just shifters."

"I can leave," Kit said uncertainly.

"What?" Will looked alarmed. "I didn't mean you, Kit. Really, it doesn't bloody matter where the assassin goes."

"It does when Ember's in love with him," said Cori.

I went scarlet. "Nope. Not even close."

If my sister had been trying to alleviate Will's obvious embarrassment, she'd succeeded. He snickered. "Well, last night sure wasn't nothing."

"It's a... shifter thing." My argument was unconvincing.

"And we owe him a debt. I'd have thought he'd wait before leaving. Astor—"

"Yes?" said Astor, poking his head in from outside. "Did someone say my name?"

"Yes," said Will and Cori, as I said, "No."

"I thought you'd gone," I added. "You're not coming with us?"

"Didn't you say you needed someone to watch that?" He nodded to the Moonbeam, without acknowledging the rest of our conversation. "Also, there are gargoyles flying over the street. They aren't landing on the roof this time, but I know that thing has an effect on shifters."

"Damn." I studied the Moonbeam's innocuous shining surface. "This isn't a great place to keep it, but we don't have a backup option."

"I'll glamour it invisible," Kit offered. "I'm not sure if it'll work if I'm not here, though."

"I'll hide it," Astor said, "but I won't be able to stop anyone approaching the house. Don't forget that Malkin will want the Moonbeam back, and the hunters already know this address."

"I know." Where else could we possibly go, though? Giselle's house was compromised, to say nothing of our other shelters. "Wish we could ward this place like the mages do."

"I can enhance our defences," said Will. "Don't forget I still have plenty of spells left from the ones I nicked from the mages."

"That's true." I still wasn't sure we were making the right choice, but the hunters *had* gone through the mirror. The other dragon shifters were in danger even if Lorne wasn't.

And if he'd forced them to submit to his control, I was all too happy to knock him off his pedestal and set them free.

———

BY EARLY EVENING, we were ready and so were our supplies. Will had brewed some fresh shadow spells in case we got too far away from Kit's glamour, and we had plenty of defensive spells to use in case of an attack. Lorne would find it harder to stab me this time, whether I fought as human or dragon.

That just left the problem of protecting the Moonbeam while we were gone. The sound of shifters flying overhead had noticeably climbed in the past few hours, and gargoyle shrieks penetrated the otherwise quiet street. They didn't know the Moonbeam was in our possession, but it wouldn't be long before someone noticed their odd behaviour. Such as any hunters who might be roaming around the area.

Astor, for his part, had taken the car back to Samuel's house and returned an hour later with the unwelcome news that both mirror and Malkin had vanished.

"And you weren't seen?" I asked him. "There weren't any other hunters nearby? Malkin tracked us before."

"Yes, and that means he knows your current location," he said. "Not only that, he might well be waiting on the other side of the portal."

"We'll risk it," said Cori. "We *have* to. Isn't the whole reason we needed the Moonbeam in the first place because we needed to find the other dragons?"

"I only wanted to wake you up." My heart twisted. "But this *is* what Rhea trained me for. To help the others fight the Orion League."

Astor's lips pressed together. "I wouldn't risk it."

"What else should we do? Wait for them to come here?" Cori fired at him. "What the hell is it to you, anyway? Just because you're boning my sister doesn't give you the right to boss us around."

"Whoa," said Will. "Tone down the drama. I'm happy to

come along and make trouble for the hunters, but this is Ember's choice."

"I know." I looked to Astor, tried to catch his eye. "If I see the hunters, I'll come back right away and warn you. Deal?"

"Fine," he said, "but I might have to move the Moonbeam underground if this racket carries on."

"Just don't get caught by the mages," said Becks.

"I won't." His gaze passed over our group without lingering on me for longer than a moment. "Try not to get into trouble."

"Likewise." I wanted to say more to him, but not in front of the others. Urgency pressed on me, and I had the sinking sense that our time to help the other dragon shifters was already limited. "I'll need to touch the Moonbeam to activate it."

Astor held out the gleaming stone, and a static shock went through my palm when our hands brushed against one another. Emotions flickered in his eyes, too quick to read, then the Moonbeam's glow slid over my skin, bleaching the whole room in white light. Swiftly I handed the stone back to Astor and took Cori's hand, turning on the shadow spell as I did so and picturing the sloping hillside over which we'd flown.

The light expanded to cover my friends, too. Then came sweeping darkness, and the carpet slid from beneath our feet as the bright flare was replaced by the dim glow of the sinking sun. Carpet became grass, and the dirty white-washed ceiling turned to open sky, bathed in a golden sunset.

"Pretty," said Will's voice from next to me. "I can see why the dragons chose to live here."

"Quiet," Kit whispered. "They might be listening."

"I don't see any dragons." Becks hissed out a breath. "Ow. Someone stepped on my foot."

"Sorry." Cori shuffled closer to me. "This is a hell of an impractical way to travel."

"Better than getting ambushed."

At the foot of the hillside, stone houses were arranged in a slapdash fashion, and there were no streetlights by which to navigate when the sun had fully set. We'd need to reach the mirror quickly to avoid getting lost in the dark.

"All right. I'll lead the way to Lorne's first. Then Cori and I will find the others."

My skin prickled. Even hidden by the shadow spell, I felt as if I was watched by unseen eyes, but nobody accosted us on the way along the cobbled street to the large stone building we'd entered the last time.

"Here," I whispered, using my voice to guide the others. "Don't make any sound until Cori and I are back."

"Sure," whispered Becks. "Damn, this place is old. You weren't kidding."

"There's got to be a reason nobody's on the streets," Will murmured. "This place has 'town under siege' written all over it."

"C'mon," said Cori impatiently. "We only have an hour's use in these shadow spells."

"I know. Let's go." I reached for her hand. When she grumbled, I whispered, "We can't lose each other."

Cobbled streets wound between the houses, all well made yet without any modern adornments to speak of. It was a wonder they even had window glass. The chill in the air was palpable, as was the sense of trespassing somewhere forbidden. My doubts multiplied with each minute we spent here. What if the other dragons were all as unwelcoming as their leader?

A door on my left opened. Holding my breath, I tugged Cori after me, resisting the urge to look back when the door opened wider and someone came out.

It's okay. We're invisible. I continued to walk, careful to avoid making a sound, but the shuffle of footsteps behind me told me they hadn't been fooled. Cori squeezed my hand.

I halted and turned my head. The old woman who'd exited the house slowed her pace, beckoned to us. "I can see you, child. Come in."

13

"Come in." The old woman beckoned to us again. She spoke with a Scottish accent, more distinct than Lorne's. "It's dangerous out there."

No shit. How could she see us? I'd wanted to talk to someone other than Lorne, but the ability to see through illusions wasn't a dragon shifter trait and she didn't smell like one either. She must be an uncommonly talented witch, or a mage with an ability I hadn't encountered before.

"Come on," she whispered again. "I can help you. I know what you're looking for."

"How can we trust you?" asked Cori, without turning off the shadow spell. "Lorne tried to kill us the last time we came here."

"I'm no ally of his." She lowered her voice. "My name is Madison, and I'm a friend to the true dragon shifters. That's you, isn't it?"

I hesitated. She was certainly no shifter, but Lorne had been open about his disdain for humans, and doubtless that extended to mages or witches, too. Moreover, every second she spent outside risked drawing attention.

"All right," I whispered. "We'll hear you out."

Her house was much smaller than Lorne's, but also more homely. The floors were carpeted, albeit worn and tattered, and damp seeped through the walls of the narrow hallway. I kept close to Cori, scanning the dingy living room for any signs of danger. A lone candle burned on a table, but the old woman lit another as I switched off the shadow spell.

Cori turned off hers, too, and we seated ourselves in two of the sagging armchairs. The woman gingerly lowered herself onto an equally threadbare sofa, the candle offering a better view of her face. Her features were crinkled with age and hardship, her thin grey hair pulled into a knot. Though I didn't know her, she seemed familiar somehow. So did her house.

When she surveyed us, sorrow creased her forehead. "Ember, is it?" she murmured. "And... Coriander. You're sisters."

"You know us." A chill raced through my blood. "I thought you would."

"Are you a witch?" asked Cori. "How did you see us?"

"I'm a witch by practise, but one of my grandparents was a mage," she said. "I inherited some of the knack for detecting the presence of other living beings, in a similar way to how a shifter can sense one of their own. Also, we don't get a lot of strangers here."

"I gathered." My fingers drifted towards my thigh, and the healed spot where Lorne had stabbed me earlier. "Lorne attacked us, twice. Without any reason. What's his problem?"

She sucked in a breath. "I'm afraid he sees you as an outsider and a threat."

"To whom, exactly?" I queried. "We only came here for answers. We used to live here in this village, right?"

"Did you know our parents?" Cori broke in. "Do you know why they sent us away?"

Her sorrowful countenance deepened. "They did not, for they were already dead."

Dead. The word rang out like a gong, with a finality that brought the sting of tears to my eyes and a tightening in my chest that had me reaching for Cori's hand. She ducked her head, a tear leaking from her eye, then another.

"I thought so." My voice caught. "How?"

"They were killed in a battle with a rival dragon clan."

Her words sank in slowly as my mind grappled with the truth. *Another dragon killed them? Not the hunters?*

"Who sent us away?" Cori wiped her eyes on her sleeve. "Someone put us on a train with that notebook. Was it you?"

"Yes." She spoke quietly. "It was I who made the final decision, but your parents had already raised the suggestion. They feared for your lives and wanted you to grow up away from the violence until you grew strong enough to shift. I was instructed to take care of you."

Regret pierced my chest. Our parents had got their wish, in a way, but at a terrible cost. "Are there no other dragon shifters aside from the ones who live here?"

"No longer," she murmured. "This village is our oldest, an ancient dwelling that has always belonged to the dragon shifters. There were once several clans, but after years of bloodshed, there is only one left."

"And Lorne is the leader," Cori guessed. "But you're not a dragon shifter."

"I am not, but my family has always been an ally to the dragons and played a role in ensuring they maintained their secrecy from the rest of the world," she said. "However, most of the others left a long time ago as the violence escalated. Now Lorne has tightened his grip, enforcing laws forbidding us to leave the village and interact with the outside world. Since the invasion, the restrictions have only grown worse."

My throat tightened. "I don't get it. The notebook never

said the other dragons were the threat. Just the Orion League. The hunters. Where do they fit in?"

"The League is the reason we're in this sorry state," she said. "At least, according to Lorne. They were a more active threat to us at the time you were sent away, and Lorne's initial bid for power revolved around promises to keep us safe from them."

"They aren't here now?" What of the hunters who had come through the mirror? "The notebook didn't even mention Lorne."

"I am sorry for that," she said. "I hoped by the time you reached adulthood, this feud would be over and we would be free. I'd be able to explain how your parents died—the battle between the clans is too brutal a story for children to grow up with—and it was easier to blame the League than to burden you with the knowledge that some of your fellow dragon shifters are merciless killers."

My hands fisted in my lap. I didn't agree with her, but I understood. If I could have spared Cori that knowledge a little longer, I would have.

"Then the invasion happened," said Cori. "Did you know Samuel?"

"I did." Anxiousness layered her voice. "I haven't heard from him since before the faeries came. How is he?"

"Dead," I said, with a pang to my chest. "The League killed him."

"I'm terribly sorry to hear that," she said, with seeming genuine sadness. "But you were able to use the mirror?"

"Yes," lied Cori. "We came straight here."

My mouth parted, but I didn't contradict her. If Madison didn't know the mirror had broken, she wouldn't have assumed we'd used the Moonbeam. She might not even know we'd taken it from the hunters, and while her remorse seemed genuine, Cori had evidently decided that we didn't know the old woman well enough to entrust her with that information.

My sister might well be right. We'd been duped in the past, and who was to say how she'd react if we admitted the hunters held the other mirror and not the Moonbeam?

Madison frowned. "If Samuel is dead, who told you how to use the mirror?"

"He only died this morning," I said, regret clenching inside me. "I injured the hunters' leader and escaped. Do you know of him—Malkin?"

"Yes." Her eyes closed for a brief moment. "I know of him and his family. His grandparents were hunters—not in the League sense, but hunting animals, particularly rare ones. Malkin's grandfather became obsessed with the notion of dragons hiding in the modern world. Perhaps he'd heard a rumour or spied a dragon shifter who got careless and exposed themselves to humans. In any case, when he discovered there was an entire supernatural world living alongside the one he knew, it became his new obsession."

Bile burned my throat. "He's the one who founded the Orion League?"

"Yes, alongside a few of his most trusted friends." She spoke softly. "Their ranks grew gradually, attracting a range of individuals from conspiracy theorists to those who had witnessed a piece of the supernatural world with their own eyes and wanted more. And, in addition, many people who had committed other crimes and sought refuge from the law with someone who promised them protection and a new purpose."

"Their founders were conspiracy theorists and criminals. How apt." Cori's tone dripped with venom. "But that wasn't enough, was it? They didn't just want to kill us. They wanted to take us apart and understand how we worked."

Madison inclined her head. "That is why he opened

several bases across the country to hold the shifters he'd captured to experiment on. Most were shut down over time, as the mages and other supernaturals learned of their existence, but they've become almost as adept at surviving as we ourselves have."

"And there was a base near here?" I guessed. "They used to be active in this area, right? But they aren't anymore."

"It is Lorne who is the true danger at the present time. I wish... I wish things had been different."

"Don't we all." Cori fidgeted in her seat. "I have a question. If we were supposed to go to Samuel when we shifted, why make it so hard to find him?"

"The text in the notebook," I clarified when Madison looked confused. "You know, part of it was written in the faerie language, and the rest was invisible. How were we supposed to find a translator?"

She frowned. "Why, your guardian should have put you in touch with them."

"She died in the invasion." The day I'd first shifted—but telling Madison that would involve admitting that we'd lied to her. "But she told us enough to get us to Samuel. Were you the one who took our memories?"

It was a clumsy diversion, but also a question I wanted the answer to.

"Not I," she said. "Your memories were erased to protect you, on your parents' orders."

"There's something else I don't understand," said Cori. "You said a rival dragon clan killed our parents. Who?"

"Why, this clan." She lifted a hand to gesture at the surrounding room. "All the survivors were assimilated into one. It was the only way we could survive."

Cori and I looked at each other, both coming to the same conclusion.

The Orion League hadn't killed our parents. Lorne had.

14

Incandescent rage ignited inside me. A wave of fire roared through my bones, demanding to be released. *He killed my parents.* I caught Cori's eye and saw the same flame flickering back. Never mind the hunters, Lorne was the reason my parents were dead. The reason we'd lost our home.

Madison leaned forward in her seat. "I see your rage and I understand it, but it's very unlikely you would survive challenging him directly. Besides, his death would create complications."

"Like you being allowed to walk free?" Cori said incredulously. "Yeah, I don't buy it. The guy's a tyrant."

"Agreed." So help me, I'd find the bastard and make him pay for what he'd done. He didn't know we were in the village, so we had the element of surprise on our hands.

"You won't get near him, Ember," Madison warned. "He's surrounded by allies at all times, and he's told every dragon loyal to him to strike without questioning the next time they see you."

My nails bit into my palms. Inaction was unacceptable.

Lorne had taken our home away from us. Everything we'd suffered since could be traced back to him.

"Nice of him to give us a fair chance," Cori muttered. "We might have been allies. Not that I'd join his little cult if he was the last dragon on earth, but still."

"After the way your parents challenged him, he never would have accepted any child of theirs."

A heartbeat later, her head snapped up, and then she was on her feet with speed I wouldn't have expected of her. Crouching, she extinguished the candles with one breath and then shuffled across the room to the window. The curtains were already pulled closed, but she tweaked the edge to cover any gaps.

"Someone outside?" Had my friends come back? Their shadow spells only had an hour's use, and while Kit could use glamour to compensate, Lorne might have picked up on the presence of intruders.

I switched my shadow spell back on and trod over to the window to peer over her shoulder. A chill seized my blood at the sight of several figures walking past the house. All human, dressed in black.

Hunters.

I let the curtain fall and turned back to Madison. "Did you know?"

Sadness filled her gaze, which was clue enough. Crossing the room to Cori, I turned off the shadow spell and fixed a glare on our host. "The hunters are outside. She knew."

"If I was on their side, why would I have helped you?" Madison whispered. "I knew, because—"

"Lorne is working with them," said Cori. "I knew it."

So had I, even though on a surface level, their alliance made no sense. The hunters had killed our ancestors, forced us into hiding, and taken away our future. Moreover, it would have been far more logical for Malkin to kill Lorne and silence the dragon shifters forever. Or vice versa. Lorne was far stronger than a mere human, even with the supernatural advantages Malkin had given himself. Right?

"You have to leave," Madison said. "Now."

"Oh no." Cori planted her feet on the floor and stared her out. "I want to know why you lied to us. I knew you weren't telling the full truth, but this? What does Malkin have to gain by working with one of the dragons he hates so much? A willing test subject?"

"No," Madison said. "It's an uneasy alliance, if one exists at all, though I've long suspected the hunters played a part in Lorne's rise to power. As to what Malkin gains, it's access to the last group of surviving dragon shifters in the country."

"He wanted *me* as his test subject." My skin crawled. "He said he wanted to use me as a weapon. Against the Sidhe, maybe, but against other supernaturals, too. But the League isn't what it used to be. We already destroyed their Stronghold."

Shock flitted across her face. "You did?"

"Yes, so we're more than a match for Lorne," said Cori. "And if you're telling the truth, *you're* probably one of the people he'll hand over to the hunters first, given the chance. He's worked with witches, too."

She shook her head. "Lorne sees me as a harmless old woman, nothing more. Regardless, I cannot leave. I have too many promises that I am loath to break."

Maybe she was telling the truth after all. I took in a breath. "You can leave. In fact, you can come with us right now. We can send you somewhere safe. We don't have the mirror from Samuel's house at all. We have the Moonbeam."

For the second time, her mouth sagged with shock. "You stole it back from the hunters?"

"We did," I confirmed. "It's in London."

Her face clouded. "But the hunters do have the mirror?

That must be how they got here—and if you have friends on the other side of the portal, they're in danger, too."

Astor. I looked at Cori in alarm. "She's right. We need to get back to the others."

"We can't leave these people to the hunters' mercy," she protested. "It's not right."

"I know." The hunters wanted them *dead.* Every last one. That Lorne had been willing to make a deal with the enemy who'd hunted us to near extinction spoke to a level of callousness that I could barely comprehend—but I couldn't risk my friends either. We didn't have an army, not like Lorne did.

I can still kill him. He didn't know we were here, and if I had surprise on my side, I'd gladly slit his throat with my claws. He'd never see me coming.

More footsteps pounded outside. Madison sucked in a breath. "Go. Please. This isn't a fight you can win."

"We'll see about that," Cori murmured.

"Careful." Anger and fear churned inside me. "Don't show yourself, Cori. We'll find the others first."

Whatever happened then depended on what we found in Lorne's house.

I swivelled back to Madison. "Thank you for talking to us. For telling us the truth."

However devastating it might be. This village was living in a state of terror and facing enemies on multiple fronts. The dragons on the inside, faeries on the outside, and the hunters colluding with their leader. Could I blame them for not resisting, for not offering us any help?

We checked the street was empty before we left. With the shadow spells back on, we slipped out of the house like ghosts, tiptoeing down the cobbled street. When we reached Lorne's house, I hesitated, wondering whether to risk signalling to my friends. I couldn't see if they were around, but they'd have had the sense to hide as soon as the hunters had shown up.

I couldn't see any more black-clad figures roaming the streets, but murmur of voices from inside the house drew me closer, straining to hear. A deep-seated instinct urged me to leap in through the window and sink my claws into Lorne, but he had the hunters—the entire Orion League—on his side. Who knew what other weapons they might have given him?

I couldn't make out what he was saying to the hunters, but when I neared the door, an unmistakable white flash seared my eyelids.

Cori clutched my arm. "Ember," she hissed. "They used—"

"The mirror, I know."

Damn. There was no way to tell from here whether they'd been transported to the other mirror back in London… or through the Moonbeam. To Astor.

Caution fled. I let my shadow spell flicker off for a brief instant, just long enough that any of my friends who might be near the house would see me. Hidden again, I waited a few moments, and then walked straight into something solid and human-shaped. "Kit?"

"Quiet," he hissed. "I'm not here."

"Calm down, Kit," whispered Will from my right. "We were waiting for you. Becks is hiding inside the house."

A gasp caught in my throat. "She's in there? With—"

"The hunters, I know. She's there to make sure nobody gets in the way of the mirror."

"*They* went through the mirror." My mind free-fell. "They might be waiting when we go back."

"We'll risk it," Cori murmured. "We have to. If Malkin's there, we'll deal with him. Finish him off this time."

My chest knotted. I wished I could hug her fiercely and tell her everything would be okay, but I'd never tell a lie that cruel. And as much as I wanted to make Lorne suffer, starting a fight with him now would put the lives of everyone on the other side of that portal in jeopardy.

"All right. Will, get ready."

A blast went off at the street's end, followed by a shower of sparks that erupted over the rooftops and shattered the silence in an instant. Movement stirred behind the windows, and then, as I'd hoped, the door to the house opened and Lorne stormed out, looking for all the world like a dragon trapped in the body of a human. Rage was etched on his every feature, and the same was true of the two, three, four dragons who prowled out of the house behind him. Their bodies were coiled to attack, their heads lifted to sniff out their prey.

A second blast followed the first, closer, rising over the rooftops as if someone had tossed a lit match into a box of fireworks. Lorne shifted into a dragon so abruptly that his wing nearly clipped me in the face as he took flight. Two of his companions did the same, but the others remained in front of the house, blocking the way to the mirror.

A flash of purple sparks went off, and the dragon shifters both startled, claws sliding out. One began scratching his lower back, while the other snarled and twisted, trying to reach his shoulder. *Itching spell, is it?*

Silently thanking Will's ingenuity, I took Cori's hand and pulled her into the open hallway. The mirror was in the same place as before, but the fact that Astor waited on the other side wasn't as reassuring as it might have been. If anyone would be ready to fight hunters materialising from the walls, it was Astor—they were probably begging for mercy by now—but that didn't stop me worrying about him all the same.

When I was certain the others had all joined me, I reached to touch the mirror's surface, picturing the Moonbeam in my mind's eye. A pillar of light expanded to cover the hall, and within seconds, we fell into darkness.

An elbow rammed into my back. I stumbled forward a step, switching off my shadow spell to better get my bearings. From the low ceiling, we must be in Will's basement, and the Moonbeam lay on the floor, casting fractured lights on the walls.

And the bodies. Cori tripped over the first: a hunter, female, blood soaking her chest from a deep stab wound.

"Astor?" I asked uncertainly.

Silence.

"Astor!"

He didn't appear. I stumbled past another body on my way to pick up the Moonbeam and shone its light on the opening to the underground tunnel—and Astor, blood staining one side of his face and a knife in his hand.

"Oh, good, it's you," he said, as if we'd run into each other at the grocery store and not in a room full of bodies. "I ran out of bullets."

"Fucking hell, Astor." I blew out a breath. "I hope that was the last of them. I guess that answers the question as to whether the hunters have the mirror."

"And they're working with Lorne," Cori added. "Which you already guessed."

His jaw tightened. "I hoped I was wrong."

Cori tripped over one of the dead hunters' bodies, grabbing my arm to steady herself. "Let's get upstairs. There isn't anyone in the house, is there?"

"No, but there will be, if I take that thing upstairs." Astor jerked his head at the Moonbeam.

"We'll be ready."

Will climbed the ladder, and Becks followed in cat form, shifting into a human once she reached the top. Kit joined them, and I resigned myself to following, if just to find somewhere to talk that wasn't a dusty basement full of corpses. There was no doubt that the Moonbeam placed a target on all our heads, but what was the alternative? Any attempt we made to get it off our hands would run the immediate risk Malkin stealing it back.

I put the Moonbeam carefully on the coffee table and gave the others a brief overview of our chat with Madison.

"What happened out there?" I asked. "At Lorne's house, I mean?"

"We didn't see much more than you did," said Will. "I heard voices in the hall, a lot of them, but it wasn't until they came outside that I realised it was the hunters."

"Some of them are still on the other side?" I surmised. "I wonder what they were doing."

"Threatening everyone they met, probably," Cori said. "Lorne and Malkin on the same side? How are we supposed to best that?"

"Uh, *why* would the dragons team up with the hunters?" said Becks. "I don't get it."

"Neither did I, but Lorne and Malkin are cut from the same cloth, despite being different species," I said. "They're both too fond of power to care what bridges they have to burn with their own allies to get there."

"Bastards." Astor picked up the Moonbeam. "What do you want to do with this? Throw it in the river?"

"Not with the other dragons trapped over there," I protested. "If we throw it away, we're condemning them to death. Not all of them are on Lorne's side."

"Also, if we throw it in the river, Malkin will just fish it out," Cori said. "We can't give up our one advantage."

"An advantage that spits dead bodies at us," said Will. "Interesting definition."

"We'd also be surrendering our only chance to take the hunters by surprise," I said. "Before they do the same to us—"

A rattling noise sounded from the hall. All eyes turned that way, and Astor took the lead, opening the door first. The closed trapdoor trembled, as if someone was trying to climb out.

"Shit." So much for all our enemies coming from an expected source.

My claws slid out as I leapt over, yanking the trapdoor open.

A hunter waited on the other side. To be precise, one of the hunters Astor had killed, one ear still hanging off and a hole in his chest revealing his rotting innards.

15

The undead hunter stuck a bony arm out of the trapdoor, pawing sightlessly around. Astor strode over and stamped on its hand hard, causing its grip to break and the dead man to slip off the ladder into the basement.

"I knew we should have got rid of the bodies," he said.

Will made a noise of disgust. "As if trespassing in my house once wasn't annoying enough already."

"Everyone grab some salt," I called to the others, reaching into my pocket for my own salt canister and finding it empty. Swearing, I ran into the kitchen in search of backup and found Cori had already opened the cupboard.

"We're almost out," she said.

"Shit." Will appeared behind us. "I should have bought more. I was too focused on preparing the spells."

"We'll have to burn them… with real fire, I mean." Shifting into a dragon inside the house wasn't an option. "Or take them to pieces."

It wasn't a terribly appealing idea, but it was that or let

them run amok in the basement. Of all the timing. Was this Malkin's doing, too?

Astor made to climb down first, but Will held out an arm to stop him, dangling a gleaming diamond-shaped spell over the open trapdoor. "This'll make it easier."

A blue flash ignited, setting off a blast that screamed through my eardrums and ended in a wooden crunch that sounded suspiciously like a door falling out of its frame.

Will winced. "Okay, that was stronger than I thought. Let's check on the damage."

Astor descended the ladder, or what was left of it. The bottom half had been blasted clean off and so had the door to the tunnels. Bits of dead hunter lay amid the debris, twitching limbs embedded in shattered wood.

"Will, did you steal that one from the mages, by any chance?" I landed behind Astor, grimacing when I trod on a severed finger. "You should have saved it for the hunters. The living ones, I mean."

"I have a spare." Will climbed in to inspect the broken door frame. "I can put this back on, no problem. Let's see what's happening in there."

I stepped over a twitching limb and peered through the hole that had once been a door. The narrow tunnel was littered with body parts, but a distinct shuffling noise echoed further in.

"Someone has been busy raising the dead down here," Astor said in a low voice. "I'd say those are the least of what we can expect."

Malkin? I let my claws slide out, following the sound of movement. "Everyone, get ready. We have company."

I refused to the Moonbeam fall into the hunters' hands again. Living or dead.

I rounded the corner into the oncoming undead, claws

severing decaying flesh from bone. One dead hunter fell, but another took its place, and the confined space made it impossible to take out more than one at a time. Astor fought, too, his knife cleaving into every undead he could reach. The battle's clamour echoed off the cave walls and made it hard for me to hear if anyone living was among the dead.

Cutting two more undead down, I climbed over their bodies. My nose told me more waited further in. "I think our necromancer is ready to make a move."

"Or already has." Astor's tone was grim. "I bet we'll find Malkin lurking down here, too."

"Bring it." Better that than him walking through the Moonbeam into our living room. "Who's coming?"

"I think Kit's staying with the Moonbeam," said Will. "Becks, too."

My instincts rebelled, but the Moonbeam was safer in the house than in tunnels swarming with dead, and I wouldn't make it any easier for Malkin to steal it from my hands and use it against me. *Not this time.* "Cori?"

"I'm coming. I owe him a good kick or three."

I took the lead, following my nose. Though my senses were clogged with the stench of the dead, I soon found myself familiar with the route. We were moving south, in the direction of where the first dead hunters had been dragged out of the tunnel before being dumped in the river. But we hadn't found any traces of the ritual site on our last search. Where had they come from?

A hollow echo, like a stone being dropped into a hole. I stepped forward, hearing the same echo again, again.

Then the ground gave way beneath my feet. I flailed for a moment, claws scrambling for a ledge but finding nothing. My claws sliced the earth with too much ease. Dirt fell on my head and into my mouth, making me cough uncontrollably, and layers of ground gave way beneath my feet as my legs flailed to gain purchase.

Then my body smacked against hard earth, knocking the air from my lungs. I rolled over, coughing, heaving, then came to an undignified stop.

"Fuck." I groaned, coughed again, and rolled onto my back. Above, more soil fell from the half-collapsed ceiling, and based on the rough-hewn nature of my surroundings, someone had dug this tunnel out recently. Either they hadn't the common sense to realise that digging under an existing tunnel would end in the ceiling eventually falling through, or they didn't care.

Or, of course, they'd done it on purpose.

I scrambled to my feet, squinting around me. There was no obvious light source down here, and I had to half-feel my way through the tunnel, glad of my enhanced hearing. Not so much my sense of smell, though, since the place smelled of a combination of blood and something far more unpleasant.

The tight space sent panic fluttering through my chest. I moved swiftly, hoping my friends had had ample warning not to fall after me. They might not be lucky enough to survive the drop.

A high-pitched scream rent the air, jolting through my bones. My head smacked the tunnel ceiling. Wincing, I walked at a crouch, the smell intensifying until I didn't need to be able to see to know there was a dead body in front of me.

I gagged when my hands brushed against fabric and chilled flesh. The body lurched at me, and I brought up my claws, aiming for where I thought the undead's legs should be. A heavy weight landed on my feet, and I kicked it aside, shuddering.

Beyond the undead glowed a faint light that might have been a candle. Or several. The tunnel opened out into a wider cave in which gleaming candles had been placed at intervals, forming a circle.

A necromancer summoning circle.

Within its boundaries lay several bodies, their clothes stained in fresh blood. Some in hunters' uniform, some not. Malkin had been busy. But what was the point in all this? Why sacrifice hunters just to raise them as mindless corpses without the advantages that made them such deadly killers? No, there must be another purpose to this ritual.

My gaze caught on a stalagmite within the circle's boundaries which stretched almost from floor to ceiling. A man slumped against the stone, ropes binding his hands and feet and his clothes soaked in so much blood that I startled when his leg twitched. Was he alive, or undead? He twitched again, and a thrill of horror ran through me. Alive or not, he wore a long black cloak that pointed to him as the ritual's source. A necromancer, tied up within his own summoning circle.

I knew better than to step into the boundaries of a necromancer's ritual, but someone had to shut this down. I kicked dirt onto the nearest candle, but not a speck touched the blue-tinged flame.

I lifted my foot to kick the candle instead, and a familiar voice rang out: "Stop, Ember."

Malkin emerged from behind another stalagmite with a bloody dagger in his hand, displaying no sign whatsoever of the broken bones I'd left him with at Samuel's house. *I should have gone back and finished the job.*

"I knew it was you screwing around with the dead." Damn. Facing him alone, without the Moonbeam, had not been on my plan. "This isn't as nice as your last hideout."

"I have to admit I expected you to stumble in here sooner," he said. "I suppose you've grown too used to spreading your wings to return to your underground domain. I can claim some level of credit for that, I'm sure."

"Like hell," I spat. "You've been under my feet all along? Well, it's where you belong, I'll give you that."

He moved closer, pulling a gleaming gun from his belt. He didn't need me alive, as he'd demonstrated already, but if he shot me here and now, would I count as a sacrifice, too?

"Is there any particular reason you're killing your own recruits when you're already running low on supporters?" I asked. "Because they're even more useless as undead than they are when they're alive."

"They're doing what I intended all along," he said. "Every hunter is happy to willingly give their life for our cause. They know that their sacrifice will be rewarded with our victory."

"Pity for them." Dying in a summoning circle didn't seem like a worthy goal to me. But then again, I wasn't a brain-washed cultist. "Seems a shame to kill me down here without an audience. I thought you wanted to make a huge show of it, to make up for all the trouble I've caused you."

"Oh, it will be." He indicated the necromancer. "He tells me that the blood of supernaturals is more potent when used in a sacrifice than that of an ordinary person... and I have an inkling the blood of a dragon shifter is something special indeed. When your lifeblood is taken into the circle, so shall this world be cleansed."

"You don't know shit about necromancy," I said. "You don't have the faintest idea what you're meddling with, do you? Was your grandfather into practising human sacrifice in his spare time, too?"

"So you did speak to... what was her name again? Madison?"

Ice slid through my veins. I'd feared Lorne would suspect we'd spoken, but I hadn't guessed that word would have already reached Malkin, too.

"I worked it out," I lied. "You seemed to know the shifters, and this has been your goal for ages. It's not hard to guess that it's a family trait."

"Perhaps, Ember, but I know how busy you've been today," he said. "It must have been quite a blow to find your fellow dragon shifters colluding with the enemy."

You don't know the half of it. I wished I had space enough to shift and turn him to ashes. If only I'd brought the Moonbeam. I never should have left it behind.

"Mostly I'm concerned for their sanity." I did my level best to keep my voice steady. "Since you've already demonstrated you're happy to sacrifice anyone for your cause, not just your own people. Unless you promised to spare anyone who takes your side?"

I'd been trying to gauge whether his and Lorne's relationship was built on a shared goal or if it was more centred around mutual manipulation, but Malkin didn't take the bait.

"One of the more perplexing traits of your kind is your inability to know when it's time to quit. Like now, for instance." He gestured at the summoning circle and its captive necromancer. The man clearly wasn't here on his own volition and looked to be in terrible pain. Killing him would be a mercy, and without a necromancer, Malkin would have a hard job completing his ritual.

No, I thought, sickened. *I can't kill an innocent man—a prisoner—just to slow Malkin down.* Besides, it might already be too late to stop the ritual's effects unless I tore the whole circle apart.

"Yeah, we don't give up easily," I said aloud. "If you think you have Lorne under your control, you're wrong. Tyrants don't tend to play nice with other tyrants."

"Is that what you believe?" The hint of a smile nudged at his mouth. "Lorne is a willing puppet. He is no threat to my power."

"Pity he didn't finish you off a long time ago." Fury

threaded through my veins. "What I don't understand is why you spewed all that bullshit about using me as a weapon to face the Sidhe if they invaded again. You wouldn't need to do that if you already had allies among the other dragon shifters."

"I mistakenly believed you would be easier to mould into my weapon than the wild dragons serving Lorne. You swiftly proved otherwise."

"Glad I could be of use." My heart thudded in my ears. "I guess the only other thing you needed me for was to use the Moonbeam for you."

"Correct." His smile widened. "Your predecessor was unwilling at first, too, but I had years to convince him to adjust his behaviour. I have less patience now."

"Good for you." Heat boiled in my blood, a growl rumbling inside me. Maybe it'd be worth shifting after all, to see if I could bring the ceiling down both on him and on his summoning circle.

"You came here too late, Ember." Malkin moved deliberately, skirting the circle's edge while maintaining his grip on the gun. When he reached another tunnel opening, he ducked inside and vanished from sight.

"Running away, Malkin?"

I hadn't taken two steps before the candles around the summoning circle burned brighter, twelve blue-tinged flames leaping up in unison. Then grey smoke filled the space between the candles in the circle, masking the necromancer and the bodies from view.

Within the grey, dark shapes stirred, indistinct yet chilling to behold. Beings from the other side of the veil that defied description. My teeth rattled as an icy breeze slapped me in the face with a smell like nothing so much as the scent of Death itself.

I hadn't seen that kind of fog since the day of the faeries' arrival. The day the veil had split open and the dead had been wrenched back to the land of the living.

Malkin's voice drifted back into the cave. "Once your blood is spilled in the circle, your sacrifice will instigate a second breach of the veil. One that will spell the end of the Mage Lords' rule over London."

Then he was gone, and I was alone with the dead.

16

The fog closed in on me like a mass formed of layer upon layer of living, pulsing darkness. I fought and thrashed, fighting for air like I'd fallen into the sea, except greyish shadows filled my lungs in place of water and fog seized my arms like slippery tentacles.

Pushing aside the seizing panic, I swiped and slashed, my claws easily slicing through the fog but unable to dispel my fear. With my sight smothered in grey, I couldn't see the way out.

The candles. Take out the candles.

Dead hands seized my legs, and my feet slammed down on decaying fingers and toes as I fought my way through. Something brushed against my face, more solid than smoke. Earth. The ritual had shaken the already disturbed tunnel ceiling, and if I wasn't careful, the whole thing would collapse on me.

Dammit, I have to get out. Kicking at solid darkness, I caught a flicker of light that showed me a small flame burning near the ground. My claws dug in, ripping through solid stone, and knocking the candle askew.

The shadows receded, the smoke clearing enough for me to see the way out of the circle, but the earth continued to fall in solid clumps and a warning tremor beneath told me the ground underfoot wasn't stable either. Did Malkin want to bury me alive?

"Get back here, you bastard!" I spat out earth between each word as I trod through the darkened space until I found the tunnel Malkin had left through. I picked up one of the remaining candles to light the way ahead. It had a bluish tinge more like an artificial light than a true flame, but it did the job.

The thud of falling earth accompanied me into the tunnel but lessened the further I walked. The light only showed me a small area in front, making it hard to see how far the tunnel went, or whether Malkin was waiting on the other side. He hadn't been carrying the mirror with him, but it wouldn't be far away. It was his ticket to getting the Moonbeam back—if he hadn't already stolen it from my friends. Who was to tell what the other hunters had been up to while he'd been taunting me in the darkness?

A growl tore from my chest as the urge to shift came over me, but the tunnel was too unstable and even a dragon might suffocate beneath a pile of falling earth. Malkin hadn't cared about collapsing the ceiling on top of his summoning circle, but he'd already caused enough of a disturbance in the veil that the dead had started rising of their own accord. I didn't need to make his life any easier by letting myself get buried alive.

I'm coming for you, you bastard. I ran through the darkness, my shifter speed clearing ground fast, until I left the sound of falling earth far behind. Light gradually filtered in from above, and I put the candle down, noting that the path sloped upward, suggesting that I was drawing nearer to one of our own shifter-dug tunnels, not Malkin's recent creations.

With the light came the smell of rot. As the ground levelled off, it became notably damper, a dripping sound from ahead suggesting this was an old sewer tunnel or similar. The tunnel widened, and I quickened my pace, hurrying towards the source of the light. The rotting smell clogged my nostrils, and my ears picked up on a faint echo elsewhere in the gloom. *More undead?*

"Hello?" a hoarse voice rang out.

That wasn't Malkin. "Who's there?"

"Ember." I startled to hear my own name reverberating back through the tunnel. "It *is* you, isn't it?"

I gasped. "Giselle?"

Either it was another trick of Malkin's or Giselle, like Astor, had been transported underground when Cori had accidentally sent her through the Moonbeam's portal. But this wasn't a tunnel I was familiar with, and the dim lighting made it hard to make out what lay ahead.

The tunnel gradually widened into a cave, around the same size as the one in which I'd found the summoning circle. This one also contained candles, positioned around the edges of a set of cages suspended from the low ceiling.

Giselle peered out of the nearest, her face dirt-smeared and a sardonic smile on her face. "Took you long enough."

"How long have you been there?" I hurried forward, my feet splashing in water that now swirled up to my ankles. More trickled in from gaps in the ceiling, the constant dripping setting my dragon senses on edge.

I held up the candle, my eyesight adjusting enough to see the other cages. Cori and Will were in one and Becks, Kit, and Astor in the other. All appeared to be unconscious.

The candle slid from my hands as a choked gasp escaped me. The hunters must have brought the others here while I'd been with Malkin, and based on the volume of water pouring into the room, the entire cave would be submerged within half an hour at most. While that would also spell the end of the summoning circle, necromantic candles were no ordinary flames. How did I know for sure if they wouldn't keep burning on, absorbing the lives taken within the boundaries of the circle?

Shit. I had to get them out. How long did I have—hours? Minutes? The candles had to go first, so I kicked at the nearest, but the floor was more solid than the previous cave had been. I'd need to use my claws.

"I wouldn't bother, Ember." Giselle's rasping voice sounded tired. "There's no way out. I heard the tunnel behind you cave in, and there isn't another way out of here."

"Malkin got out." I didn't need to ask who'd been responsible for their imprisonment.

"He climbed." She sagged against the cage bars. "If you move fast, you might make it, but not if you touch those candles. They're booby trapped."

"I'm not leaving my friends to die." I pointedly didn't include her in that, though Giselle's attitude problem didn't mean she deserved to drown here in the darkness. "Now, quiet. I'm trying to focus."

I shifted my feet to claws, ripping at the earthen floor until cracks spread underneath the candle. At the same time, water bubbled upward from below, mingling with the murkiness already swirling on a level with my ankles. When the candle gave way and tipped sideways, the other flames dimmed, and the trickle became a steady-flowing stream.

I ran to the cages, splashing with each step. "Is anyone else awake?"

No response. Swearing, I reached for Cori's cage first, finding a padlock that was easy to snap off with my claws. The sound of gushing water filled my ears, and I shuddered as it crept up to my knees. We didn't have long.

"Cori." I reached for my sister, shaking her shoulders. "Will! This isn't the time to be napping."

"Been trying that for ten minutes," Giselle remarked.

"What did Malkin *do*?"

"Those darts."

Of course he had. Thanks to Malkin's drugs, none of the others would be able to shift even if they woke up. It was all on me.

I broke the lock on the second cage, water sloshing above my knees and coldness seeping through my jeans. Nobody woke up, no matter how hard I rattled the cages. I tugged each captive into an upright position to prevent the water from getting in their mouths and then made for the third and final cage.

Giselle's flat eyes met mine. "Give up."

"No." I waded to the door and snapped the lock off. "You said Malkin *climbed* out?"

She pointed up at the source of the water trickling into the cage. The narrow gap in the wall above looked to have recently been blocked with small rocks, but if I moved them, I might be able to crawl through the gap and bring help. No —there wasn't time. My friends would drown long before anyone could reach us.

It's all on me. My dragon instincts reacted with revulsion to the slimy water. The fire was out, drowned in water that stank of death, and my wings had nowhere to expand. But I refused to give in. "Damn you, Malkin. It's *not* over."

"What're you yelling about?"

I slipped, nearly losing my balance on the unsteady ground. Astor sat up, between an unconscious Becks and Kit eyes wide as he took in the rising water creeping up on the cage.

"Wake the others!" I called to him, running to the cage

containing Cori and Will. My sister slumped against the metal bars, her arm dangling in the water, and I pulled her upright so that her face wouldn't get submerged. "Cori. *Cori.* Wake up."

No response. Swearing, I checked Will wasn't in danger of imminent submersion and then returned to Astor. He was shaking Kit's shoulders, but the half-faerie's body was limp, his pointed face paler than ever.

"Ember." Astor let go of Kit. "We'll have to climb out. Before it's too late."

"I'm not leaving them here." Could we carry four people between three of us, assuming Giselle deigned to help? She'd finally climbed out of her own cage but didn't look to be in a hurry to get out. Rather, she perched atop the metal cage and watched the rising water with an expression of light indifference.

A new surge of water rose to my shoulders. Astor swore when the sudden current carried him out of the cage altogether. Catching himself, he trod water beside me, lifting his head to the ceiling. "Ember, climb up there. Get those rocks out. I'll bring the others."

"You—" *You'll die,* I thought. There was no way in hell everyone would make it. As I looked up, I saw Giselle was already climbing towards the tunnel opening. It really shouldn't have surprised me that she'd gone back on her advice to give up on escape now she was freed from her own cage.

With one kick, I propelled myself back to Cori and Will's cage. I lifted my sister out first and pulled her onto the cage's roof, draping her arm around the chain securing the cage to the ceiling.

Spluttering came from below as Will disappeared under the water, and dread surged when I saw Becks and Kit were in a similar state. Astor was trying to reach Becks, but their cage sagged more than the others and it wouldn't be long before the whole thing sank altogether.

"Will!" I checked Cori wouldn't slide off and lowered myself into the water again. As I reached out a hand, Will surfaced, spitting out water and gasping.

"Ember!" he said hoarsely. "Where's—"

"Help me with the others!" I saw his eyes widen as he took in our dire predicament.

Astor had managed to pull Becks onto the cage lid, but Kit still lay floating inside. Noticing, Will gasped. "Kit!"

As he swam towards the half-faerie, more water rushed over my head. I kicked my way to the surface, coughing on the filthy taste, and saw Will had Kit draped over his shoulder and Astor was swimming towards the far wall with Becks's arms looped around his neck. That left—

"Cori!"

My sister had been submerged again as the cage sagged under the weight of the water flowing in. Panic sparking, I swam over, my eyes trained on the gap in the tunnel wall. With the water at this height, I'd almost be able to reach it. Giselle was already there, treading water with her good leg, tugging at the rocks blocking the way.

"Ember!" Will spluttered when the water flowed over our heads again. "How do we get out?"

"That way!" I gestured towards Giselle. She'd moved one rock, but her human hands couldn't match a dragon's claws and she was clearly exhausted already. "Leave this to me."

I kicked my way over to her, each movement painfully slow as my inexperienced swimming technique was hampered even further by my attempts to keep Cori's head above the water. My arm and shoulder ached with the strain, my lungs burning with each stolen breath. Elbowing Giselle's hand aside, I shifted one hand into a claw and swiped at the piled rocks.

Water gushed into my own mouth, hitting me in a torrent that momentarily blacked out my vision. A roaring sounded in my ears, and my legs turned to lead weights as I swiped blindly into the dark, searching for a handhold.

Then my claws dug into solid earth, and in a final desperate lunge, I pulled myself upward.

The heaviness dragging me down vanished as I crawled out into the now exposed tunnel. Heaving coughs racked my body, and I doubled over, gasping for air. Water lapped around my knees, but the air was blessedly clear. I checked on Cori. She was still unconscious, but her pulse fluttered against my fingertips.

I pulled my sister aside when Giselle appeared through the tunnel entrance, swearing when her bad leg knocked against the wall.

"The others," I said hoarsely. "Are they—?"

"Behind me."

Will came through next with Kit slumped over his shoulder. Collapsing onto his knees, he broke into an uncontrollable coughing fit and choked out, "If he's dead, I'll kill him."

"Kit?" I reached to help him lay Kit down on the tunnel floor. The half-faerie's eyelids flickered, then he rolled onto his side and started vomiting up water.

"Astor?" I tried to see past Will into the flooded room, but the water entirely filled the space beneath the tunnel opening. "Astor!"

He surfaced, pulling himself out of the water. Becks tumbled off his back into a heap. She groaned, wheezing out a waterlogged breath. "Never again."

"Cori. Shit." I crawled over to my sister, the only one yet to wake up. "Cori!"

Kit reached her, his hand aglow in green light. "I think I

can wake her up. I've never used my healing magic for this, but it should work the same."

"Better hurry," Astor warned. "The water's coming in here, too."

Kit held out his palm. Green light shimmered over her chest, and Cori stirred to wakefulness. Heaves overtook her, and she rolled onto her front.

"Ember?" She looked blearily at me, then she spat out more water. "Ugh. That tastes foul."

"I'm never going underground again after this," Kit groaned.

"Likewise," Will said. "Everyone here?"

"Just about," Astor said from the back. "Now, move, before we end up submerged again."

Giselle took the lead. I stuck close behind her. Filthy water clung to my clothes, slowing me down, but the trickle of light from ahead told me that we must be closer to the surface than before. My hands were numb with cold, my teeth chattering, but I was more worried for Cori than for myself. Nobody spoke for a very long time, and the only sound that accompanied us was the ceaseless dripping from above. Since the trickle didn't become a flood, I managed to hold my panic in check.

Then came daylight. A grate lay above, confirming my suspicion that Malkin had used an old sewer tunnel for his machinations. I let Giselle climb out first and then followed, using my claws to reach for the opening above. I then helped lift Cori out and she half lay in my lap, burying her face in my shoulder like we were kids again.

Will came next, carefully carrying a semi-conscious Kit, and Becks and Astor brought up the rear.

"You know," Will said, "I'm starting to go off tunnels."

"Likewise," Becks croaked. "Also, flying is growing on me,

believe it or not. At least there's less chance of a cave-in or a flood when you're in the sky."

Giselle grunted. She'd pushed to her feet, half leaning against a dustbin, eyes squinting up at the night sky. Darkness had fallen while we were underground, and no sane person wanted to be out on the streets after sunset.

I rose to my feet, shivering as the cool night air penetrated through my soaking wet clothes. "Where to now? We can't go back to the shelter."

"I know somewhere," said Giselle. "Remember that old place near the waterfront?"

"Yes," Astor said shortly. "I remember. It's also known to the hunters."

"They aren't using it. I've been hiding in there for more than a week."

"Where?" I asked suspiciously. "None of us are in the mood for more of your bullshit."

"What would be the point in tricking you?" She coughed. "I deceived you about my intentions for the Moonbeam, yes, because that thing is an abomination that should have been destroyed a long time ago."

The Moonbeam. Fuck. I'd been so occupied trying to get my friends to safety that I'd forgotten their capture also meant that Malkin had stolen the Moonbeam back.

"We don't need your judgement, thanks." Becks pushed a handful of bedraggled hair from her face. "We'll find somewhere else to stay."

Giselle made an impatient noise. "Would you rather spend the night underground? It'd be a damn pity if you all got eaten by death fae due to your own stubbornness after all the effort you made to get out of that tunnel."

She wasn't wrong. I looked to Astor. "You know this place? Is it safe?"

"It was," he said. "I think she's right. Malkin won't lower

himself to staying in our old accommodation. He might not even be in the city, if he used the mirror to escape."

The mirror. He had both that *and* the Moonbeam now, and the hunters controlled every connection to the dragons in the city.

We no longer had any way to reach them.

17

As it turned out, Giselle's destination was one of London's less affluent areas which had escaped suffering too much damage in the invasion, possibly because it wasn't all that appealing-looking to begin with.

"You stayed here when you were with the League?" I eyed the tower block, noting the number of broken windows and the general air of neglect.

"The League used to own a bunch of places in the middle of the city," Giselle said. "They still do, technically, but most are out of use."

"I always forget Malkin is loaded enough that owning several buildings isn't a big deal," Will muttered. "If you're sure there aren't any hunters lurking in there, we'll take you up on the offer."

"And before you say we owe you, I'd say it's a fair exchange for getting us all arrested," I added.

"You're the one who dumped me several miles underground," she retorted. "It's lucky I didn't starve to death down there."

"Actually, I'm the one who sent you into the tunnels," Cori said, eyeing her with open dislike. "And the mages would've shot you if I hadn't. You're welcome."

Giselle glowered back but didn't respond. Maybe she remembered that it was Cori who would have been stuck in an indefinite coma if Giselle had succeeded in destroying the Moonbeam before we could wake her, but past grievances would have to wait until later.

Astor went into the building first to check for lurking Unseelie and returned a short while later. "Coast's clear."

"Good." I traipsed after him into a dingy entryway. The flat was on the ground floor, to my relief. I hadn't the energy to climb stairs after our ordeal.

Giselle unlocked the door, and we crowded in after her. A flick of a light switch revealed bare floorboards and a single threadbare sofa. A small kitchen nestled in one corner, and a short corridor led to an equally tiny bathroom and bedroom.

"Cosy," Will remarked. "Well, this is going to be uncomfortable."

"I can see if there are spare blankets in the other rooms." Astor slipped out of the flat, while the rest of us crossed the room in varying states of exhaustion.

It took all my energy to make it to the sofa before I fell into a seat, shuffling over to make room for Cori.

"Oh, that's right, drip filthy water everywhere," Giselle grumbled. "I'm going to shower first, since this place is mine."

"Go right ahead." I leaned against the sagging cushions as Becks perched on the sofa arm and Will slumped against the side, his eyes closed.

"I'm starting to think there's something to the rumour that cat shifters have nine lives," Becks mumbled. "Though the same would have to apply to gargoyles, and dragons."

"And faeries." Kit's bright eyes scanned the flat. "Do you think we can trust her?"

"Nope." Cori yawned, looking too tired to pick a fight. "But I'm not moving from here."

A haze of tiredness settled over me, broken when Astor came back into the room, carrying a pile of blankets and a bag of clothes and various other items. I rolled my eyes when I saw two knives among them. "Can't forget the weapons, can we?"

"I expect Giselle's already brought in a few." He began laying blankets on the floor. "Also, she'll turf you off the sofa when she's back."

"She's welcome to try," Cori mumbled, half-asleep. I didn't move either, but Becks sprawled out on a blanket while Will crouched down and fussed over Kit, pulling bits of dirt out of his hair.

"Are you sure you're all right?" he said. "You nearly drowned."

"I'm fine." The faerie pushed his hand away. "I have natural healing abilities. *You* don't, though. What were you thinking, fighting off five undead at once?"

"I wasn't." Will spoke quietly enough that I was pretty sure he hadn't meant for the rest of us to overhear. "I just didn't want them to take you again. I wanted to give you a chance to get out."

"That wasn't very sensible of you."

"Do I look like I make sensible life choices?" Will looked up, realised he had an audience, and moved away from Kit. "What?"

Nobody spoke. Kit himself seemed oblivious to the stares. Lying down on the blanket he'd selected, he closed his eyes and was instantly asleep.

"Wish I could do that." Will dragged a hand over his face. "What are you all looking at?"

"I'm not," Becks said without opening her eyes. "But we all nearly died, so I'd say now's the perfect time for romantic confessions."

"Romantic what?" Will said, unconvincingly.

Cori stirred, lifted her head. "Ooh, is there drama?"

"No!" Will glared at Becks, who sat upright, her eyes glittering with amusement.

"Everyone knows, Will," she said. "Even Cori does, I'm betting. It's possible Kit doesn't know, but I'd be worried if he didn't."

"What in the world are you talking about?" said Will, even less convincingly. "I'm too tired for this. I'm going to sleep."

"With Kit?" Cori said, and he blushed up to his hairline.

"Have you actually spelled out that you're interested in him?" Becks cut through Will's protest. "Because faeries— well, I've no experience with what faerie courting rituals involve, except I've heard rumours one of them involves naked dancing under the full moon."

"That," said Will, "is a myth. At least, I think it is. Yes, Kit knows. It's up to him to decide what to do about it. Never mind being a faerie, he was imprisoned and tortured for years and I'm not going to pressure him to commit to anything. Can you all go away now?"

"Nope," said Becks. "You've spent the last two years teasing the rest of us about our lousy love lives. Now it's your turn."

"Lousy?" he said indignantly.

"Oh, so he's that good?" Cori snickered. "Have you already—?"

"Keep it down," Will hissed with a glance at Kit.

"At least neither of you has traumatised Cori for life yet," Becks added, to my total mortification. Cori herself cackled, while I buried my head in the cushion and groaned. At the foot of the sofa, I heard Astor, of all people, quietly laughing to himself.

Giselle chose that moment to come back into the room. "What in the world happened this time?"

"Nothing," said five voices.

She rolled her eyes. "Shifters. Well, the shower's free. Who's next?"

Once everyone had showered and changed into relatively clean clothes, we faced the inevitable question of what to do next. Malkin might not yet know of our escape, but his own plans would continue regardless, and I doubted those two summoning circles were the extent of it. To say nothing of the mirror, the Moonbeam, and his apparent alliance with Lorne.

Astor went to get takeout because nobody else would, and the rest of us turned to other subjects to avoid treading on the live wire that was the topic of the Moonbeam. I'd have to get the full story of how Malkin had stolen it back later. Giselle didn't know anything about his current movements, but she reacted with her usual indifference to the revelation that Malkin had been dabbling in amateur necromancy.

"So that's what he was doing in the tunnel when he caught me," she said. "It's my own damn fault for going back down there to look for Astor."

"You two never ran into each other?" I asked Astor when he came in carrying bags of Chinese takeout that instantly revived me from my lethargic state.

"I was at your house most of the time." Astor nodded to Will. "Since there were undead in the tunnels."

"I saw a few of those." Giselle snatched the takeaway bag from him. "I didn't realise they'd been raised from death on purpose. *Necromancy*, really."

"He said his goal was to break the veil, like in the invasion," I said. "Not sure how the dragon shifters fit into it, but he was convinced I'd make a particularly worthy sacrifice because of that."

"Why can't rich people like him ever have normal hobbies?" Will remarked. "I also don't think he's doing himself any favours by involving himself with that Lorne guy. Seems a good way to get himself decapitated by another would-be tyrant."

"I wish they'd finish each other off." Seeing Giselle watching me curiously, I dropped the subject of the other dragon shifters. "Malkin's lost his mind if he thinks he can keep the dead under his control, too. His necromancer already died down there in the cave."

"I bet he has a backup somewhere." Will grabbed a box of noodles from the bag. "And on that note, I'd like to stop talking about dead shit. I'm starving."

So was I. It'd been a long-as-hell day, and if our house on Magic Avenue was compromised again, it looked as if we'd be stuck here for the duration. Admittedly, our living situation wouldn't matter for much longer if Malkin did unleash the apocalypse by the morning.

When we'd finished eating, I broached the subject of how the others had got caught.

"They got me first," said Will. "I was trying to keep the dead away from Kit, and the next thing I knew, someone shot me with one of those darts."

"There were living hunters amongst the dead ones," said Cori. "One of them grabbed me during that earthquake and jabbed me with a dart, too."

"Earthquake?" I thought back. "Uh, I think that was when I fell through the floor. Malkin's digging destabilised the tunnels. That's why the ceiling nearly came down on our heads, too."

"And they got Kit and me when they came swarming into

the living room," Becks added. "There must have been a dozen or more. I tried to fight them off, but…"

"I know." My chest tightened. "It's not your fault. None of you."

"Astor came in last," Giselle said. "He said he was trying to find you. Arsehole."

"It's lucky he didn't," I said, thinking of the cave-in. "I'm surprised Malkin didn't kill you on the spot."

"He didn't have time," said Astor. "Water was already coming into the cave by then. He wouldn't have risked drowning."

Giselle snorted. "Now he has more important targets than the likes of us. Such as the Mage Lords."

My mouth went dry. "Has he attacked them again?"

"If he hasn't, he will," she said. "He wants that Moonbeam back."

Oh boy. A prolonged pause followed, and Giselle's eyes narrowed. "Fuck. He stole it from *you*, didn't he?"

"Don't act like leaving it with the mages would have been any safer," I said. "Also, Malkin already had a substitute long before he took it back." And I told her about Samuel and the mirror.

Giselle still didn't look impressed. "So, instead of blaming you for losing the Moonbeam, you want me to blame you for letting that old guy get killed? I can do both."

"I'd rather you didn't," Cori said. "We have enough enemies."

Giselle tilted her head at her. "I have to admit I'm surprised your older sister's letting you run around fighting zombies after how many close calls you've already had."

"My sister doesn't dictate my life," Cori retorted. "I don't know you, but I already think you're a miserable piece of shit who takes her personal issues out on other people."

Giselle disarmed all of us by bursting into laughter. "I hope your claws are as sharp as your tongue, kid."

Before Cori could add to the argument, I broke in. "Malkin was already in contact with the other dragon shifters. He's the reason Lorne ended up gaining power in the first place. I've no idea how the dragons fit into his master plan, but I *do* know he'll figure out we aren't dead and come after us. That includes you."

"I doubt he gives two shits about me," said Giselle. "My money's on the mages being his first targets."

"And then the whole city," I said. "He mentioned using my blood—as a sacrifice—to *cleanse the world.* Whatever the fuck that means."

"Ugh." Becks shuddered. "Does he think a second invasion is really what everyone needs?"

"That or he plans to set himself up as the saviour of humanity," said Will. "That seems like his sort of thing. Though he's unpredictable as all hell, and it's hard to figure out what's next from someone who changes his plans on a whim."

"I don't know, it seems like he's been plotting with Lorne and the other dragon shifters for a while," said Cori. "Also, if his plan is to wipe out all life on earth, he does realise that includes himself, doesn't he?"

"He thinks he's beyond ordinary humans," I said. "What he doesn't seem to grasp is that it's one step from there to, well, us. Supernatural. The very thing he's willing to destroy all other life on earth to remove."

"You still don't get it," said Giselle. "In his mind, there is nothing he can't do to justify his ends, including to himself. He doesn't care about hypocrisy. And when you destroyed the Stronghold and stole the Moonbeam, you pushed him over the edge and removed all reservations he might have had about the consequences of a mass purge of supernaturals."

"I'm honoured," I said with an eye-roll. "So, essentially, his aim is to wipe out all other supernaturals—and decimate the humans, too, it's all the same to him—and then build a new Stronghold out of the ashes?"

"Then we have to stop him," said Cori. "I don't care if I die in the process—don't look at me like that, Ember. I was his prisoner. I know there's no line he won't cross."

"Me, too," said Kit quietly.

Their gazes met, an unreadable message passing between them that spoke to a shared horror they'd both experienced there in the Stronghold. Similar bonds linked us all, forged in spite of the League's attempts to divide us. For all the times they'd tried to wipe us out, they'd never succeeded.

I had to believe Malkin's current gambit would fail, too.

The silence that followed Kit's words broke when he jumped to his feet, exclaiming, "Oh! I know how he plans to survive the veil splitting open."

"What, Malkin?" I frowned. "How?"

"The fortress is made of the same stuff as the Stronghold, isn't it?" He looked around at all of us, his eyes bright. "I remember the ghosts never came into the Stronghold during the invasion. I didn't even know the veil had been disturbed at first."

"Not a single ghost got in?" After all the lives that had been taken inside the Stronghold, the place should have been swarming with ghosts. "It's made out of metal. Iron, I bet. That will have held off the invading faeries, too."

"I thought he abandoned the fortress," said Becks. "Since he's been spending all his time in the city instead."

"He might have gone back," said Will. "Now he has those two portals in his hands, he can easily move back and forth between locations."

"Yeah." He had no limits now. "He can't set up a summoning circle inside an iron fortress. Also, undead aren't fond of water."

"If he tries another ritual, he'll do it in London," Cori agreed. "Then he and his top Elites will hide in there while the faeries and the dead overrun the planet. If the dragon shifters all kill each other, too, that's a bonus."

A grim silence descended over the room. I wasn't entirely sure how the dragon shifters fit into Malkin's plan. They did still have their own mirror, and Lorne didn't seem the sort to cede authority, but right now, Malkin seemed to hold all the cards.

"Right." Giselle stood up decisively. "Now we've established we're all going to die horribly tomorrow, I'm going to bed."

Somehow, her departure lowered the mood even further. I did take the chance to ask a few more questions of my friends about the loss of the Moonbeam, but there was little that they hadn't already confirmed.

"She took the news better than I expected," added Astor. "Then again, she's had over a week to get over her temper tantrum, and nearly drowning might have mellowed her out a little."

"I doubt it," Cori muttered, getting up and taking Giselle's place on the sofa.

That left the rest of us to try to sleep on the uncomfortable wooden floor. It didn't seem to bother Kit, and Becks could sleep everywhere, like pretty much every cat I'd met, but despite the blankets, the floorboards dug in too sharply for me to relax.

"I've had enough of this," Will muttered from the other side of the room. "Astor, were there any flats in here that actually have beds to sleep in?"

"Yes, half of them are empty," Astor said. "I can't speak to whether they're in a liveable condition, though."

"I'll find one." Will paced over to the door and opened it.

I sat up, rubbing the back of my neck. "You know, I'm going to do the same."

I might not have high standards, but if tomorrow went wrong, this might be my last night alive. And besides, Astor had heard me, and when our eyes locked, he subtly motioned to the door.

I joined him outside. "You have somewhere in mind?"

"It's not a five-star hotel suite, but it'll do." He beckoned me down the hallway to another vacated flat in a similar condition to Giselle's current haunt. Good enough for me.

"There." He closed the living room door but didn't seem in a rush to follow me to the bedroom. "You can sleep in there."

"Huh?" I frowned. "Why not you? Unless there are bedbugs you didn't warn me about?"

Or he didn't want me after all. It was ridiculous for that to bother me when we'd nearly *died* earlier, but it did. My face burned.

"No, it's…" He paused, then spoke without looking at me. "When Malkin shot me with that dart, it removed the spell hiding my tattoos."

Oh. *Oh.* "I know they're there, Astor. I did tell you I didn't care."

"That was when you couldn't see the evidence."

"So?"

"I asked Will what they meant. The tattoos. Because they look like…"

"Witch marks?" Some spells used glyphs, but I wasn't clear on what language it was. Neither was Will, the last I'd asked. And Astor had, too. What had that cost his ego? He must like me a lot. "I guess they do. Did he know?"

"No." His jaw tensed. "Even a witch can't identify what the League did to me."

"That's hardly your fault," I said. "Also, I doubt Will's ever read a book of witchcraft in his life. Most witches learn by intuition, not studying. They don't need to know all the symbols to create and use spells."

He still didn't look convinced. "I could try to find out myself."

"If you wanted to," I said. "Listen, do you think that I'm in any position to judge? The last living leader of the dragon shifters is a raging tyrant. And we might all die in a second faerie apocalypse tomorrow, so if you have any desire for me whatsoever, come in here and fuck me, or else fuck off."

His brows shot up. Then a smirk crept onto his face. "That's how it is?"

"Yeah." I took a step closer to him. "Astor, I don't give a shit what kind of supernatural powers you have. I mean, I'd appreciate a warning if you're going to sprout wings, but only so I can do the same."

"Unfortunately, I doubt I'll develop any other new abilities at this point."

"I think one of us being able to fly is enough." As he leaned in closer, I forgot to breathe, forgot everything except the narrowing distance between us.

"Though..." His lips bushed mine. "I can't say where I got my powers of seduction."

"You're talking to a shifter," I murmured. "I could be turned on by an automaton if the mood took me."

"But can an automaton do this?" He kissed me with enough force to obliterate my last coherent thought. When he pulled back, I growled impatiently and pulled on his shirt, crushing his mouth against mine. He was rock-hard between my legs, apparently wanting to skip the seduction part as badly as I did.

"By the way," he said, his breath tracing a pattern from my ear to my throat, "I hope you know I want you now."

I growled as he nipped the skin behind my ear, my claws sliding out and gripping the wall behind me. If anything, that seemed to turn him on even more, his hands sliding over scale and skin and then tearing at my borrowed clothes. Desire flared to life between us, all words left behind as he drove himself into me.

It wasn't gentle or slow, but that wasn't what either of us needed. We knew we might both die tomorrow, and I was happy to surrender to instinct and leave all thought behind. Dragon and human were one, and now our desires had combined into an unquenchable fire, a heat that could never be satisfied except with the man in front of me. He rode me to the brink and over it, until sensation overwhelmed me and I broke apart.

Later, when we lay in a tangle on the bed, I had a closer look at his tattoos. There was a kind of harsh beauty in the sharp lines interspersed with swirls etched all over his chest and arms.

He arched an eyebrow, seeing me looking. "I'll get another spell tomorrow."

I weighed my words carefully. "It's up to you. You can't choose how other people see you, Astor."

"I'd worked that much out for myself, Ember. I can only assume that right now, you don't see me as a hunter."

"I haven't seen you as one of them in a long time. Even when you pissed me off."

A smirk flickered across his face. "So you wanted me from the start? I did wonder why you tied me up in the basement."

"I'm not the one who originally tied you up."

"You would have if you hadn't swooned at my feet."

I scowled. "I passed out from blood loss, remember? Don't muddle the facts. I still hated you."

"I didn't. Hate you, I mean."

"I suppose you did stalk the hunters across half the city to make sure they didn't kill me." I poked him in the shoulder. "It's kinda sweet."

"You weren't my only motive. I wanted to make Malkin suffer."

"Don't ruin it." I poked him again, and he caught my wrist, pulled me underneath him so that I looked up at his face. "Making Malkin suffer is a win for me, too. See, we were always on the same page."

"If you say so." He kissed me again, the molten heat in his eyes the polar opposite of the blank expression he usually offered to the rest of the world. The look was for me alone. A thrill chased through my nerves.

We moved against each other, slower this time, but with equal passion, hot enough to burn.

18

ime to stop the end of the world. That was my first thought when I woke up early that morning, curled in Astor's arms.

That thought was followed by a second, more immediate one. *Oh, shit. I don't have any clothes.* The ones I'd briefly borrowed from Giselle had been torn to shreds during mine and Astor's amorous activity the previous night.

Astor was in the same position, but while I was in the bathroom, he unearthed a spare bag from somewhere, containing more pilfered clothes.

"You think of everything, don't you?" I fished out a pair of jeans that looked like they might fit.

"I try to, little dragon." He gave me a kiss on the shoulder blade, and the heat within me stirred to life again. *Not now. Focus.*

The time for distraction was, unfortunately, over. Astor must have picked up on my mood, because he went quiet for a long moment and then said, "Is it the other dragon shifters?"

"No, but you were right," I said. "Lorne is evil and allied

with the hunters. Hell, maybe all the others are, too. The only reason Cori and I didn't end up the same is because we were sent away before he could corrupt us."

I wasn't sure if I actually believed that, but then again, I didn't know the dragon shifters, either. Not really. As much as it hurt to know I might not ever be accepted by my own kind, our priority was stopping Malkin and Lorne both, regardless of whoever else they drew into their schemes.

"I don't think that's true," Astor said. "Not every dragon is loyal to Lorne. That witch you mentioned, too…"

"Madison." I grimaced. "She was hiding from Lorne. I'm not sure she's even still alive." Not now Malkin knew her name. I was sure Lorne would have tightened his grip on the village even further after Cori and I had sneaked back through the mirror. There might not be any other dragon shifters left who gave a damn about us at all.

And yet for all that, I still mourned the life I might have had.

"It's so fucked up," I murmured. "I shouldn't want anything to do with those people. But I do. You can tell me I'm being ridiculous."

"No," he said. "I can't begin to understand what it's like, but I know you, and your attitude isn't like theirs. You want to be free. What you saw in that village… did that really look like freedom?"

Like the dragon soaring over the mountains in my vision? No. Not in the slightest. *But it could be. One day. If we defeat them.*

Astor went to see if Giselle was awake while I made myself presentable. When I slipped out of the room, I spied Kit leaving the flat opposite Giselle's. Not a minute after he'd gone in, Will poked his head out of the door.

"Morning." I grinned at him. "Sleep well?"

"What's got you so cheery? The assassin?"

Two could play at that game. "I just saw Kit come out of there. Will, you're about as subtle as a dragon in an antiques shop."

A flush appeared on his cheekbones. "Guess I deserved that one. Though I still think it's weird. I mean, he's a hunter."

"He really isn't."

"I'm just messing with you," said Will. "He's not a hunter. He's weird, though. Hot, but weird."

"Okay. I'll let that one slide. Seeing as we're all weird. Including Kit."

"All right, you've got me there." He grinned and sauntered over to Giselle's flat.

Inside, everyone was awake and ready for the day. In theory. I'd come up with a plan in the dead of night, but I hadn't mentioned it to Astor. If we wanted to survive, I might have to do something that would really, really piss him off. Giselle, too, but I'd taken it as a given that she wouldn't be coming with us.

"I think it's safe to say Malkin's strategy will be centred on London," I began, when I had everyone's attention. "But I don't know for sure. He'll be using the Moonbeam and the mirror to move around, and it's impossible to keep tabs on someone who doesn't stay put."

"Unless we have someone on our side with connections all over the city." Astor looked sideways at me. "Someone like the Mage Lords."

Shit. He guessed.

The others reacted with a similar lack of enthusiasm.

"Don't they want to arrest us?" said Will.

"They also want to stop Malkin," Cori said. "Maybe we should leave them a note instead."

"That won't get across the urgency." I drew in a breath. "I don't like this idea, but the mages are the only people in the city who have any idea Malkin's dabbling in necromancy at all."

"There's a big leap from there to a second invasion," said Becks. "But… shit. You're right."

"No," said Astor. "Contacting them won't just put your own freedom at risk. They're as unlikely to spare the other dragon shifters as they are the hunters, given the chance."

My insides twisted with guilt. "They don't even know the dragons exist. Imagine if Lorne got loose in London without anyone being prepared? People would die."

"Lorne might not be part of his plan," said Will, but he sounded doubtful. "I mean, he'll have his hands full hopping around between the fortress and wherever he's doing this ritual of his, if that's his plan."

"The mages haven't found the fortress yet," I reminded him. "They also don't know he has the mirror as well as the Moonbeam."

"And what exactly are the rest of us supposed to do?" Astor challenged. "You know what the mages will do to Giselle and me if they find us."

I forced myself to speak through the tightness in my chest. "Then I guess you should make sure they don't catch you."

A grim smile stirred. "I see. Enemy of my enemy and all that."

"I don't want to do this." I had to make that clear. "If Malkin's plan works, there'll be a second invasion. We owe it to the other supernaturals to warn them, and the mages have the biggest reach."

"Will they believe you?"

"They'd better," I said. "They did fish those dead hunters out of the river. They know he's been dabbling in necromancy."

That didn't mean they'd have guessed his true intentions,

but they already knew the scale of Malkin's ambitions went far beyond a few dead bodies.

"All right." Astor's expression smoothed out. "You know the Mage Lords will shoot Giselle and me down as soon as they see us. Even if they were prepared to give us a chance beforehand, they're in the middle of a major crisis. That means they're more likely to act rashly."

"I know." The knowledge sat heavily upon my shoulders. "We'll meet you later."

If we avoid a jail sentence.

THE UNIVERSE WAS NOT on our side. The first person I saw when my friends and I approached the mages' headquarters was none other than Lady Clare, who stood in conversation with the teenager I'd assumed to be her apprentice. She wasn't my first choice, for obvious reasons, but if anyone would be forced to see the truth in my warning with one peek into my thoughts, it was her.

Here we go. When she dismissed the apprentice, I approached her, steeling myself.

"Hey," I said. "We have information."

"It's them." Lady Clare raised her voice, and several other mages came out of the headquarters to join her. "Bring them in."

"Oh, crap," Will said, reflecting the general sentiment.

I suppressed the instinct to summon my claws and spoke up, loudly. "We have information for Lord Smyth. On Malkin and the League."

Lady Clare stepped forwards. "Ember, you have been lying to us for a long time. Tell me that if I probe your memories, I won't find you committing crimes against us. To say nothing of your role in sheltering a fugitive, against

Lord Smyth's direct orders. I will not hear a word from you."

So much for hearing us out.

I'd expected no less, but that didn't quell my frustration to see my friends separated and escorted to jail without anyone listening to a word we said. Lady Clare didn't even come with us. If she knew of Malkin's upcoming gambit, I didn't know, but she'd clearly decided we weren't worth her time.

The same was true of Lord Smyth. Within minutes, I found myself corralled into a cell without speaking to a single Mage Lord, and at least an hour passed before I saw a familiar face. Lord Smyth's apprentice, Roger, stood guard outside my cell, but the man himself was absent.

"Hey!" I called out. "I want to talk to Lord Smyth, or someone who'll listen. It's serious. I'm talking about something on the same level as the invasion. I'm not kidding."

The apprentice glanced at me. "I'm not supposed to talk to you."

"You just did." In the background, I could hear someone else shouting. Cori? "Whatever you think I've done, I guarantee it can't be as bad as Malkin starting a second faerie invasion. Which he's planning to do, if he hasn't already started."

"How do I know you're telling the truth?"

"You don't. Either you believe me, or the zombies come here and prove my point."

I heard a tremor in his voice. "I don't believe you."

"If Lady Clare had read my thoughts, we wouldn't be having this conversation," I said. "I have nothing to gain from lying. If I wasn't willing to risk my own freedom to give you all a fighting chance, I wouldn't have come here. Malkin is planning to break the veil with a necromantic ritual. Your boss already knows he's been raising the dead. This is the next step."

Roger shook his head, his face pale, frightened. "I can't trust you. Sorry."

"Are your boss's orders more important than the lives of everyone in London?" I asked. "Malkin's planning to break the veil. He already tried to sacrifice me. I barely escaped alive. It's the truth."

Roger looked away sharply. I could see his shoulders shaking, hear his panicked breaths. Then he withdrew, and there came the sound of retreating footsteps. *Hope he's gone to tell his boss.*

Within two minutes, Lord Smyth himself entered the cell, closing the door behind him.

"Well?" he said expectantly. "You'd better have a good explanation, Ember."

"I've been waiting to give one to you." I swallowed my frustration and ploughed ahead. "Malkin plans to use necromancy to conduct some kind of ritual that'll trigger a second invasion."

"Really." His tone was as sceptical as I'd expected. "When?"

"We don't know exactly," I admitted. "He came close yesterday when he tried to bury me alive inside a summoning circle. Once he realises he failed, he'll try again. He wants to break the veil open, like in the invasion. He claimed my death will cleanse the world."

"Cleanse the world?" he echoed, sounding as if he wondered if I had a screw loose.

"His words, not mine." I spoke quickly. "We never did find his fortress, but I think that's where he's currently hiding. He has a way to transport himself around the city using a mirror that works as a portal. It links to the Moonbeam."

"The Moonbeam." His voice lowered dangerously. "I've heard rumours that the shifters around the part of London that holds Magic Avenue were behaving very strangely yesterday, and Malkin wasn't seen there."

"I stole it from him, briefly, after I dropped a house on him." That much wasn't worth concealing. "Unfortunately, his hunters caught up with me before we were able to take it to safety."

"She's lying," said another voice. Lady Clare approached the cell door, and my heart sank in my chest. "She planned to keep it for her own. That's why she and her friends tried to steal it from us themselves."

No. Oh, no.

"Is that so?" asked Lord Smyth.

"Yes, and I dread to think what else she is concealing from us."

Anger and despair rose in equal measures. We were finished. Whether she found out about Astor or not, stealing from the mages carried a death sentence on its own.

Don't think about him. My mind filled with the image of water gushing into a cave, choking, dragging us into the deep. I forced the thoughts at Lady Clare, projecting my own terror at facing death inside a necromancer's circle.

"We wanted to keep the Moonbeam safe," I said aloud. "We knew Malkin would steal it back. Like I said, it's a portal, and it can only be used to its full extent by a dragon shifter."

Lady Clare gave no reaction. "Then you played a part in enabling Malkin to gain access to the power he desires."

My hands curled into fists. She was right, but damn, I didn't need to hear it from her. "Malkin was using the Moonbeam for years before I took it from him. I barely had it a day. And you're the ones he initially stole it back from, not me."

"If your purpose is to apportion blame, Ember, far more lies with yourself than with us," Lady Clare said. "Now, I think we've heard enough from you. Lord Smyth, I believe we should send an envoy to the necromancers."

At least she believed my warning, but it was difficult for anyone to argue with an image I'd projected directly into their mind. "Can the necromancers find out where he's hiding? He might be planning to use this ritual anywhere in the city."

"If you speak true of his goal to break the veil, the Ley Line is his likely destination."

"The Ley Line?" The name rang a bell. I'd heard the term used by witches sometimes, referring to an invisible line that ran through the middle of the city and that amplified any magic that was used in its presence.

"Yes, the Ley Line," said Lady Clare. "It's common knowledge, among those who had a front-row view, that the Ley Line is where the invasion started."

Shock slapped me in the face. "The invasion…"

I'd never had cause to ask exactly where the origin point had been. After all, the effects had soon spread across the entire city, the country, the world. And while I might have responded to the clear insult implied in the term 'common knowledge'—as if the rest of us hadn't seen the invasion close-up as well as the mages—it hardly mattered at this point.

Lord Smyth nodded, his face grim. "The Ley Line, like all spirit lines, is a seam where this realm overlaps with the spirit world. For that reason, it's particularly volatile, and prone to disturbance. This city has seen a lot of death, and if Malkin chooses his spot carefully, it wouldn't take much for the balance to tip again."

"Damn." My mind reeled. "But if the Ley Line runs through the whole city, how will you know whereabouts Malkin will pick as his spot?"

"We'll root him out," said Lady Clare. "Send out patrols to

all the key points. Lord Smyth, if you're done with the prisoners, I think we need to hurry."

Dammit, I can't stay behind. The mages didn't know the extent of Malkin's ambitions.

"Wait!" I called out as the mages began to retreat. "There are dragons—other dragon shifters. Malkin plans to use them, too."

Maybe I was betraying them, or Madison at least, by telling him that. Astor was right. The mages would never spare anyone they viewed as the enemy. I might be fooling myself for believing that any of the dragon shifters were innocent at all—but sickening guilt seized me the instant the words left my mouth.

Lord Smyth stopped in his tracks. "Excuse me? You've seen other dragon shifters?"

Lady Clare's gaze cut to me, and I knew the instant our eyes locked that she'd seen the village in my mind's eye. "Yes. Yet again, you concealed the truth."

"I don't have time to tell the full story," I said, "but Malkin has been terrorising the other dragon shifters for decades. He put his own puppet leader in charge, and there's a chance their battle will spill over into London, too. I figured you should know that any other dragon shifter that might appear probably isn't an ally."

It hurt to acknowledge that the dragon shifters were no friends of ours, but until I saw proof otherwise, I'd have to assume every dragon I encountered was on Lorne's side—and Malkin's.

"Really?" Lord Smyth's tone didn't give away whether he believed me or not. "How did you learn this?"

"With the Moonbeam." I braced myself for Lady Clare's approach and projected an image of Lorne—in dragon form, fearsome and scaly and terrifying—at her, obliterating all other images she might see in my thoughts. "I didn't know it at the time, but the portal function is only usable by dragon shifters. As soon as one of us laid our hands on it, the portal opened, and sent us to—this village."

"When you stole it, you mean," said Lady Clare. "You should have told us at once."

"What business is it of yours?" I knew the instant the words escaped that they wouldn't help my case in the least, but I was so sick of the Mage Lords trying to claim owner-ship over something that had never been theirs. "The Moon-beam was created by the dragon shifters, who were driven to the brink of extinction because other people thought they had the right to control their lives. I'm not claiming it's mine any more than it's yours, but you would never have been able to use it the way I did. There are three portals—the Moon-beam and two mirrors—and now Malkin has two of them. The third is in the dragon shifters' village."

Lord Smyth took in my words with an expression of stern watchfulness. "You believe Malkin intends to use the dragon shifters as his personal army?"

"Not exactly. I think he believes he can control their leader, but there's an equal chance that the dragons will see through the act and declare war on the hunters."

"With London as the battleground. I see." A soft sigh escaped. "You put me in a difficult position, Ember. You're very lucky you don't have substantiated connections to the League, except through your friend Astor. A significant portion of the council want you to face a heavy jail sentence, and your friends, too."

"Yes, your friends." Lady Clare pursed her lips. "I think I shall ask your sister to confirm your story."

My heart sank. "She's a teenager. She doesn't deserve for you to torture her with your powers."

"And she was complicit in stealing the Moonbeam," said Lady Clare. "Her age will be taken into consideration when she is sentenced. I will make contact with the human authorities in due course, to see if there's a place at an orphanage for her afterwards."

No. "You can't *do* that. You—"

Lady Clare gave me a thin smile, turned her back and walked away without another word.

I glared at Lord Smyth. "That was a dick move. Breaking into a teenager's mind should be illegal. And you can't stick her in an orphanage. If you cared for her wellbeing, you'd be helping to house all the teenage shifters living on the streets, not taking my sister away from people who love her."

An emotion that might have been remorse travelled over his face. "We shall see what our options are in due course, but you should know better than to expect us to let the crimes you've committed go unpunished."

"Then keep my little sister out of it," I growled. "She's not a bargaining chip, and everything I've done has been to protect her. Those other dragon shifters are supposed to be the ones who raised us. Instead, the League and their allies destroyed our home and murdered all of our other family members. We have nobody left but each other."

His response was quiet. "I sympathise with your argument, Ember, but I simply cannot set you free."

"Damn you," I said quietly. "I won't die in a cell while the world burns. I can't."

"You speak as if the mages are entirely helpless in this," he said. "We've been preparing for another attack from Malkin for weeks."

"Not on this scale," I said. "You were as unprepared for the invasion as the rest of us. Even Malkin doesn't know what will happen if he breaks the veil."

"Who told you that, your friend?" Disappointment resounded in his voice. "I confess I find your dishonesty to be a personal affront. You told me to your face that you would hand him over to me if you saw one another again. Whatever else he is to you, Astor is a fugitive of the law."

"There won't *be* a law by the day's end if your people don't fucking listen to me."

My words left a ringing silence behind, shattered when thunder crackled above his head and lightning sizzled in his eyes. "Don't push me, Ember. You said yourself that you aren't an essential part of Malkin's plan. He thinks you're dead, and we can fight him without your assistance."

"Ouch." I meant to sound sarcastic, but real hurt crept through. Did all the mages really think the dragons weren't worth saving? That *I* wasn't worth it, after all the times I'd tried to help them? No wonder the dragon shifters had retreated to an isolated village if this was how the rest of the magical community treated them.

"I've faced opposition continuously for giving you the benefit of the doubt before," he went on. "If I allow you to walk free again, the mages will divide at a time when we cannot afford to be anything but united. Stay here, and we'll revisit your claims shortly."

And that, it seemed, was the end of our conversation. He and Lady Clare retreated, and as the voices outside quieted and the corridors emptied, my last hopes of finding someone to listen trickled away.

Minutes crawled by with excruciating slowness. I cursed the mages, cursed their ridiculous laws, and cursed the apprentice standing outside my door and studiously ignoring everything I said.

"Dammit, Roger. Have some sense," I hissed. "Your boss is going to get killed."

He turned his head. "I'll let you out in a minute. I'm just waiting for Will."

"Er, what?" That wasn't Roger's voice. A flicker of green revealed Kit's pointed ears beneath the apprentice's face, and

I gave a double-take. "Kit?" He'd glamoured himself to look like Roger?

"I stole the idea from Malkin himself." He sounded proud of himself. "Almost there."

There came a thud, and then the lock clicked open.

"Ready for a jailbreak?" asked Will. "Sorry it took so long. Had to wait for that slimy mind-reader to leave."

"What did you do to the real Roger?"

"Tied him up and shoved him in an empty cell."

"Poor kid." I stepped out of the room. "And the other security guards?"

"I'll explain when we're out of here. Give it five seconds—"

There came a muffled bang from somewhere upstairs.

"Okay, three seconds. Let's run."

I did so, following Kit and Will down the warded corridor. Becks and Cori waited at the end, where Will motioned for us to stop. Kit raised a hand, and a green haze settled over all of us.

"That'll get us past the guards," Will said. "Kit, you do the honours."

On the next floor up, we found a commotion. Mages ran in all directions, shouting at one another, while the reception area was all but deserted. We didn't need a diversion to get us out of the door and onto the street.

When we'd put enough distance between ourselves and the mages' jail to risk turning off the glamour, I slowed my pace. "What had all those mages in a frenzy upstairs?"

"Kit." Will nodded to him.

"I glamoured some of the other prisoners so they turned invisible," Kit explained. "The mages just about lost their minds thinking everyone had escaped."

"It was brilliant," said Becks. "I bet they'd never arrested a faerie before him. They have no clue."

I found myself smiling despite myself. "Where to? Magic Avenue?"

"It'll have to be," said Will. "It's where we left all our stuff, assuming Malkin didn't steal it when he took the Moonbeam."

"The mages will expect us to go back there," said Becks. "And don't forget the hunters have access, too. Malkin will have told them. If he figured out that we survived drowning, I bet it's the first place he went to look."

"If he cared enough to," I added. "I wish we had somewhere else to stock up on spells."

"Here." Kit opened his jacket, revealing pockets containing what looked like half a shop. "The mages ought to guard their confiscated items better."

Will grinned at him. "Kit, you're a genius."

We found a park bench on which to sit and distribute the spells between us. Will claimed any whose purpose we didn't know, saying he'd be more than happy to test drive them on the hunters.

That left us with an obvious problem: how to find them.

"The mages seemed certain that he'd set up that ritual of his somewhere on the Ley Line," I said. "Which is invisible. Isn't it?"

"More or less," Will said. "I'm not sure I'd trust the mages' expertise, either."

"What *is* the Ley Line?" asked Cori. "If Rhea taught us, I think I slept through that lesson."

"It's an invisible line that divides this realm from… others." I gestured vaguely at the city in general. "It's also an amplifier for any kind of magic. I know witches avoid using spells on it because they have a tendency to explode."

"More than usual, that is," added Will. "And it does weird shit to faerie magic, too. Necromancers have the hardest time with it, though. Half the troublesome ghosts in the city are around the Ley Line."

"And Malkin plans to set up his sacrifice there." A chill raced over my skin as I thought of the summoning circles he'd set up belowground. "I bet that cave he trapped us in overlapped with the Ley Line, if it goes through the whole city."

"Then how're the mages expecting to find the right place?" Cori queried. "They can't fly, or teleport, I don't think."

"They're mages. They'll find a way." *We* could fly, but we didn't have the mages' contacts with the necromancer guild, and besides, the skies were far from clear. Above the rooftops, a large number of winged beasts flew closer to mage territory than I usually saw them. "What're they doing?"

"Fighting?" Will tilted his head back, observing a pair of winged gargoyles that appeared to be grappling in mid-air. "Shit, that doesn't look good."

"Might Malkin be using the Moonbeam on them?"

Something had certainly drawn them away from their usual haunts. I kept an eye on the sky as I moved closer, hearing enraged shrieks that signalled a supernatural showdown.

At first, I thought the gargoyles were warring with each other, but when one of them skimmed the rooftop of a nearby building, I caught sight of a screaming woman dangling from its claws. As we moved closer, another gargoyle swooped down on a car, crashing into the windshield, claws reaching for the people inside.

"Holy shit, they're attacking humans," said Will. "Is that Malkin's work?"

"The Moonbeam." I swore, my claws sliding out as I sprinted down the road. A gargoyle swooped down, one claw gripping its human captive and the other reaching towards me.

"Hey!" I yelled. "Cut that out. Fight me instead, you big feathery bastard."

I didn't know if we'd met, but the madness staring out of the gargoyle's eyes confirmed my worst guess. The human—male, late teens—screamed as they plummeted down. I flew in to intercept them and drive my claw into the gargoyle's throat, catching the trembling human in my other hand. As I placed him on the ground, he gasped out a thanks, eyeing me with terrified awe.

Another gargoyle flew in and snatched him up before he'd reached the street's end. I ran in pursuit, shifting as I did so. Mid-run, wings sprouted from my shoulders, carrying me into the air. I rose, colliding with the bulky gargoyle who held the unfortunate human. The impact juddered through my shoulder—even a dragon couldn't crash into a giant heap of stone without feeling pain—but it also caused the gargoyle to lose its grip on its captive.

Quickly, I reached and caught the man by the scruff of his neck. My other claw locked with the other gargoyle's. A growl ripped from my throat, and as I stared into the madness gleaming in the gargoyle's eyes, I focused on the impression of pure terror.

Fly away. Flee for your life.

The gargoyle's grip on mine broke under the raw power my dragon side projected, and it stopped mid-flight, transfixed.

I descended, deposited the terrified human man at the street's end, and caught the falling gargoyle by the throat before it hit the ground. Hurling the gargoyle onto its back, I then landed on my feet and shifted into human form. "What the hell are you doing?"

The gargoyle stirred, tried to take flight, and I shifted my hand to a claw in warning. "Turn human and talk to me or I'll rip out your throat."

This one understood my command. Turning into a heavyset man, he squinted at me through eyes half-aglow with the Moonbeam's power. "You should be dead, little dragon shifter."

"Malkin told you that, did he?" I queried. "We both know he'll kill you, too, when he's done with you. Why's he got you capturing humans?"

Wingbeats sounded above, and I glimpsed more gargoyles flying over the rooftops, each carrying a struggling human. With a brief glance up, the man before me began to shift again, stone-grey sweeping over his skin. "Their deaths will cleanse the world."

Malkin's words. The humans were sacrifices.

The man shifted into a gargoyle. I lunged forward and grabbed his leg, managing to lock my hands around a taloned foot as he left the ground. The gargoyle spun in mid-air, screeching, trying to pry me loose. I held on, my claws digging in hard enough to draw blood.

"Take me to Malkin, you bastard."

A talon narrowly missed my forehead, but I hung on tight as we flew higher over the rooftops until I had a clear view of the gargoyles' destination. Hyde Park. One of the biggest havens for half-faeries in the city, due to the abundance of magic in the area. *Damn. I bet that's because it's on the Ley Line.*

The gargoyle growled, trying to shake me loose, but I ignored him, trying to make out what was going on below. The gargoyles swooped over patches of bright forest that belonged to the Summer faeries, and colder, more threadbare areas more suited to Winter fae. Their magic had warped the surrounding area into more of a forest than a park, but despite the overgrown greenery, I made out several bright lights shining at the trees' edge. Not the Moonbeam, but almost as bright.

When the gargoyle flew lower, I recognised the bluish sheen of a necromancer's flame. A massive one, more like a bonfire than a candle.

It wasn't alone. More surrounded the park's perimeter, glowing at intervals. I was willing to bet that if I counted them, I'd get to twelve.

The park itself was the summoning circle.

19

Oh, shit. He's going to sacrifice the whole park? Did the faeries inside the boundaries have any idea that they were even trapped? I doubted it. The place was vast enough that it would have been all too easy for Malkin to set up those giant candles without most of the park's inhabitants being any the wiser. Few other people ventured close to faerie territory if they could avoid it.

My grip finally slipped free of the gargoyle's foot. I shifted as I fell, but my wings barely had the chance to beat before a torrent of blue light slammed into me. My vision blacked out as icy cold pain roared through my limbs, and when my sight cleared, it was to see the ground lurching towards my face.

I crashed through the trees into a net of branches soft enough to break my fall but hard enough to hurt all the same. I shifted into human form and slid through a gap in the branches to land in the bushes below. I sat up, shivering, feeling as if I'd run headlong into a jet of concentrated cold air. Which pretty much summed up getting hit by Unseelie magic. Ow.

I scrambled out of the bushes, teeth chattering with the cold. Dark, twisted trees crowded around me, a kind of forest that hadn't existed in modern England for centuries before the faeries had invaded. In here, nobody would have the faintest idea they were inside a summoning circle which might switch on at any moment.

"Human!" screeched a voice, and a winged half-faerie dived out of the trees.

I stepped back, raising my claws warningly. "Sorry I dropped in on you." I didn't need to start a fight, not least because any bloodshed inside a summoning circle would only bring Malkin one step closer to victory. "I'm just leaving. You should do the same."

Three more half-faeries flew in. Two also had wings—delicate, gossamer-thin—and their pointed ears and glowing green eyes marked them as Summer faeries. The third had a long monkey-like tail and a pale face dotted with patches of what looked like snakeskin.

"Guys, you're inside a summoning circle," I warned. "This place is about to explode."

"You're trespassing." The long-tailed faerie threw a handful of green light, which I dodged. Unlike the Winter magic, the effect was more of a warm breeze that hit the ground, conjuring up a wall of thorny branches where it struck.

"Seriously, you need to leave." My claws swiped a layer of thorns away, and I broke into a sprint, wishing I'd taken note of the way out. The place was warped by faerie magic, covered in a mass of tangled forests and creeping plants, and I saw no signs of any glowing candles when I emerged from one thicket of trees only to find myself in another.

Damn. How many lives are contained within the circle?

The scent of blood ignited my shifter senses a moment before I tripped over a body. A hobgoblin or similar creature lay beheaded amid the bushes, and a flurry of redcaps tore into another, screaming with bloodlust. I must have crossed into an Unseelie section of the territory. Winter faeries tended to be more overtly violent—though that wasn't to say Summer ones didn't pack a nasty punch of their own—but the fae might well kick the ritual into action all by themselves without Malkin having to do a thing. So much magic filled this place that I dreaded to think of the amount of power already inside the summoning circle. And generally, when two incompatible magical forces slammed against each other, they had a tendency to explode.

I sidestepped the bodies, kicked a redcap out of my path, and emerged from the swathe of trees onto a battlefield. Magic filled the sky in vibrant green and blue currents, but the faeries weren't fighting against each other. Rather, winged beasts descended upon the park, eyes glazed with the familiar blankness of those controlled by the Moonbeam.

Malkin's shifters. There were gargoyles among them, too, but the majority of the beasts attacking the faeries resembled the enormous furred creatures that Malkin had created and enslaved to his will. Both Summer and Winter faeries fought against the intrusion on their territory with vicious fury. The shifters were huge, but faeries were stronger, possessing magic that no shifter could hope to match. The shifters' huge bodies flew through the air, lanced through with thorny attacks or caught in blizzards of icicles.

When a blue-eyed Winter half-faerie took aim at me, I shouted, "I'm not with them! Stop fighting and run. This place is a giant summoning circle."

My warning went unheard, but a half-dozen fae heard my shout and turned on me, too. Green light clashed with blue, and I dodged a shower of thorns as I repeated my warning. It was hopeless. I hadn't a hope in hell of convincing them all to leave before they turned me into a human—or dragon—pincushion.

Fire roared through my chest as I shifted into dragon form and launched into flight, no longer encumbered by the trees. I gained height quickly, half my attention on the faeries hurling attacks up from the ground.

A whirring noise above was my only warning before a heavy net slammed over my wings, driving me downward. I snarled, beating my wings an attempt to dislodge the net.

Piercing light drew my gaze upward. The Moonbeam shone like a beacon in Malkin's outstretched hand. He stood braced against the open door of his helicopter, apparently unconcerned with the risk of falling out.

"I suspected you'd defy me again, Ember," he called to me. "I suppose you did ask me for a more dramatic end."

Not if I can help it.

I tried to shake off the net, but the webbing tangled around my wings and refused to budge. Worse, the Moonbeam's glow had drawn several monstrous shifters into its orbit. As they flew at me, I dropped in height, still attempting to free myself.

A solid wave of blue light hit me with the force of a truck. The resulting chill crept beneath my scales and sent a shock through my nerves that threatened to drive me into unconsciousness. One of the monstrous shifters froze solid and fell out of the sky, and for the second time that day, I found myself in a downward descent towards the forest. The net encasing my wings made it impossible to slow the fall.

This is gonna hurt.

The second collision shook my whole body down to the bones. My vision momentarily blacked out. I came to, draped over a tree with my human limbs bloodied and the net half-crushing my back. My human body felt like I'd broken at least five ribs. I groaned, whimpering in pain. I tugged at the net with clumsy hands, trying to pull it off me.

Green light filled my vision. The pain vanished outright with a suddenness that nearly made me pass out again in relief. I looked for my saviour and spied Kit perched elegantly in another tree.

"Sorry," he said. "I wasn't fast enough to catch you, but I healed you."

"Thank you." I lashed out at the net with my claws and sliced it to ribbons. "Fucking Malkin. Kit—did you see him? Is he above us?"

"No, he flew away." He bounded lithely out of the tree. "The others are coming."

"Kit, we need to get the hell out of here," I said. "This park —it's the summoning circle. Malkin plans to sacrifice everyone in it. Including us."

The colour drained from his face. "I didn't know. Will, Becks and Cori are already in here."

"Oh god." I scrambled out of the tree and landed beside Kit.

He looked up at me, distress stark on his face. "A third of London's half-faerie population lives in here, too."

"I know." I pushed branches aside, having once again lost all sense of direction. "Where'd you last see the others?"

"This way." He motioned for me to follow, navigating the winding forest with the natural ease attainable only to a Summer faerie. Bushes didn't tangle around his feet, and I could have sworn even the trees moved their branches out of his way. I, however, tripped over every root and bough that crossed my path and would have lost sight of him if he hadn't stopped at the forest's edge to wait.

Ahead, the ground had split in two as though hit by an earthquake, jagged cracks shredding the earth. From within, a pair of huge hands reached for the surface, sending a ripple through the area that shook the trees to their roots.

A giant. The disturbance must have woken it from slumber. Once out of the pit, the colossal beast dragged its huge body upright, lifting a menacing-looking spiked instrument in its hands that was longer than my whole body.

Kit let out a frightened squeak. "This way!"

We kept running, skirting the pit and passing behind the giant, until we reached an opening to the forest. The others crouched amid the branches. When she saw me, Cori ran over and hugged me so tight I could barely breathe.

"Ember, you're bleeding."

"Kit healed me. Guys, you need to get out. We're inside the summoning circle right now."

"You've gotta be kidding me," Will said, horrified. "Is that why Malkin took off?"

"You saw him?"

"Nobody else would wave the Moonbeam around from a helicopter above a battlefield."

"We need to move!" Kit insisted. "The realms are fracturing again. I can sense it."

"How?" Becks lifted her head to the sky. "I can feel *something* in the air, but I thought it was the faeries' magic."

"It's all linked," Kit said in a quiet, tortured voice. "The Ley Line connects *all* the realms. The spirit world, the human world, and the realm of the fae. None will be spared."

"That's how the invasion happened," I said, the pieces slotting together. "All three worlds clashed, and everyone in this realm paid the price for it."

"This is what Malkin wants." Cori's face had paled. "I bet he's on his way to his iron fortress right now as we speak."

"Then we'll have to catch him first."

I ran over the fractured ground, shifting into dragon form. Cori climbed onto my back and hung on tight as I rose into the air. Will flew underneath with Kit and Becks, while the ground continued to split open with each of the giant's thunderous steps.

The giant looked up at us and roared, arms flailing in an attempt to reach us. Blue and green light arced through the sky some distance away, but every other fae had fled in the giant's wake and so had Malkin's monstrous shifters.

There came the clear, sharp sound of a hunter's gun. Two hunters approached the giant on either side, guns trained on the huge creature's head. The giant roared, its enormous body shuddering as the bullet reached its mark.

The second shot skimmed overhead as I dived, searching for the circle's edge. A blazing candle beckoned, showing me the way, but the hunters had willingly walked *inside* the circle. Did that mean Malkin planned to use them as sacrifices, too, or had they cared more about spilling supernatural blood than their own lives?

It didn't matter either way. The giant's body hit the ground with a resounding thud that knocked several trees over.

I flew on, towards the burning flame marking the circle's edge. The air shimmered as I slammed into an invisible force. Cori screamed from my back, gripping my scales tight. I reached out a claw and swiped at the air. The same unseen barrier blocked me. The rippling air suggested a dome encasing the circle's boundaries, whether external or a result of the ritual itself.

God. How are we meant to get out?

One of the hunters fired at me again. I flew to the right, the bullet missing by mere inches as the unseen wall slammed into me again. I glimpsed more hunters forming a guard around the circle's edge, one hunter every ten metres or so, all with their guns trained on Cori and me.

I have to land. In human form, I'd at least make a smaller target. I flew higher, trying to keep Cori out of their reach as I aimed for one of the few tree thickets left within view. I landed and drew Cori close to me, shielding her with my body.

"Why the hell can their bullets get into the circle but we can't get out?" she gasped.

"Maybe because the bullets negate anything magical." Pity they didn't seem to have any negative effect on the barrier created by the candles. "Stay behind me."

Drawing Cori close to me to shield her, I ran in a zigzag pattern, whipping one of the spells Kit had stolen from the mages out of my pocket. The smoke bomb went off in mid-air but only hit the hunters on this side of the barrier and not the ones outside. Even witch magic couldn't bypass the circle's boundaries. Billowing smoke filled the air, obscuring our vision but also making it harder for the hunters to hit us.

We ran for the circle's edge. The invisible barrier slammed against my human body as forcefully as it had my shifter form, and I staggered away. "Dammit."

"Abomination." On the other side of the circle's boundary, a masked hunter pointed a gun at me. "Time to die."

20

As the bullet soared towards us, a wave of green light encased me from head to toe and rippled over Cori, too. I sidestepped, tugging at her arm, my heart lurching into my throat.

"Kit?" she said.

The faerie's voice spoke from my shoulder. "I glamoured all of us, but it doesn't mean they can't hit you."

"I figured as much," I said out of the corner of my mouth. "Can your magic break the circle? We need to take out the candles. Just one will do."

"You'd think that earthquake would have done it," Will said.

A bang cut through the air, and green light flared an instant later. The hunter disappeared with a shout as Kit's power engulfed him, and Will followed up by hurling a spell. A flurry of sparks went off, sending the hunters ducking for cover.

A second bang split the air, but it came from the other side of the circle. A hunter dropped to the ground, clutching his bleeding arm. *Is that a bullet wound?*

Wait. Someone else had crept up on the circle's barrier. I caught a glimpse of the shooter ducking behind a parked car as she fired again, one leg slightly crouched. Giselle. Another shot hit the hunter immediately next to the candle straight between the eyes.

Astor. I didn't need to see his face to know it was him, and that he and Giselle were picking off the hunters from behind. Yet even they couldn't make an impact on the candles, nor on the barrier separating them from the rest of us.

Smoke crept in from behind me, thick and grey. At first, I thought Will had let off another spell, but Kit's scream made me turn around. Creeping tendrils brushed against my skin, more like mist than the billowing clouds that came from a spell, and a lot colder. A gasp caught in my throat when I saw a *face* staring out of the greyness, insubstantial and wispy.

"It's a person!" Kit's voice whimpered from beneath the glamour.

"Ghosts," Cori murmured. "We're too late. The dead are already rising."

"You fly," Will told me. "We'll deal with the League."

"But…" *Cori.* As if she'd sensed my objection, Cori herself stuck her tongue out at me. "We will. Go and do your badass dragon shifter thing."

"We'll look after your sister," added Becks. "We won't die easily. If you fly, you can cover more ground and can more easily take aim."

"Take Kit with you," Will said. "Dragonfire and faerie magic stand a better chance of destroying the circle than anything else."

"Are you sure?" Kit briefly flickered into view. "Will, I—"

"Yes," Will said. "Don't let anyone hurt him, otherwise you'll have to answer to me."

"I'll be fine." Kit gave him an anxious look and then vanished beneath the glamour. With the creepy smoke hiding us from view, I risked reappearing long enough for him to see me shift into a dragon and climb onto my back.

Cori. Leaving her behind felt like ripping out my own heart, but being up in the air made me far likelier to get hit and she'd be marginally safer on the ground. I took flight, aiming for the nearest blazing candle and the Elites stationed beside it.

Fire erupted from my lungs, searing the air and hurtling towards the hunters. They cried out as their bodies were consumed, turning instantly to ashes. Yet the candle blazed on, not to be bested even by a dragon's flame.

I dived, Kit clinging to my back, and breathed fire again. The tongue of flame ripped up the ground both outside the circle and within but still made no impact on the candles.

Coldness brushed against me, stifling the fire within my chest. Grey smoke filled the corners of my vision, bringing a bone-deep chill. Ghosts were normally harmless, but not here, inside a circle fuelled by death. Iciness crept beneath my scales like freezing cold hands pressed to my bare skin, and the smoke made the ground appear fuzzy and uncertain. Within, the candle flame seemed to distort and split into two. Then I looked closer and saw that the second light wasn't a candle at all but the Moonbeam, held aloft in Malkin's hands from where he stood safely outside of the circle.

What is he doing? Wasn't he supposed to be in hiding, far away from here? Even his magical protections wouldn't save him from the very realms being ripped apart at the seams, but not a trace of fear showed on his face. His expression was still, calm.

"This is your doing, Ember," he called to me. "You will be the one who brings about the end of the dragon shifters."

Lifting an arm, he hurled the Moonbeam into the circle.

I stared, uncomprehendingly, as the gleaming stone flew towards me, circled in a halo of white. There was the slightest buzz as it hit the circle's boundary and then passed through, rolling to a stop on the cracked ground.

The dragons. I dove, claw outstretched, ready to pick up the Moonbeam.

A pillar of light spilled over me, swallowing me whole.

———

A LOW CEILING blocked my wings, crushing them against my back. Kit groaned, and I turned human again, scrambling off him. "Sorry."

"Ember?" He stared around in confusion. "Where *are* we?"

"We're on the other side of the mirror." Stone walls indicated we'd landed in the dragon shifters' village, but someone must have moved the mirror from Lorne's hallway into an empty room that might have belonged to any house in the village.

An open door led into a hallway, and on the threshold lay a body. Madison was sprawled on her back, blood fanning out from a wound in her head. A bullet wound. I stared, numb, at the chilling evidence of a hunter's kill.

Madison. She'd died for helping Cori and me. I might not be able to remember the days I'd spent with her as a child, but she'd been our friend, our guardian, and Lorne had killed her.

"You bastard." My voice echoed hollowly in the empty space. "You murdering bastard, Lorne."

Searing rage seized me. I launched to my feet and stormed across the room to a half-open wooden door. Yanking it open, I stared out into an equally empty hallway.

"Ember, *wait!*" said Kit. "We can't be here. This is what Malkin wants."

Malkin. My heart wrenched, torn in two directions. One side dragged towards my own kind, and on the other, a stronger pull urged me back to my friends, whose lives were in peril.

Malkin wanted me to bring the dragons through the portal. To London. But where *were* the other dragons?

"I just want to check if anyone's alive out there." Madison had died from a hunter's shot, after all. The killer might still be in the village.

I pushed open the door with shaking hands. More bodies lay in the street. Blood pooled between the cobblestones and formed trails from the open doors to houses, as if the inhabitants had been shot while trying to escape.

It was a massacre.

Horror choked my throat, and tears burned my eyes. I was too late. I counted at least twenty dead, none of them known to me. Not Lorne or his allies. Had they already evacuated the village and left everyone else to die?

Kit cried out in warning. A giant green dragon appeared over the rooftops, flying towards us with a great sweep of its vast wings. Not Lorne, but another of his henchmen I recognised from the last time.

The dragon's claw shot out, snatching Kit around the waist.

"Let him go!" I shouted up at him. "Where the fuck is Lorne? Did he allow this?"

The dragon's claw tightened, then Kit vanished. The dragon lifted his claw in obvious confusion, pawing at the air.

I leapt in, shifting into a dragon myself. My claw locked with his, my other hand swiping at him with a brutality that barely dented the fury brewing inside me. I managed to knock several scales loose, and he roared as I tore through the vulnerable flesh beneath.

A shadow above warned me of another dragon's arrival, this one with obsidian-tinted scales. The dragon descended over the rooftops, releasing a roar that drew an echoing growl from my own chest. *Bring it on.*

Kit yelled a warning. A jet of flame shot over my head, barely tickling me. If I'd been in human form, I'd have laughed. *As if fire could ever touch me.*

The first dragon's claws wrenched from mine and stabbed me in the leg, ripping through scale, through muscle. I roared in pain, blood dripping down my side. Their claws were as deadly as mine, and even my tough scales couldn't protect me against my own kind.

I swiped back in retaliation, blood spurting as I tore into the open wound I'd already left in the green dragon's side. I dug my claws deeper into the skin beneath. The dragon bellowed in pain.

The second dragon grabbed my tail and yanked me back, but the weight lifted almost at once when a green light flashed below. *Thanks, Kit.*

Freed from the weight, I flew at the first dragon and tackled him. Pinning him down, my claws found his throat and pierced through the scales to the flesh beneath.

The dragon's breath guttered out. In the moment he died, he turned into a human, his mangled throat working as his last exhale escaped.

"Ember!" yelled Kit. "Look out!"

The second dragon dived at me again. I whipped my head around, my teeth sinking into his neck. Kit shouted again, and a voice screamed in the back of my mind, urged me to hold off on the killing blow. The human voice inside me finally gained dominance, and I landed and shifted back, spitting out blood.

"Turn human," I rasped at him. "Tell me who put you up to this. Where's Lorne?"

The black dragon landed, blood pouring from his ruined

neck, and shifted into a human, too. "Gone," he choked. "They're all gone… dead."

"They've already gone through the mirror?" Lorne had left? Was that Malkin's plan? Why had he opened the portal —to get me killed by the other dragons? Or had he hoped they'd follow me into London?

You will be the one who brings about the end of the dragon shifters, he'd said, after he'd thrown the Moonbeam into the centre of his ritual. A powerful magical object that even the dragon shifters scarcely understood, thrown into a magical circle already overflowing with magic, right on top of a Ley Line… shit, that alone might have been enough to tip the balance into a second invasion.

I had to go back.

The dragon gave one last heaving cough and fell silent. Dead, like the other. I'd killed them. I blinked furiously, refusing to let myself cry. They'd betrayed all our fellow shifters by siding with the hunters. Yet deep sorrow dug its claws in. In other circumstances—had they made better choices—we might never have been in this position.

"Ember?" said Kit. "We need to get out. The others—"

"I know," I said through numb lips. "Hang on. I need a healing spell. So do you."

"It's okay. I can heal us." He placed a hand on my arm. The pain faded, my breath coming easier, but the hole in my heart only grew bigger.

The mirror. I ran back to Lorne's house, my feet slipping on the cobblestones. My shoes were covered in the blood I'd spilled, but the sight of Madison's body kicked my disgust at my own actions to the back seat. I wished I could give her and the others a proper funeral, to mourn the family I'd never had. I wished I'd had the time to truly know her… but wishing wouldn't bring back the dead. Nor would it save the people in London who needed me, too.

Reaching the mirror, I turned to Kit. "Should I use the portal in the Moonbeam, or the mirror? I can't guarantee the hunters won't be on the other side."

I also wasn't sure the mirror would let me pick the destination the way the Moonbeam had. I'd never tried before, and it was the Moonbeam that held the deeper connection to the dragon shifters.

"The Moonbeam is where our friends are," he said. "We should go to them."

"I know." My heart twisted. "I'll try my best."

I stepped into the pillar of light emanating from the mirror and pictured the gleaming stone in my mind's eye.

The flash enveloped me, and the floor dipped beneath my feet, like stepping onto a rickety seesaw. I fell sideways into Kit, my head spinning with the sudden change, and the light fled, leaving us in darkness. Another rocking motion made nausea sweep over me.

"Are we on a ship?" Kit grabbed my arm to steady himself as we were both thrown sideways. "Why aren't we in the park?"

"Because of that." The second mirror rested against the wall, the sole spot of light in the otherwise dark room. Malkin must have taken the mirror offshore, as I'd thought he planned to do with the Moonbeam, but the rocking was more reminiscent of a smaller vessel than the giant metal fortress. "Shit. I can take us back through, but this place..."

If the mirror from the dragons' home led here, that meant the survivors must be somewhere on this ship. Did that include Lorne? I took a tilting step, glad the ship was making enough noise that our appearance had yet to be noticed by anyone outside the room. The space was wider than I'd expected, and past the mirror, a hulking shape lurked in the darkness.

A large body lay sprawled inside a cage, blue scales marked with vicious cuts, clawed feet bound in iron cuffs.

Lorne.

He must have been drugged, because he didn't stir even as I trod over and examined the cuffs binding him. I didn't pity him—after all, he was the reason my parents were dead—but it couldn't be plainer that Malkin had come out on top. And he'd left Lorne here... why? Because he hoped that I'd either finish him off myself, or that I'd set him free? Or that I'd bring him through the portal like Malkin intended and let his death be the final catalyst for the second invasion?

I wrenched my gaze away. "I don't think so."

"Ember?" Kit said questioningly. "Is that...?"

"Lorne. Yes. Malkin wants me to finish him off. I'm not taking the bait."

"I didn't expect you to hesitate." Malkin walked into view, looking directly through my glamour. "Yet again, you disappoint me."

"So do you," I said. "You didn't even have the balls to kill Lorne yourself?"

"Isn't this way more satisfying?" A cruel smile curved his mouth. "I don't *need* to sacrifice a dragon shifter to complete the ritual, but I think the two of you deserve to see your grudge through to its bloody conclusion.

"And look, your friends are ready for him."

My gaze snapped over to the mirror. Through the glass, I glimpsed the park, the grey smoke filling the circle... and my friends, surrounded by the dead. Without Kit's glamour to hide them, they were out in the open, exposed.

Malkin reached the mirror first and pulled it closer to Lorne's cage. The unconscious dragon stirred, a claw twitching. *He's awake.*

The mirror's light ignited, and alarm rang through me. "Don't."

The light formed a pillar, extending towards the cage. Kit and I stood directly in its path. At once, the rocking ship became solid ground beneath us, and Malkin disappeared.

Kit and I emerged into cold fog above earth cracked from the giant that had fallen dead some ten feet away. I squinted through the grey haze and spied my friends, all corralled into a tight space with hunters surrounding them on all sides. Seeing my sister alive and unharmed didn't stifle my horror at the hunter's gun pointed at the back of her head.

"Where the hell have you been?" Will called out. "I thought you were bringing backup."

"I wish." *Lorne.* He hadn't followed us, but he'd likely be groggy from the effects of Malkin's drugs and might not be aware of the open portal. Yet. "Do your captors know they're going to die if they stay inside this circle?"

"We tried telling them," Cori said. "They won't listen."

Kit approached the hunters at a fast stride, his eyes fixed on Will. The hunters lifted their guns, and he slowed down with his hands raised in surrender. I didn't blame him. There were at least twenty hunters within my view as well as the five or six circling my friends.

They don't get that we'd rather die beside one another than watch each other die. They'll never understand.

My claws slid out, stained in dried blood, and I faced the hunters.

"We can do this the easy way or the hard way," I told them. "If you're willing to sacrifice your lives for Malkin's ritual, it doesn't matter if you let my friends go or not. We're all trapped here in the same way."

No reply. Maybe Malkin had ordered them not to speak. Losing patience, I shifted into dragon form and fixed the hunters with my fiercest stare.

Fear me, hunters.

Fear washed over them. They swayed on the spot, some freezing with their hands halfway to their weapons.

None had the chance to shoot before I torched them.

Dragonfire surged across the cracked earth and devoured every hunter in its path. Some of them cried out as they burned alive, every inch of them consumed by the flames. Malkin wouldn't be able to raise them as undead if there were no bodies remaining.

The flames faded, revealing Malkin. He was back, standing in a pillar of light, and a body lay sprawled at his feet.

Astor.

The fire died in my throat. Malkin took a deliberate step forward, the Moonbeam's glow spilling over to him and over Astor, who lay face-down in the mud with Malkin's foot resting on his back.

A rumbling growl echoed, not from me. A dragon's head appeared within the pillar of light. Blue scales, sharp teeth, the Moonbeam's glow reflected in his blank eyes.

"You really should have killed him, Ember," said Malkin.

21

Lorne roared, jaws unhinging, and unleashed a fireball. I shifted into a dragon myself, landing in front of my friends, and the wall of fire hit me head-on.

Though it didn't hurt, my breath flew from my lungs and dazzling white light filled my vision as Lorne's fire mingled with the current of brightness streaming from the Moonbeam.

Within the blaze, I glimpsed two human figures grappling with one another. Astor's hands were at Malkin's throat—had someone turned off the shield preventing anyone from touching him?—but as soon as I tried to get closer, Lorne flew across my path. His claws grasped at any living creature that got in his way, and even the surviving hunters scattered before him.

The Moonbeam's effects prevented Lorne from telling the difference between enemy and ally, but I doubted he'd ever seen the hunters as real allies at all. Malkin didn't care about sacrificing his people. Not when he needed as many sacrifices as possible as fuel for his ritual.

I flew straight at Lorne, knocking his flight path away from my friends. Our scaly bodies clashed, claws gouging between hard scales, teeth snapping and tearing. Warm blood flowed from a wound on my shoulder, but I hardly felt it. Rage consumed me. *He killed my parents.*

Lorne's armoured body was tougher than the other dragons I'd faced, and the scales on his neck blocked what might have been a fatal blow from my teeth. Snarling, I breathed fire, not to set him ablaze but to blind him. As his eyes screwed up against the glare, I dodged his claws and went for his throat again.

My teeth locked around his armoured neck, digging through the scales, drawing warm blood. His tail lashed and locked around my legs, and my grip slipped, releasing him. His claws slashed up, and agony tore through my left arm. I roared, letting go, blood streaming down my scales where he'd clawed me.

Fog brushed against my wings, bringing a deep chill and reminding me of the necromantic trap ensnaring us. My human side urged me to look down. My friends were completely obscured by fog. Astor and Malkin had also vanished amid the grey.

In their place, ghostly figures rose up, seemingly unafraid of the two grappling dragons. Why would they be? They were on the other side of the veil, untouched by the living.

The urgency of the aerial battle slipped away. This was what Malkin wanted, a fight to the death, destined to end in both of us becoming sacrifices. Our blood spilled within the summoning circle would benefit him alone. Not us.

My dragon side roared in the back of my mind as I dropped in height, protesting that the fight wasn't over. That Lorne had to die for what he'd done to my parents. But he'd done the same to Cori, and in pursuing him, I'd left her behind. The thick fog obscuring the ground made it hard to make out the bodies below, but my friends were nowhere in sight and neither was Malkin. Had Astor triumphed over him, or the other way around? *I shouldn't have left them.*

A dragon's roar came from above. Even Lorne had vanished behind a wall of fog, and his audible frustration suggested he'd lost sight of me, too. I shoved aside the rising bloodlust upon hearing his roar and flew low over the ground, scanning for any sign of my friends. Had Malkin taken them through the portal? Where *was* he?

Lorne slammed into me, claws slicing the delicate skin on my wings. I screamed and thrashed, kicking at him until his hold loosened. Blood streamed down my wings, and agony spiked when I tried to take flight again. Hands grabbed at me from within the fog, ghostly and insubstantial yet solid enough to brush my scales. They grabbed Lorne, too, and he roared, his claws unable to repel the dead.

Unfortunately, the ghosts seemed to see both of us as fair game. Cold hands grabbed at my body, and the fog thickened until it was like flying through icy soup. Shivers rattled through my chest, cold air creeping beneath my scales and into my bones. I roared, but even my dragonfire couldn't vanquish the persistent ghosts.

Dammit, Malkin, where are you? Who had even kicked off this ritual in the first place? Even a necromancer couldn't keep the lid on a park-sized summoning circle containing enough faerie magic to level a city, but Malkin had already proven he was more than happy to sacrifice as many lives as necessary, including the person responsible.

Plenty had died already. Screaming ghosts materialised and vanished just as quickly into the swirling haze. My gaze snagged on a bright light, but it belonged to a candle, not the Moonbeam. The candle meant I was near the circle's edge, but the fog made it impossible to see the invisible barrier encasing everything inside it. Worse, it looked as if the fog was outside of the circle as well as inside, and the dead had started to materialise throughout the rest of the city. Not just ghosts, but undead, too, crawling out of the fissure created by the giant's waking.

Two dragons flew above, drawing my eyes to the sky. Lorne, locked in combat with a second dragon.

Shit. The other dragons must have come through.

Malkin had got his wish. More winged forms were visible in the sky, soaring amid the grey to rip and tear at one another with teeth and claws. The other dragons, engaged in a bitter struggle to the death. Like Lorne, the Moonbeam had incited them to madness.

But where was it? Had it fallen into one of the cracks splintering the earth? I turned my back on the circle's edge and flew beneath the battling dragons, despair clutching at my weary limbs and crimson droplets falling with each beat of my torn wings.

Cori's face flashed before my eyes, urging me on. I needed to know she was alive. My own injuries didn't matter.

Lorne collided with me again, his weight sending us both plummeting downward. The impact split the already fracturing earth. I tore at him, my claws loosening some of his scales. Bloody gouges wept tears of blood all along his back as he wrenched free, but the damage to my own wings kept me from flying out of range of his retaliatory blow.

Agony ripped through my right shoulder as his teeth sank into the flesh, dislodging scales and biting through muscle and sinew. My arm went limp.

I'm going to die. The realisation travelled through both halves of me, dragon and human alike—then light bloomed, vibrant green, and the pain lifted as the faerie healing magic kicked in. Kit must be glamoured nearby, but the fog was even thicker on the ground and the only solid thing I could see was Lorne.

Someone else—someone much smaller—dove at Lorne from above. Will, in gargoyle form, holding something shiny in one hand that I guessed to be a witch spell. I wriggled free from Lorne, my injured wings throbbing in pain. With the path clear, Will took aim and hurled the spell.

A blast ignited in a shower of sparks that caught Lorne in the mouth. Bits of broken tooth went flying in all directions, and Lorne roared, spitting out blood.

Green light washed over me again, and I sighed in relief as the rest of the pain faded from my battered body. Now recovered, I relaunched my attack on Lorne. Before he could shake off the effects of the spell, I jumped on him from behind with the full weight of my dragon form. Leaning forward, I grabbed his wing and twisted, rewarded with a scream of agony as the joint gave way in my grip.

Another green flicker prompted me to lift my gaze from my enemy. Kit appeared, followed by Becks, and then Cori. My little sister ran up and kicked Lorne viciously in the leg.

"Had to do it at least once," she said, firing a grin up at me. "Nicely done."

I slid off his back and leapt down to the earth, turning human as I did so. Leaning down, I hugged her. "I was so scared for you. You just disappeared."

"We hid underground." She gestured at the cracked earth. "Kit's magic was a huge help."

"I'm sorry I left."

"Hey, you vaporised those hunters. That helped."

"Where's Malkin, though?" And where was the Moonbeam? Malkin himself might be waiting on the other side of the portal for the danger to pass, but the last I'd seen, he and Astor had been doing their level best to kill one another.

"What do you want to do with that guy?" Becks had turned human again, looking warily at Lorne's hulking, scaly body. "Kill him?"

"Leave him," I said to her. "Malkin wants me to kill him. His death will fuel the ritual, and we don't need to do him any more favours."

"Looks like he has plenty of power already." She gestured at the swirling fog. "How do we shut this thing down?"

"Knock the candles over."

"Or stop the person who originally kicked off the ritual," Will suggested. "Shouldn't there be a necromancer somewhere in here?"

"Good point." The necromancer might be anywhere within the circle's boundaries, though, and their death wouldn't necessarily spell the end of the ritual. Not after so much blood had already been spilled.

A roar shook the sky, a reminder of the brawling dragon shifters above. I winced. "They're all under the Moonbeam's effects. At this rate, everyone will think the dragons are the real villains, at least for the five seconds the city's still standing before it's swallowed by the dead."

"I mean, it's still standing at the moment." Cori shuddered when a ghostly man brushed past her back. "The circle hasn't blown up yet. How many lives have to be taken before it does what Malkin wants?"

"Too many lives," whispered a male voice from within the fog. "Already, all the dead in the city are being drawn to this spot."

"You sound familiar." Cori spun to the ghostly man. "Hey—it's you."

The blurred figure resolved into an old man with white hair.

I gasped. "Samuel."

"Ember." His gaze travelled to my sister. "Cori. I'm sorry I was unable to help you before Malkin took my life."

"I'm sorry for what he did to you," I said. "I don't suppose you know how to turn this ritual off? Or at least find the necromancer responsible?"

He nodded, his ghostly form flickering around the edges. "The dead can move where the living cannot, and I can sense him. He's close."

"The necromancer?" I wasn't sure the necromancer would be able to stop this from within his own circle any more than the poor guy in the cave had yesterday, but I was all out of any better ideas.

Samuel glided ahead of me, his ghostly form easily navigating the thick mist. My instincts screamed against leaving the others behind again, but Lorne was no longer capable of harming them and someone had to shut down the circle. Someone had to stop this.

And one person hadn't been with my allies. *Astor. Is he dead? Is Malkin?*

Samuel's movements quickened until I had to shift into a dragon to keep up with him. My swift wingbeats easily kept pace. After a few short minutes, he slowed above the gaping hole in the ground near where the giant had surfaced.

A sharp light caught my eye from deep within the fissure. I dropped into a dive and then slowed when I realised my dragon form would never fit into that gap. I'd have to shift into a human.

I landed on the cliff's edge, peering down at the glowing light. There was someone crouched down there in the darkness, too, a man dressed in a long, ragged cloak.

A necromancer.

I wasn't sure he was even alive, but he must be. Back in human form, I half-lowered myself onto a jutting ledge and called to him. "Hey. Are you all right?"

The necromancer lifted his head, displaying a pale, bloodied face. Then he jumped at me, hands closing around my neck. The motion propelled both of us out of the fissure and I gasped when we landed on the edge, his fingers cutting off my oxygen supply. My eyes watered with pain as my hands shifted to claws, trying to pry him off me.

As his fingers loosened, I gave him a shove in the chest. He stumbled back, caught his balance, and smiled at me, a disarming expression that didn't quite fit on his face.

"What the hell?" I croaked. "Who are you?"

"I have… become more than human." The voice was Malkin's, but the mouth he spoke through wasn't his. The man was younger, dressed in a ragged cloak and bearing injuries that suggested he'd been tortured and dragged into the circle against his will. But how had Malkin gained control of his body?

Because he's a ghost.

The realisation slid into me, and a burst of hysterical laughter escaped. "Tell me how you died. Was it Astor?"

"I wouldn't laugh, Ember. I am stronger than I ever was in life."

My eyes watered as I fought to get the hysterics under control. It was so ridiculous that this man had unleashed a ritual upon London in the name of kicking off a second invasion and then fucking *died* before he could complete it. Yes, he'd possessed the necromancer's body, a feat not every ghost could attain, but he was seriously grasping at straws if he thought that made him any more powerful than he'd been as an enhanced human.

Malkin waved a hand, and the fog moved in, a hundred or more angry spirits swarming around me. My amusement faded as the chill bit in deeper. He commanded the ghosts? Did they take him for the real necromancer?

"It's like I said, Ember." His voice echoed within the fog. "The world will be cleansed."

"Not if you burn first."

I shifted into dragon form and exhaled a stream of fire.

The ghosts screamed and fled as the fire rippled through them, but it left no mark upon the dead, and when my vision cleared, Malkin was untouched.

"Is part of you enjoying yourself?" he asked. "Being allowed to unleash your fire openly? I'm sure you hate to admit that you wanted this, somewhere deep within your core. Permission to destroy with impunity."

"That's you, Malkin, not me." I landed, shifting into a human again. "Ghosts aren't invulnerable. Nobody can live forever, not even as a spirit. You should know that."

"That was never my goal," he said. "I always planned to give my own life for the mission, too."

"That'd be a nice sentiment if you weren't pretending you aren't just a twisted version of the very supernaturals you hate so much. You've become what you feared the most in the name of destroying them."

"It seems we shall disagree to the last, Ember." Fog swirled around him, obscuring him from sight. "Once the faeries came, once this realm became a sanctuary for unnatural monsters, I knew I had no choice but to destroy it."

Malkin was gone, and the ghostly beings from beyond the veil took his place. Hands reached for me, striving to claim me as one of their own.

22

The ghosts' frigid hands latched on—not to my body, but some non-physical part of me that turned to ice under their touch. As if they were grasping at my very soul. Maybe they were. Ghosts could rip someone's spirit out of their body if they were strong enough. I'd only ever seen it in the invasion. And once the two were parted, there was no reversing it. I'd be as dead as they were.

"Let go of me!" I shouted, shoving at the ghostly hands. "Attack him, not me."

Maybe they had, and that was how he'd died in the first place. Then Malkin had stolen someone else's body, and he didn't seem to know or care that that union would never be permanent. There was no bringing back the dead, not even for a necromancer. If the ghosts tore me out of my physical form, I'd be severed from life and forever trapped on the wrong side of the veil.

I shifted into dragon form, the sudden change in size dislodging the ghostly hands. Then I turned human again and landed on my feet. Changing forms had broken their hold on me, but not for long, and non-shifters wouldn't have a hope of fending them off. Had even Malkin seen this consequence of the veil breaking, or did he not care that the dead might overwhelm the living?

All this because the Orion League wanted control over who was allowed to live. No, who was even allowed to be born. I'd sooner die here than live in the world Malkin wanted.

I roared, exhaling a stream of fire that left no mark on the ghosts but drove them back from me all the same and exposed the crack in the earth. The fissure seemed larger, more extensive than before.

"Take that, you bastards!" Will shouted, his voice distorted beneath the sound of a thousand shrieking spirits. A spell rippled through the air, a blast striking the cracked earth and blowing another chunk out of the soil.

What was he trying to do? *The candle.* My gaze locked on the writhing flame at the circle's edge. As the trench expanded outside of the barrier, the earth beneath was splitting open, and with each tremor, the candle came closer to tipping over.

"Will." I landed beside him, seeing Becks in cat form darting in and out of a horde of spirits while a flicker of glamour concealed Kit from sight. Being hidden wouldn't stop the ghosts from grabbing him but made it easier for him to dodge their grasping hands.

The candle fell, toppling over the edge, and carried the flame with it. There was no visible change to the circle, but the seeping grey fog filled the air both inside and out and made it hard to tell if anything was different.

"The dead aren't leaving," I said. "Why?"

"Because Malkin caused too much of a disturbance in the veil." Kit's voice spoke from near my shoulder. "I think we're too late to stop it."

"Oh, god." Will sounded faint. "The ghosts... they're escaping."

He was right. Ghostly bodies crossed the invisible barrier around the summoning circle and surged out into the streets beyond. It didn't matter that *we* could get out now, because we'd also unleashed the dead in the process.

Becks turned human again, shaking off a persistent spirit grabbing at her arm. "Is everyone here? Where's—?"

A scream, a familiar one, jarred my bones.

"Cori!"

I spun around and saw her beneath the dragons still fighting in the sky. Lorne had risen to his haunches where he'd fallen, wings hanging limply at his back, his claw grabbing my sister around the ankle.

"Let go of me!" she screamed. "Hey! All of you! You're being manipulated!"

"Stop, Cori!" I shouted. "You can't, not without the Moonbeam."

She couldn't hear me. She kept yelling, both at Lorne and at the other dragons, heedless of the ghostly forms closing in on her.

I launched into a run. The ghosts seized me with each step, hands slipping through me as I shifted from dragon to human and back again. Lorne was still in the form of a dragon, but he was *alive*, the bastard. I never should have spared him. Cori struggled, her leg hooked inside his claw.

"Let go of my sister!" I screamed at him.

One ghost stood back, watching the scene. The necromancer, Malkin's face overlaid with his and a cruel smile on his mouth. This was his doing. He'd singled out Cori on purpose and set the dead upon her. Ghostly hands grabbed Cori's shoulders as she fought to free herself, unable to shift and shake them off like I had.

Cori's body shuddered. I shifted, shook off ghost after ghost in my efforts to reach her. I saw my friends trying to do the same —Will hurling spells that had no impact on the dead, Becks darting in and out of the fog in cat form, Kit's outstretched hands aglow with green healing light unable to reach its mark.

"Get off her!" I swiped and slashed and finally hit solid scale. Lorne's claw released Cori, and her body fell to the ground.

She didn't get up.

"Cori." I crouched down, trying to feel for a pulse, shuddering at the cold chill of the dead around me.

"Ember!"

My head snapped up. Cori's face stood out in the mass of ghosts, as transparent as the rest of them.

I'm too late.

She's dead.

A strangled scream escaped me, half human, half dragon. After everything—breaking her out of jail, facing the hunters again and again—Malkin's cruelty had found a way to take her from me after all.

I kept screaming. Cori's ghost cried out, too, perhaps telling me to stop, but I was beyond hearing, beyond thought. Shifter instinct overwhelmed me, rage and grief colliding.

I failed to protect her.

I let her die.

All I can do is burn.

I heard several people shout my name, but I ignored them as I shifted back into my dragon form and launched into flight in search of the monster who'd killed my sister. My vision turned to cinders and ashes, and even the ghosts fled from the oncoming wall of fire.

Except one. Malkin endured, a cruel smile fixed on his mouth as the flames passed through his body with no effect.

"You cannot destroy me, Ember, only yourself."

I dropped to ground level, shaking down to the tips of my wings. I knew, in the back of my mind, that driving myself to exhaustion would do nothing, that even my dragon form had a limit—but the realisation that Cori would never have the chance to shift at all tore another cry of anguish from my raw throat. My body trembled as I fought for control. All around was scorched ground, ashes raining like snow.

In the sudden quiet, I heard a voice.

"Ember." Someone spoke, closer than they should be. I hadn't seen them coming with all my senses consumed in rage and fire. What foolish human dared to get this near to an enraged dragon?

Astor. Of course it was him.

I growled a warning. He ignored me and stepped out in front of me, extending a hand to reveal the Moonbeam. White light spiralled upward, and the dead retreated, their ghostly forms repelled by its unnatural glow.

Even Cori.

My rage faded to weariness as bone-deep pain took hold of me. I'd been so caught up in tearing through the army of ghosts that my sister had been lost amid the sea of other spirits. A whimper escaped, and tears burned my eyes only to be consumed by the heat sizzling from my skin. I hardly felt the impact as I slammed down on human knees, my hands splayed onto the earth scorched to ruin by my fire.

My head lifted, my eyes drawn to the mesmerising glow of the Moonbeam in Astor's hand. A shudder racked my body as the rage threatened to return, as though the Moonbeam called to the fire within me. Like the other dragons, raging and battling in the sky above.

"Malkin." My voice shook with hate. "He…"

"I killed him."

My gaze snapped to Astor in shock. Of course he'd dealt the final blow. I'd missed his moment of triumph, and he'd missed mine, but it didn't matter when my sister was dead, when we'd lost in every way that mattered.

The glow caught me again, as the power of the Moonbeam beckoned, destructive, infinite. Text flitted across the surface, not written in English yet somehow readable to me.

I am fire, the Moonbeam said.

More words followed, blurred beneath a fresh wave of tears as grief rose to quell my rage. Cori should be reading this, too.

I was forged in dragonfire.

Each word brought new understanding. The Moonbeam had been forged in dragonfire itself. Dragons had created it, and it was ours by right. It was never meant to be wielded by a human.

I was forged in dragonfire, the Moonbeam said. *I was made for you.*

Whether the stone itself was somehow communicating with me or the words had been imprinted on it by the long-dead dragon shifters who'd created it, it didn't matter. The Moonbeam was dragonfire incarnate, and as long as it was in my possession, it would never control me or my people. Malkin had twisted its original purpose, desperate for domination over forces he'd never be able to control. Its true power would never have revealed itself to him. Nor Lorne, neither.

This was the only way to calm the warring shifters, to stop the raging magic threatening to crack open the Ley Line, and to quell the storm about to break over London.

I held up the Moonbeam and let its light spill out across the scorched ground that had once been a park. The bright penetrated the fog and rose upward to encompass the brawling dragon shifters in the sky.

I couldn't have explained how I knew what to do. The Moonbeam seemed to have a will of its own, and everyone, dead and living, began to circle around its glow. I held it aloft, capturing every stare. While I was in human form, they didn't attack, as mesmerised as if I'd fixed them with the glare of a dragon.

"Stop!" I roared, and the word rang out like an echo in a vast canyon. "Stop fighting. Now."

Nobody had listened to me before, but the Moonbeam carried its own presence and amplified my voice far beyond its usual boundaries. All eyes were drawn to the glow, dead or living. Even the mages outside of the circle's boundaries moved towards me, towards the light.

"The Orion League is your true enemy," I continued, "and they met their end today. They're done. Malkin is dead, and the League is finished. The battle is over."

The Moonbeam's glow dimmed, as if to emphasise my point, and the world seemed to release a long-held breath as the spell lifted. A dragon landed on the ground, then another, and although they were no longer held under my command, they didn't resume the fighting, either.

In the dimming glow, I saw the fog was still seeping out of the gap between the candles. The ghosts remained, albeit less solid-looking than before. They were losing their strength, both due to the broken circle and from the absence of the shifters' fury adding to the torrent of magic building in the air.

The Moonbeam's glow lingered. Malkin had brought it into the circle to fuel the ritual, and perhaps removing it would be enough to bring an end to the power keeping the ghosts in this realm.

But that included Cori.

I faltered, my hand clenched around the stone, seeking my friends. They'd all gathered in one spot near the fissure in the earth, standing around a small body.

Cori. Above floated her ghost, hands reaching out as though to grasp mine from a distance.

I dipped my head to the Moonbeam and whispered, "Please. Help me bring her back."

The Moonbeam had told me itself: it was forged in pure dragonfire, from the very essence of our kind. You couldn't bring back the dead. I *knew* that. But her body hadn't died. She'd been ripped out of it, and her spirit was still in this realm, a mere touch away. She hadn't moved on yet.

My friends parted around Cori's body to let me reach her. She looked so small, lying there on the ground, her own spirit hovering close enough to touch my hand.

"Ember," she whispered. "I…"

"You're alive." I crouched down, pushed the Moonbeam into her pale hands, and wished for the impossible. "Please, bring her back."

The Moonbeam's white light bathed her spirit and body both, calling to the dragon inside her. *Wake up. Wake up, Cori.*

The light turned to a blaze until the fire seemed to shine from within her very skin. I heard my friends shouting, and Cori herself let out a startled yell as her ghostly form blazed all over.

An image briefly flashed into my mind's eye of a woman suspended within the flames. Not Cori, but someone else, a stranger whose fiery eyes seemed to stare out of the stone itself.

A whisper tickled my ear. *"Yes… I thank you, Ember, for offering me a host."*

I recoiled, half-certain I'd imagined the voice, and a roar of pure rage cut through the air. Not a dragon's roar, but a human. Specifically, Malkin.

All around, the ghosts had begun to disappear, one by one, called beyond the veil. As each vanished, the fog thinned, and it took a moment for me to spot Malkin trying to reach me, his ghostly face screwed up in concentration.

"You will not defy me!" he screamed.

"Told you death was permanent." I didn't need to breathe fire, to rip off his head, to tear him to pieces. He was nothing, a mere whisper, and each instant consumed more of him until his last furious scream vanished into the void.

One ghost remained. Cori, hovering above her own body with a smile on her mouth. "Hey, Ember."

My heart clutched. "Cori."

She winked. As she vanished, the Moonbeam's light went out. I dropped to my knees beside Cori and opened her hand to touch the lifeless piece of rock. It had turned back to its obsidian shade, as cold as Cori's palm.

Then Cori's hand closed around mine.

An exclamation cut through my stupor. Becks jumped to her feet, Will swore, and Kit gasped aloud.

Groggily, Cori spoke my name. "Ember?"

Eyes blurred with tears, I looked into my little sister's eyes. I couldn't even say her name, only sob in relief until exhaustion claimed everything that was left of me.

23

I didn't remember losing consciousness. Only waking with a soft bed cushioning my back and Astor's face looking down at me. Fire stirred in my chest, luring me to wakefulness.

"Astor," I mumbled. "Why is it always you?"

"Because I've been given bed rest duty. I'm not good enough for anything else, according to Lord Smyth."

I blinked up at him. Something was very much out of place, but I was too sleep-drunk to make sense of what, exactly. The last I could recall, the battle had been over, and my friends had survived. Including my little sister. "Cori?"

"She's fine. Better than you are. You exhausted yourself so thoroughly that even Lady Clare couldn't wake you up."

"Lady Clare?" I sat bolt upright. "Fuck. She... wait... you're not in jail?"

A smile tugged at his lips. "Well observed."

"Am *I* in jail?"

"I don't see any bars or handcuffs. Though if you want me to procure some, I'm game."

I leaned forward and hugged him. My whole body ached

in protest at the sudden movement, and I half-fell against him, buried my head in his shoulder.

"Was that a yes?"

I punched him feebly in the arm. "I feel like hell, actually, but considering hell itself nearly intruded on the land of the living, I guess that's a good enough reason."

"Yes, it is." Astor drew back and gently pushed me down onto the bed. "I'm amazed you can speak after breathing so much fire."

"Huh." I thought back to my last coherent memories. "What happened after I passed out? Where's Malkin?"

"Where do you think?" Satisfaction gleamed in his eyes. "He disappeared along with the other ghosts. With a little luck, he won't come back."

"He'll have to face the angry ghosts of all the hunters he killed. He deserves it."

A smile nudged at his mouth. "He does. Also, the Mage Lords got onto the boat Malkin put the mirror on, set all the prisoners free, and claimed it as their own."

"Wait, they did?" I sought to find the questions I needed to ask. "And the dragons?"

"I don't know about the survivors in the village, but the mages rounded up the ones who were fighting in London and hauled them into custody. I gather that's why they haven't had much time for us. You're a tame prisoner to deal with, by comparison."

"Lorne." My hands clenched on the bedsheets. *He* was the one who'd held Cori down while the ghosts had claimed her on Malkin's orders. "I wish I'd finished him off."

"I think that would have finished *you* off, Ember," he said. "You've been unconscious for three days."

"And the mages have held off arresting you for all this time?"

"I killed Malkin."

My mouth parted. "Oh. So you did. Sorry. I forgot."

"It's less of an achievement when he caused so much trouble as a ghost, I know," he added, "but it was enough for Lord Smyth."

"He actually let you go. Fuck me."

"Really?" His brow arched. "I wondered if you were too tired, but if you insist…"

"Arse." I grinned. "In all seriousness, tell me more. Where's the Moonbeam? The mirror?"

"Both with the mages, naturally."

"Figures." I scowled. "I mean, the Moonbeam's safer in the mages' hands without the League actively trying to steal it back, but I hope they've learned some lessons. And I hope they keep Lorne well away from it."

"I'm sure you'll make sure they do."

"Do I really have that level of influence on them?" I snorted. "Don't tell me they're trying to recruit me. Or—they didn't force Cori to sign anything, did they?"

"Of course not," he said. "She and the others have been voluntarily helping with the clean-up effort, but nothing official. I think they're waiting for you to wake up before they try again."

"Then they'll just have to wait a little longer." I pulled his mouth down to mine.

———

CLEANING UP AFTER A BATTLE, as it turned out, was a more involved effort than actually participating in one. I was happy to help out, partly to avoid the inevitable moment when we'd all have to face the looming question of what to do next. Lord Smyth hadn't offered me another job trial, but I doubted I'd take him up on it if he did. As was clear, our principles didn't always align. But I wanted to mend bridges with the mages, if I could.

The morning after I woke up from unconsciousness, I found myself outside Lord Smyth's office, assuming a job offer waited on the other side and readied for pushback should I refuse.

"Come in, Ember," called Lord Smyth.

"Lord Smyth." I entered the office. "I'm free to help with the cleanup later, but I figured the faeries wanted a turn." Half the reason everything was taking so long was because every faerie who'd lived inside the park wanted to have a say in the restoration of their territory, and the mages kept having to mediate arguments between the Seelie and Unseelie fae over who got to claim which parts. I wouldn't lie, I was glad to have slept through most of that.

"Oh, it's not the cleanup," he said. "Lady Clare is handling that today."

I suppressed a grimace. Lady Clare might have been forced to accept my freedom, but it was plain to me that if she'd been head of the mages and not Lord Smyth, I'd still be squatting in a jail cell. Luckily, she'd had plenty of new prisoners to occupy her attention, including a fair few of the Fanged gargoyles who'd come out in the open in the fighting and promptly got themselves arrested for inciting violence. That had pleased all of us, especially Will.

"Then what is it?"

"We brought the mirror back from the hunters' ship yesterday," he said. "As we've had time to examine it, I've decided to grant your request."

My heartbeat kicked into gear. "I can use the mirror to see the other dragons?"

It had been one of the first questions I'd asked, once I'd established that my friends and I were free to leave without being tied to any contracts. I'd expected it would take much longer for him to agree for me to visit the other dragon shifters, if ever.

"Of course," he said. "We did travel through once to check that no rogue dragons were attacking the nearby human habitations."

"As though we're all uncivilised monsters." Oops. I probably shouldn't have said that aloud.

"Lorne's influence spread widely," he said. "It was necessary to protect ourselves."

"How'd you use the portal without a dragon shifter around?"

Surprise flitted across his face. "I thought it worked for everyone."

"Huh." Maybe it just required a dragon shifter to switch it on in the first instance and otherwise anyone could use the mirror as a portal. Unlike the Moonbeam—which, according to the little I'd managed to learn in the past day, had remained in its lifeless black state since the battle and didn't even seem to have affected the shifters imprisoned in the nearby jail. "I guess it does. Just try not to break it again. Only a dragon can repair it."

"We will treat it with care, of course." He sounded mildly insulted at the very suggestion, but I had to admit to some unease about the mages keeping the only means of reaching the last surviving community of dragon shifters in the country here in their headquarters.

Which brought to mind another question. "Did you speak to any of the dragon shifters?"

"Only to establish that Lorne was in our custody and that any allies of his would face the full consequences of crimes they committed," he said. "The dragon shifters are free to act as they see fit, and we will treat them like any other independent population of shifters, as no local Mage Lords claim authority over them."

"Neither does Lorne, now." They'd have to elect another leader. Hopefully a fairer one this time, though I didn't know how they made those decisions. "Or Malkin. He was the one really calling the shots."

Without either of them, the other dragons would finally be free. That didn't mean they'd accept Cori and me. They'd lost so much to the hunters, and we'd lived happy lives in full ignorance of it all. The recent massacre might have been the last straw.

But we had one chance to see them again, even if it turned out that they wanted nothing more to do with us.

———

WHEN CORI and I went to meet the other dragon shifters on the other side of the mirror, I was more nervous than I'd been in a long time. Even fighting Malkin had nothing on this.

Lord Smyth had dropped in to confirm our visit and had added that the dragon shifters had chosen an interim leader who had taken over custody of the mirror for the time being. That at least meant they wanted to meet us, but that didn't mean they'd *like* us, or that they wouldn't end up being clones of Lorne and his cronies after all.

Cori and I stepped out of the portal into a room furnished in dark wood that looked a little more homely than what I'd seen of the village so far. The leader was a middle-aged red-haired woman named Azalea who'd lost her husband in Lorne's attack on the village and the subsequent violence. Although her prematurely aged face was lined with grief, she offered Cori and me a smile. "It's wonderful to finally meet you both. Ember and Coriander. Is that right?"

Some of my nervousness disappeared. "You, too. I'm sorry for the losses you suffered."

A sheen of tears appeared on her eyes, but she inclined her head. "Lorne is no longer a threat to us, and for that, we owe you our thanks."

"It wasn't just me," I said clumsily. "I'm sorry I didn't act sooner."

"We're grateful regardless. You've made this village safe again for those of us who remain." She offered us two of the seats within the room and took one herself. I noticed her hands were trembling a little. Was she nervous, too? In the silence that followed, I heard indistinct voices upstairs, followed by the unmistakeable sound of a child's laughter.

Cori and I looked at one another with mirrored shock.

"I thought Cori and I were the last children in the village before we left," I said. "Who—?"

"They're mine." Tears shone in her eyes again. "Lorne held them hostage, as leverage over me."

"Oh." I choked on a breath. "Oh, I'm sorry."

"Before the attack, he handed them over to the League." She retrieved a handkerchief and dabbed at her eyes. "He did the same to all the children in the village before he corralled us all to fight on his behalf and killed anyone who resisted. It's not an excuse—"

"No, I get it," I said, horrified that she'd ever think that I'd blame her for Lorne's actions. "Were you in London?"

"Briefly." She dabbed at her eyes. "Before you freed us. I'll never forget that. The Moonbeam offered a miracle."

"I know." I blinked tears from my own eyes.

Cori sniffled, buried her head in my shoulder, and I held her close.

A voice trickled into the back of my mind. *Yes... I thank you, Ember, for offering me a host.*

Once the aftermath of my return to consciousness had

worn off and I'd properly reunited with my sister, I'd casually asked Cori if she'd heard any voices herself when I'd used the Moonbeam to return her to life. She hadn't, except for the yells of the other ghosts, and for all I knew, that was exactly what I'd heard myself. But I'd be lying if I said some of my added protectiveness towards Cori since the battle wasn't due to that one unanswered question. She didn't *seem* any different than usual, at least. Maybe a little more cautious, but who could blame her?

Cori sniffled again, bringing my attention back to the present. "I *knew* we couldn't be the only children. Lorne didn't stamp us out entirely."

"That he didn't," Azalea said softly. "I am glad to see you again."

"You knew us?" I asked. "When we were younger?"

"Not well." Her expression clouded. "We used to be much more numerous in those days, and your parents weren't close friends of mine, but I knew Madison and her sister."

"Sister?" My mouth parted. "She had a sister? Did Lorne—?"

"Her sister left the village before Lorne made it impossible to do so," said Azalea. "But I'm right in thinking that you two have no memories of your time here as young children, aren't I?"

"Yes." Hope kindled inside me. "Do you know who erased our memories?"

"Madison's sister, Agnes, did," said Azalea. "Unfortunately, we've had no contact with her since she left shortly after you did."

The flames began to dim. "You don't know where she is."

"I can find out," she said. "It's the least of what I owe you."

"You don't owe us a thing," I insisted. "It's enough that we have access to the village and can get to know you again."

"Nevertheless," she said. "If I had the ability to help you

recall that time, I would. I did know you as a child. Both of you. I wish this had been a safe home for you."

Tears pricked my eyes. "So do I, but it's okay. London's our home now."

Even being accepted by the other dragons wouldn't erase the bonds we'd forged in the past nine years. While gaining our memories back—if we ever did—would be an adjustment, it wouldn't remove the memories we'd made since.

I might not have found my home here, but I was surer than ever that I knew exactly where I belonged.

We went back at least every other day from then on, with the Mage Lords' permission, to help the other dragons rebuild their homes. Our third visit brought the news that Azalea had tracked down Madison's sister at another village further north, named Foxwood.

The news took me off guard. Honestly, just visiting the other dragons in the village was enough of a gift. Cori and I seized every chance to learn about their lives, and any memories they had of our parents and other relatives prior to Lorne's atrocities. All the survivors bore deep scars, and I could tell some harboured a little mistrust of us, but they were ready to rebuild their lives in his absence and heal the wounds he'd inflicted. I was more than happy to play a role in that without expecting anything in return, and Azalea's revelation brought more resistance than I'd expected to feel. Yes, I'd spent years yearning for the truth, but I had a life now, and contradictory memories of a time I'd never have back might be an unnecessary complication.

Still, maybe this would bring both Cori and me some much-needed closure, and an end to the questions surrounding our arrival in London.

With Azalea's directions in mind, Cori and I flew over the Scottish mountains and valleys, heading north. Cori was a restless passenger, wanting to take detours over every peak and forest, but the views were stunning. This was a world even the hunters had never reached, a place where nature had ruled long before the Sidhe came.

Foxwood was tucked out of sight so well that I flew right over it twice before Cori spotted the tell-tale shimmer of a town hidden by witch spells. I was impressed she'd seen it from that height and told her so when we landed outside.

"Kit's been teaching me how to see through glamour," she said in explanation. "There's something... *fae* about this place. I hope this Agnes isn't a Sidhe in disguise."

"I doubt it."

The place did have a powerful aura, and looking at the village gave me an odd sense of double vision, my eyes trying to see both the buildings and the illusion of empty countryside grafted on top. We'd landed behind a cluster of trees to avoid causing too much alarm and walked to the village on foot.

From there, we made our way to the shop we'd been told belonged to Agnes and her husband. An iron bar on the door told me that the inhabitants certainly weren't fae, and the shop was stocked with magical trinkets that I might have given a closer look if not for the woman standing behind the counter. She looked unnervingly like Madison, down to the silvery hair, though her features were maybe a decade younger.

"Hi," I said, approaching her. "Are you Agnes?"

"I am," she said, regarding me with raised eyebrows. "You're a dragon shifter. I can't say I've been visited by one of those in a long time."

"But you've seen me before," I said. "Even though I don't remember you."

Understanding cleared her eyes as she made the connection between the adult me and the child I'd once been.

"I apologise," she said. "I did have some reservations about performing the spell, but I felt obliged to follow through, as your lives were in terrible danger."

"You lived in the dragons' village, too?" I asked.

"For a time," she said. "However, I made a living selling spells, and the dragons weren't regular customers, for obvious reasons. Madison was fond of them, so I often stopped by to visit her when I moved away. When Lorne started his bid for power, I decided it was the time to permanently leave, and I chose to settle in Foxwood. I'd just met my husband, Everett, so it worked out perfectly."

Not so much for Madison. I assumed she knew her sister was dead, but I wasn't entirely sure what to make of Agnes herself. She seemed entirely too sensible for someone who'd once apparently tried to sell handmade spells to the dragon shifters.

"Is this another shifter community?" asked Cori.

"It's a supernatural one, but no dragons," said Agnes. "Madison and I were born part-witch, part-mage, with added gifts."

"You don't seem unhappy she died," said Cori. I elbowed her.

"She planned to go out on her own terms," said Agnes. "In truth, it's an old grief. I already mourned her when she decided to stay behind. It's been nearly a decade since we were in touch, after all." I did pick up on a hint of sadness in her voice, and she drew her shawl tighter around her shoulders as she spoke.

I swallowed. "She did it for us."

"She did it for all the dragon shifters," she said. "Our opinions differed, but we both sought to use our abilities with purpose. As for me, perhaps I made the wrong choice. Are you sure you want me to undo the spell?"

I nodded, as did Cori.

Agnes raised a hand. Light flared in her palm, and my mind fractured in a manner similar to a mirror breaking. I pressed a palm to my forehead, reminded of when I'd first looked at Foxwood and seen the illusion placed on top of the real village. One set of memories overlaid the other, and my head was suddenly bursting with recollections of running through the village hand in hand with Cori, playing together in Madison's house, watching dragons entwined in the sky above.

Cori's eyes met mine with the same confusion, sadness—and hope.

"Thank you," I said softly to Agnes. "We're grateful."

She grunted in a manner that put me in mind of Giselle. "It's nothing. Personally, I think using magic to meddle with minds is crossing an unspoken line, but nobody ever asks for my opinion on such matters."

"There's a mage in London who can *read* minds," I said. "She's awful."

"That I expect." Her eyes narrowed. "In my opinion, the Mage Lords have entirely too much power. I wouldn't have minded them gaining a rival, but not a tyrant like that Lorne."

"Or the Orion League," I added. "They aren't still lurking around up here, are they?"

"Oh, they never threatened *this* place," she said, with a slight laugh that made me wonder just how much power *she* had, hidden away in this unassuming village, selling charms. "Give Azalea my best, will you?"

I promised to, and Cori and I left her house without buying anything. I did have to drag Cori away from a packet of chewing gum that was supposed to enable someone to breathe fire.

"I only wanted a turn," she protested. "It's not fair that you get all the firepower to yourself."

"You'll get to shift in a few years, you know that."

"Not soon enough." Her words made me wonder if that time would come sooner than it had for me. There was no telling what side effects being revived by the Moonbeam would have on her. "What?"

"Nothing." I took her hand and squeezed it. "I'm just glad we're here. Together."

The past was whole, and it was on us to make the future the same.

―――――

CORI WAS UNCHARACTERISTICALLY quiet during the flight back to the village. Like me, she needed time to process everything we'd learned. It'd take a while to sort through the memories and work out how they related to the present, I was sure, but the new recollections would also help us to rebuild our connection with the others. Memories of chasing other dragon shifter children in the woods, of watching the adults take flight in a magnificent display over the village... they seemed at total odds with a lifetime of being hunted for who I was, but now I had both, maybe I could finally reconcile the two halves of my life.

Once we'd gone back through the mirror and left the mages' headquarters, Cori and I returned to Magic Avenue. The others had decided against staying to wait for us, as we hadn't known how long we'd be in the village, and the mages could only tolerate my friends for so long. That, and Lady Clare was a menace. Agnes had been right on that one.

"Got your memories back?" asked Will, as we walked

through the front door into the shop. He'd removed the boards from the windows but had yet to restock the empty shelves, and it would be a while before we could comfortably return to business without being afraid of gargoyles landing on our roof or hostile witches knocking at the door. Still, the tales of our saving the city had spread up and down the street, and the attitude was overall much more welcoming than it had been since before the hunters had first intruded on our lives.

"We did." Cori bounded ahead of me into the corridor to the living quarters.

"And?" asked Becks from the living room.

"It's like weird déjà vu," I admitted. "I've spoken to some of these people before, yet I had no memory of that when I visited the village more recently. It's like I've met them twice."

"Lucky you don't have to do that with us." Will followed us into the room, where everyone except Astor waited. He was probably visiting Giselle again, though he spent most nights here. "We're too awesome to be forgotten, obviously."

I snorted. "Nobody's stopped by since we left?"

"A couple of witches came to apologise for badmouthing us about those fires," said Will. "Helps that the mages have dropped all idea of putting our names on any kind of list. Oh, and since they arrested half the Fanged clan members, I doubt they'll start another turf war anytime soon."

"And the mages told me the other half-bloods are starting to move back to the park," added Kit. "I won't be joining them, though."

"You could," Cori said. "I'm sure they're willing, since you saved their lives."

"Yeah, you don't have to live with us annoying humans, even if there are perks." Becks eyed Will, who made a great performance out of staring out the newly uncovered window.

"Well," said Kit, "we did kind of accidentally turn one of their parks into a giant summoning circle."

"Technically, the League did it," said Becks. "But I can see how that might make things awkward."

"That, and I'm not local," said Kit. "I can find my own place. It's not a problem."

"You're staying here," Will said firmly. "I'll get the shop reopened, and then, I don't know, we'll do freelance shit for the mages if they're willing to give us another chance. They paid so well that I feel kinda bad for all the spells I nicked from them."

"The spells did save our lives," I said. "Saved the city, too."

"I might have to ask them for tips." Will pulled a face. "Look at me, thinking of working with the mages. They're corrupting me. Anyway, you and Cori definitely aren't moving back up north now you have your memories back?"

"Of course not!" Cori said before I could speak. "Nothing's changed."

"It has, but that doesn't matter," I added. "Cori and I will visit the village as often as the mages let us, but wherever we spent the first years of our lives, this is our home now."

"Good," said Will. "Because we've grown attached to you. I'd hate to have to follow you through the mirror and haul you back to London."

"Ha." I smiled at my friends. "I'm not leaving, don't worry. Thanks to that mirror, I'll always be able to come back."

As to the Moonbeam, the portal remained non-functioning, and the mages hadn't shown too much interest in reviving it. It technically belonged to the dragons, but considering what Lorne had done, I didn't blame them for wanting to avoid mentioning the subject, any more than I blamed the mages for wanting to keep a close eye on it.

Unless the Moonbeam showed signs of life again, I'd put the matter to the back of my mind together with any worries I might have about the long-term effects of Cori's revival.

I glanced behind me at the soft sound of footsteps on the stairs. "Is someone else in?"

"Astor, of course," Becks said with an eye-roll. "He still thinks he's too badass to walk through the door like a normal person."

My heart gave a skitter, and I crossed the room to the door. Astor stood in the hall, dressed surprisingly casually in jeans and a jacket. He'd taken off the ex-hunter gear almost entirely these days, though his old habits of climbing through windows remained.

"How'd you know Cori and I were back?" I asked.

"I saw you from the rooftop." He leaned in to kiss me.

"Does Will know you've been climbing on his roof?" Kit might have decided to stay, but I hadn't put the same question to Astor. It seemed presumptuous, and besides, the house was Will's, not mine. Admittedly, I didn't think Cori and I had ever actually asked his permission to live here. We'd just moved in. Granted, that had been in the immediate aftermath of the faerie invasion when we'd all been lucky to have a roof over our heads at all, but still.

"Better me than the gargoyles."

"True. How was Giselle?"

The grumpy ex-hunter had stayed in her broken-down flat rather than moving with us to our new rental, and Astor split his time between the two of us. I figured he thought she was lonely, though she'd said she'd happily avoid interacting with any of us again as long as the bloody Moonbeam didn't cause trouble again. She didn't even seem to mind the mages had it, now that Malkin was no longer a threat.

"Same as ever," he replied. "She did ask me about the

mages. I think she still wonders if they'll change their minds and arrest us after all."

"They'll have to answer to me if they do." I smiled, but he didn't return it. "What?"

"I won't ask for the details of what you saw—"

"I'll share them anyway, obviously," I cut in. "And also, for the record, I'm not moving to Scotland. It's nice, but it's also way too quiet for my tastes."

"You're used to all the excitement." A smile tugged at his mouth. "No, I thought you might want to keep the memories between you and Cori. Some things are personal."

"Like when you lived with the hunters?" Shit, maybe I shouldn't have said that aloud. I'd never pried for the details of his time with them either, not out of any kind of avoidance but because it didn't matter. He wasn't the same person now. We all changed, whether in a literal sense by shifting or otherwise.

His expression shadowed, his hand unconsciously drifting towards his collarbone and the concealed tattoos. "I remember it all. Part of me thinks I deserve to. With the number of aliases I have, I could build a whole new identity now, but that person will always be there."

"The past is past, Astor," I said. "You've already proved a hundred times you aren't one of them. Also, you'd better not take up an alias and disappear."

"No?" One brow arched. "I think I've worn out my welcome with your friends."

"You haven't." I had to make that clear. "Kit just accepted Will's offer to live here. I'm not going to ask you to do the same, but you know, Will's used to us annoying shifters just showing up and not leaving."

"I'm not a shifter."

"You're mine," I said, and was rewarded with a wide grin. "We tend to be the protective sort. Fair warning."

"Really? I'd never have guessed."

I grinned right back. I knew the journey ahead wouldn't be a smooth one. The League might have been disbanded, but I knew that like all evil, they'd survive in some form. But we outnumbered them, and supernaturals weren't going anywhere. If there wasn't a space for us dragons in the modern world, then we'd carve out our own, with our claws if necessary.

And if the hunters rose again? We'd be more than ready to meet them.

ABOUT THE AUTHOR

Emma is the New York Times and USA Today Bestselling author of the Changeling Chronicles urban fantasy series.

Emma spent her childhood creating imaginary worlds to compensate for a disappointingly average reality, so it was probably inevitable that she ended up writing fantasy novels. When she's not immersed in her own fictional universes, Emma can be found with her head in a book or wandering around the world in search of adventure.

Find out more about Emma's books at
www.emmaladams.com.